SMILING IN
THE DARKNESS

Vitorino Nemésio, *Stormy Isles: An Azorean Tale*
Translated and introduced by Francisco Cota Fagundes

Pedro da Silveira, *Poems in Absentia* & Poems from *The Island and the World*
Translated by George Monteiro
Foreword by Vamberto Freitas
Afterword by George Monteiro

Adelaide Freitas, *Smiling in the Darkness*
Translated by Katharine F. Baker, Bobby J. Chamberlain,
Reinaldo F. Silva, and Emanuel Melo
Foreword by João de Melo

Raul Brandão, *The Unknown Islands* (forthcoming)
Translated by David Brookshaw
Introduction by Urbano Bettencourt

SMILING IN THE DARKNESS

ADELAIDE FREITAS

Translated by
Katharine F. Baker, Bobby J. Chamberlain,
Reinaldo F. Silva, and Emanuel Melo

TAGUS PRESS
University of Massachusetts Dartmouth
Dartmouth, MA

Tagus Press is the publishing arm of the
Center for Portuguese Studies and Culture at
the University of Massachusetts Dartmouth.
Center Director: Victor K. Mendes

Bellis Azorica 3
Tagus Press at the University of Massachusetts Dartmouth
Original Portuguese text © 2004 Adelaide Freitas
Translation © 2020 Katharine F. Baker
Foreword © 2020 João de Melo
Translator's note © 2020 Katharine F. Baker

Executive Editor: Mario Pereira
Series Editors: Onésimo T. Almeida & Mario Pereira
Copyedited by Sharon Brinkman
Cover photo by Emanuel Melo
Designed and typeset by Jen Jackowitz

For all inquiries, please contact:
Tagus Press
Center for Portuguese Studies and Culture
University of Massachusetts Dartmouth
285 Old Westport Road
North Dartmouth, MA 02747–2300
(508) 999-8255, fax (508) 999-9272
https://www.umassd.edu/portuguese-studies-center/

ISBN: 978-1-933227-93-1
Library of Congress control number: 2020931473

Ao Vamberto,
às suas andanças,
e à teimosia do seu retorno;
à sua crença de que a lua é redonda.
À minha família, em cujo coração
se cruzam o lamento e o canto.

To Vamberto,
to his travels,
and to his determination to return;
to his belief that the moon is round.
To my family, in whose heart
regret and singing intersect.

Luna! Luna llena, luna llena
Tan oronda, tan redonda
En esta noche serena . . .
Yo te ve, clara Luna
Siempre pensativa y buena

Moon! Full moon, full moon
So plump, so round
On this calm night . . .
I see you, clear moon
Always thoughtful and good

—Antonio Machado

April is the cruellest month, breeding
Lilacs out of dead land, mixing
Memory and desire, stirring
Dull roots with spring rain (. . .)

—T.S. Eliot

CONTENTS

FOREWORD

Adelaide Freitas:
INNOCENCE AND PAIN

The American people have always lived with the daily reality of immigrant communities that originate from every corner of the world and that over the years have chosen the country as their destiny and as a part of their history. The integration of these communities into American society is generally achieved at a slow and gradual pace according to the gains that they make: first, command of the English language, then the assimilation of new customs and habits, and then, later on, the "American way of life," and even perhaps further into the future, their own "American dream." I do not intend to analyze the problems of this integration, such as group isolation and the conservative cult of the culture of their everyday lives as explanations for their resistance to the splendors of the New World. Americans themselves know much more about this than I do, despite the fact that I watched my entire family emigrate from the Azores to Canada and to the United States. Today they are a kind of nameless tribe to me: siblings, brothers-and sisters-in-law, nieces and nephews, and great-nieces and -nephews who are "foreigners" to me.

But this is not what *Smiling in the Darkness* by Adelaide Freitas is about. This novel brings us into the reality underlying the condition of the emigrant, something that I believe is somewhat neglected in this "country of foreigners" and its natural-born citizens, the Americans. The perspective in this book is quite different, and it has fallen to me to discuss it from the double condition as a reader and as someone who has suffered this traumatic life experience—how it used to be and how it was for us when our parents left us and went to America in search of the economic opportunities that did not exist in the Azores or in Continental Portugal. The bitterness and the loneliness of the children left behind on the islands come from our having been handed over to relatives who raised us in their own way with love or with no love at all, so often missing and absent from their father and mother figures. The author of *Smiling in the Darkness* has a right to the metaphor of the title with which she confronts readers. The "smile" is opposed to the "night" of both time and memory because it illuminates it and overcomes its darkness. The triumph over adversities is achieved through the pain and intense struggle against the traumas of absence and the eternal losses of childhood.

Adelaide Freitas makes use of a concealed narrator (she is named only near the beginning and at the end of the book) to speak to us about the innocence of Xana (certainly her alter ego), a child character, sensitive, all innocence in the painful experience of her youth and abandonment by her parents who left her in the care of her maternal grandmother, who also had lived an emigrant experience. Xana calls this grandmother "mamã" throughout her childhood, because there is in her the strangeness of a nonexistent mother whose image exists only in the portraits in the home and in her grandmother's words. Later, when her hitherto imaginary mother returns to the Azores, Xana feels betrayed by an authoritarian and cold woman who forces her children to call her "mamã" but who reveals herself to be devoid of maternal love, dry and overbearing to the point of overwhelming her husband, Xana's father, and turning him into a subdued man, incapable of dealing with and opposing the arrogance of his wife.

I speak of the innocence and of pain of the girl in this book. Xana personifies the interior drama of the author, who was also a hostage of her illusions—the child who does not grow up and who refuses to be an adult within the context of the family as well as in the world of others. On the very day of her parents' arrival from America on the landing pier, Xana is taken by her grandmother to the city, not exactly to wait for them, but to meet them in real life. It is the most intensely emotional moment of the book. It is the miracle and the expression of literature against reality. The girl Xana accepts her father and flees from her mother, who does not even embrace her child. On the contrary, she frightens Xana with her excessive determination and with the power she wields within the family. The strangeness of the power of her mother over the family, including her husband, derives from the fact that she is not feminine, but rather matriarchal, something unnatural, with no correspondence to the maternal image that until that moment had occupied Xana's imagination. This image is again transferred to her grandmother and becomes the mirage of disappointment through the future failure of a relationship that ultimately opposes mother and daughter and never reconciles them. We are, thus, face to face with a psychological conflict that becomes as absolute as it is definitive, and it shapes forever the spirit of the girl—where it seems there is no glimmer of reason or feeling, no heart, no will to live. But there are other demons in the heart and mind of Xana. Her first period, for example, proves to be a personal tragedy, for the mysteries and secrets of her body are unknown to her. Here we have something similar to a mental illness that will stay with her throughout her life. A simple act of love at night in her parents' bed turns out to be terrible to her in its fictitious violence. And every time that Xana hears them secretly planning a new "flight" to America, we see her descend into the hells of helplessness and family loss, especially the loss of the understanding tenderness of her father. The America of this book oscillates between the longing of some and a curse for Xana; between the freedom of others and the confinement of Xana in the house on the island; and between the abundance and the emptiness of that which money cannot buy, give, nor compensate for on its own.

Finally, my most obvious observation: in terms of pure analysis, this book opens before us two human geographies, two countries, two systemic times—it is singular in the way in which it exposes America to the fever of our consciousness. It is not enough to read it: it is necessary to live it as well. The book was written with the poetic sensibility of pain and innocence, for the love of the author's island roots and the land of its people.

Adelaide Freitas (1949–2018) had a Portuguese and an American life story. She graduated from Southeastern Massachusetts University (now the University of Massachusetts Dartmouth), received a master's degree from the City University of New York, and completed a PhD at the University of the Azores, where she was professor of North American literature and culture. She published her dissertation on Herman Mel-ville in book form as *Moby-Dick, a Ilha e o Mar: Metáforas do Carácter do Povo Americano* (1991). In addition to scholarly studies, Freitas left us a number of publications, including literary essays, works of sociology, poetry, and travel literature. And, above all, she left us the *saudade* of her name and her person. Most of all, there endures in us the beauty of her smile, an eternal light that remains bright in the night of her death.

João de Melo
Lisbon
September 26, 2019

Translated by Mario Pereira

SMILING IN
THE DARKNESS

CHAPTER 1

Mmmm mmma mmmaaa mmmamamm mamm

It all started when Xana babbled *mammāā*.

It was spring. Drop by drop fell the first showers of April—"the cruellest month." Cruel, too, was what my grandmother had just heard.

"No, Xana dear. It's not *mamā*, it's *vovó, voo-vóó*," my mother's mother repeated with the insistence of water dripping from the eaves.

With patience and a colossal effort, Vovó would lift the little girl up onto her lap, like Sisyphus with his stone. Overhead, for the child's amusement, hung a wreath made of wildflowers; wild, too, were her dark, dark eyes.

Coming in from the backyard, Vovó would head into the kitchen, cross the open center of the house, enter her bedroom, and go straight to the dresser with a wide mirror above it—on which sat the beautiful picture of my mother. Vovó, her sublime glowing face topped by gently arching brows, would point a finger to the woman framed there at the same time she was scrutinizing Xana, looking her straight in the eye as a way of ascertaining that she understood once and for all that Mamā was not the same as Vovó.

"I'm *Vovó!* She's your mother, Xana."

❁

It was sad, very sad to see the confusion on my little sister's round face.

3

Carolina, six years older, was accustomed to such mix-ups. So whenever Xana, now eighteen months old, mistook Vovó for Mamã, Carolina would smack her, then run off to our other grandmother's house.

Carolina's behavior did not surprise me. Unlike Xana, she had known Mamã, so was unable to get it into her head how Xana could be so stupid as not to be able to tell the difference between the two women, Mamã and Vovó.

For Carolina, everything was to some extent much simpler. "She must've been born with mush for brains, that's what it is. I mean, who ever heard of mixing up those two? So Mamã's not our mommy and Vovó's not our grandma?" Decidedly and disdainfully, she did not like Xana—yet when least expected, in a sweet and tender gesture Carolina would with her tentative and delicate hand caress Xana's damp little cheek that was turned toward her in a gurgle of affection mixed with drool.

In that instant Carolina melted like American candy. She would hug and squeeze her baby Mana with twice the force of a volcano, not knowing whether she was trying to become Xana's peer or banish her and take her place—in order to feel freed from the specter that had pursued her ever since little Xana's birth, with everyone around acting as though she were a queen, a star, at that moment the center of the world, the center of all the village's attentions. Carolina felt irritated as a tear formed in the corner of her eye and her head spun, and abandoned like a rag buried in mud.

And this was how I learned early on to live with the contradictions at home. Somewhat disoriented, I realized we were being caught up in a tangled web that would ensnare our entire family.

⚙

Exposed to such a marvel of disconnected lives, I feared what might somehow befall Xana—so mixed up, and in general so different from us.

As she grew over the months, we noticed her face become more confused and filled with dread, like tree branches at the whim of strong winds, or a tightrope on the edge of an abyss.

Every time we talked about America, or about our Grandpa who had vanished into the mists, Xana would, without understanding a single thing, curl up like a snail, restlessly and almost absentmindedly seeking out Vovó's gaze. Her eyes were sunken in the oblique inclination of the waters lapping up against the edge of a vast expanse. She watched them from behind the curtains, but they told her nothing, and nothing made sense. All of a sudden her eyes would flash and their brilliance would melt my grandmother's "snow."

Across the sea, chariots of fire awaited her, making it possible to travel faster in that unknown world. And it was all so mysterious and nameless that it would leave Xana baffled, her eyes wandering.

Fearful, she ran and hid under Vovó's full skirts.

What secret waters stalked her?

And while she watched and waited for a smile as pale as the white of the full moon sitting on the threshold of Vovó's face, Xana understood nothing.

So I tried to explain to my little sister that someday Mamã and Papá would return to São Bento. They would return one day, one day they would come back from America, but no one knew when. She then gave me a glazed look of pious relief, her eyes fogged up like those of a dead fish.

In those amazing times, if our Xana had been able to perceive or understand the strange signs of hidden secrets, she would have seen them in wrecked ships laden with lost fantasies, anchored in the ocean's depths, into which she would have wanted to dive in order to decipher Vovó's enigmatic smile that little by little became pure and tender, redeemed like a white, white fleur-de-lis lying atop the simple ogive arch of the camellia bush planted in our backyard—above which flew a plane full of airsick passengers throwing up on our camellias, turning them from snow-white to clay red.

Our little sister was always like that, so innocent, so childlike. She would plant her feet together and swear with resoluteness to Carolina that while the plane was flying over our yard she had found time to drag over the doormat, place a bushel basket on it, and on top of that a half-bushel, in order to reach high enough to be able to ring the plane's bell and let Papá and Mamã know that this was the spot for them to get off.

Xana was beside herself. She exulted in happiness and clapped her palms together in an unstoppable frenzy, certain that upon waking she would find Mamā and Papá under her pillow, just like at dawn on the feast day of St. John the Baptist, when someone pried open the good luck fava bean: if the pod was intact, the person would be rich; if half open, prosperous; but if shelled, then very, very poor.

In the morning Xana opened then closed her eyes, rolling them deep down inside herself, fearful of not finding what would be her greatest treasure, greater than the unshelled fava bean, greater than anything: Mamā and Papá. The trembling of a ray of sunshine that she squeezed in the palm of her hand with all her heart was visible on her face.

"It's gotta be this time," she insisted. "Wasn't it Daniel who said so, when he read the exact date of Mamā and Papá's arrival aloud to Vovó? It's gotta be today, and only today," she squealed from inside her fragile little body. With her fingernails and teeth she clung with all her might to her pillow, clutching and clutching it until it ripped open so Papá and Mamā could come out from inside it.

She woke up. With "sleep" in her eyes, she prepared for her surprise. She rubbed her hands together, trembling with joy. Her anxiety increased at the speed of three thundering horses. And out from under her pillow came a handful of . . . nothing.

Pain rained down on a wounded heart that had been deceived by the lie. It was impossible.

Once again, empty cold—cold, cold as Vovó's "snow."

Fat tears cascaded down her face.

At her feet a puddle of muddy, agitated water accumulated; at such moments she was manic, throwing a fit. Whenever she felt betrayed or hurt she would place her hands behind her and back up, up, up until she reached the wall. Then she would slip through it and settle in between its partitions. Between the slats, only her dark eyes were visible, dark as a moonless, starless night.

Sometimes she would go off alone and disappear, hiding sometimes under the cabbage plants, other times behind the daisies, and very often within the dense garden hedge.

Xana would then go looking for her soft blanket stitched with velvety rose petals, to rid herself of the icy chill. She would wrap it around her and build a world to her liking—shouting for the sun reflected on the plane's propeller to help her climb up to the skies. And all of it with such authentic and sincere feeling.

Years later, as a young woman in the Americas, Carolina herself used to swear to girlfriends that in childhood her sister Xana—still living with our grandmother on the island—possessed the power to rise into the sky in the direction of a metal bird that from time to time flew over Nordeste, with a large visible bell in its belly that Xana would ring.

The neighbor women, agitated like hens scratching in dung, believed this and insisted it was true every time a plane flew overhead. Xana would make a mad dash to put on the same show, shouting to everyone along São Bento's streets how it was not hard to fly, how the sky was all lit up in the color of the propeller. "It came from the east," she would squeal in excitement, "and had a white, white light, flying over Pico da Vara and heading in the direction of our garden."

As the huge bird flew closer and closer, everyone came to a standstill.

❀

The hemorrhaging sunset at the end of that late afternoon still reflected on people's enchanted faces, increasing their curiosity to see the rhythm of a dead land broken once and for all. Several heads poked out the windows and doors. A warm, full-bodied early spring aroma permeated the entire atmosphere. Daisies shone like stars against the darkening night sky, while the peach tree turned its innocent-colored blossoms skyward. The incense trees that abounded there, enclosing the backyards of most of the houses, surpassed all other flowers in fragrance. Within the hedgerows, birds sang in an act of farewell until the new dawn.

A song sprang forth from who-knows-where—maybe the still hot soil, or the ocean, or the starry sky—perhaps from the sarcophagus of the Egyptian pyramids or the depths of the tides. And everything remained unsaid, in suspended animation, waiting for . . . something.

So when at the end of that very afternoon, with its incandescent perfume, the women and children saw our schoolteacher Senhor Professor striding purposefully toward Xana's grandmother's house, they followed in the master's footsteps, and their questions rained down in a cascade.

"Where'd it go? Where'd it go?"

His answer was a deafening silence, soft like spring water.

"What did you see, Xana? Say something, girl."

"What madness is this, child?" the village teacher asked Xana once more, probing the downtrodden faces and defeated bodies overwhelmed by the indignity of so many of their children leaving.

"Where is your common sense?" the teacher continued, scratching his head.

"What plane, girl? What a tall tale! Really, now, come on!"

Xana let her chin drop, and her bulging eyes turned to the floor, threatening to spiral out of their sockets in a mix of fear and hatred. She watched in defiance and, unlike on other occasions, did not go hide.

She remained standing, head held high, and did not shrink from his glare. The teacher's voice was terrifying—deep, and good for scaring his most unwary students, as well as some of the more superstitious adults. Everything about him was large: large body, large heavy glasses on the tip of his nose, large and intelligent high forehead cocked slightly to the left, with his pointer and ruler always in his hand in order to whack the least diligent and least capable students.

Senhor Professor then set his sea-blue eyes upon Xana's. To his surprise, and almost in pain from the force he felt emanating from that frail body of hers, he seemed intimidated.

Xana, taking advantage of that space she did not know how to name, stared into the large man's face, and shot a harrowing look into the pupils of her teacher's eyes.

At the moment this happened, some of those present claimed in hushed tones that they felt a heat that seemed as though a bolt of lightning had struck there that no one had noticed. But Xana must have, because her tiny body was trembling with fright. She sensed it without knowing what it was, turned around, and when she looked back, she saw that her teacher was tugging his beret farther to the left and it fell off, and then the schoolmaster bent down to pick it up from the ground.

At that moment, anyone who was paying attention saw a demonic smile spread across Xana's lips and up to her eyes. And satisfied by what she was feeling, the little girl set off running toward the warmth of hearth and home, to nestle in the skirts of her aunt, Tia Luísa.

For their part the women, with their wizened faces, grayish clothing on hunched bodies, and dreams denied, retreated to their houses in shock and awe.

As night fell, the excitement in their voices, marked by miseries and mysteries, was still audible. Then a purple cloud fell over the rooftops and no sound lingered from the voices. Their bodies lay tangled amid the husks, intertwined like vines in the orchard, in the middle of the night heading toward the dawn's new light, when no cock was yet crowing nor hen waking up.

❊

It was well into morning and the whole village commented once again, now that cooler heads prevailed, on the previous night's events. People did not know what to think anymore, regardless of the reprimand from Senhor Professor, who for whatever reason had been unable to convince them. Their voices fell into a dissonant swirl; some were more reserved, others downright hysterical.

Everyone's tongues flicked like toads', spreading opinions by word of mouth. They gossiped, and speculation grew in tone. As they drifted away, here and there they left bits of plots, scenarios, and suspicions in a hum that filled the entire village. It was like a fever or contagious disease.

"Is that girl crazy?" the women asked one another.

"She might contain the devil in her, or have inherited the wings that transported her sister Serafina"—who died at age fourteen months, yet years later was still recalled by many villagers who had not forgotten that child's beauty and intelligence—to the other world.

But, on second thought, the neighbor women continued whispering and murmuring among themselves that there were some resemblances between the two little girls, especially the broad forehead, large cunning eyes, and light, almost ethereal body. Everything led to the belief in the village that Xana would probably meet the same fate, hence the consensus on the part of family and neighbors to let the little girl do as she wished. However, to the inhabitants' astonishment, the doctor later assured them she would survive, for the worst was over. And after having almost died twice in the short period of three years, she aspired to nothing short of ascending to heaven, where her joy and secrets resided. To her, everything there was intact. She imagined, dreamed, and saw her grandparents reunited, Papá and Mamã reunited, her siblings and cousins too.

❊

Indeed, the townspeople sought to bring Xana back down to earth, to entice her with promises of bonbons, and it was even said that a certain man—with a tripod supporting an old camera covered by a black cloth, right in front of our grandmother's house—could perform magic, because the most beautiful birdie Xana had ever seen would pop out of his box.

My little sister acceded. Then we all waited for her.

Lo and behold, she suddenly returned. She was happy. The photographer prepared to take our picture, moving a few steps forward, a few back, straightening the bow in Xana's hair, and readying his camera. Xana stood in front of the old box without a wide smile, but also without sadness, gazing off at the island's ocean remoteness. She seemed wary, ill at ease. I myself felt uncomfortable. Minutes later I noticed something in her always lively eyes that bothered me: above them, on her domed forehead her brow was furrowing—the reaction of someone not enjoying the spectacle, who felt lost.

The people were a veritable swarm of bees, drawing closer and crowding together. Curiosity kept growing, while Xana's brow furrowed more and more, its crease deepening. José Serobolho—a skinny, short-legged photographer who walked like Charlie Chaplin—stood on tiptoe and raised himself up to the tripod until he reached the box. Next he stuck his head under the dark cloth, then peeked out for one last time as everyone shouted euphorically in unison.

"More to the front, a bit to the back, Xana. Look, look, right now!" Click. And click again. But no birdie.

"Where is it? Where is it???"

There was no birdie. Nothing.

"Oh, here it is, Xana. Come see your picture."

"No! That's not my photograph, and there's no birdie. You're all liars, a bunch of liars."

At that moment my sister's face went dead like a corpse's, her little body limp and helpless.

She had been fooled by the false photograph of a nonexistent bird. And I saw then in my sister not only humiliation but above all bewilderment and disillusion.

From then on Xana became a furtive, disenchanted little girl with a tendency to hide, wherever she might be. Her wings melted right then, in a matter of seconds. She wept hot tears that she brushed away. She did not want the photograph at all. She tore it up, trampled on it. Alongside the garden she poured out her pain, her immense loneliness. "No, no, those people can't be trusted," she thought to herself. So she rushed off in search of her hiding place under the tall iron bed covered with a long damask bedspread that hung all the way down. She stayed there playing in a sea of abandon, wrapped in the transparent shadows of a rainy late afternoon, until Vovó came in promising to make her some wings from the most beautiful feathers she could gather on the outskirts of the village. Vovó would not let her little girl do without wings.

⚬

A few days later new wings appeared, containing, in the words of the poet António Nobre, "threads made of light." They came with the promise never to lack the brilliance of that sublime white light from when the sky fell to earth, obscuring the horizon and filling it with brilliance, a blade stroke cutting through the entire atmosphere—just as Vovó had promised. And in order to put an end to that ill-fated event, wrapped in a pain of endless motion, Vovó prepared to tell Xana a story.

"Come here, dear. Let me tell you a story much better than the one about that little made-up birdie.

"Once upon a time there was a little girl who had no father or mother. She was poor, but always clean. Her godmother brought her up well-dressed. She was a seamstress who worked day and night. And she worked and sewed so much that one morning she was found dead, clutching a new dress for the little girl. It was the final one among ten last-minute orders. The little girl cried and cried until she filled the ocean. Then a star shot out of the sky, fell on her dress, and the girl grew up and became a woman, put on her wings, and crossed the wide ocean. She married, had children, giving them a father and mother and many siblings as well. That little girl on the other side of the choppy waters, who was now a mother, was still said to be pretty. She had gone to heaven and conquered the stars, where the angels pluck their harps."

And then Vovó finished this tale, like all of her others, always in the same way: "And that's the moral of my story."

"But where are the angels, Vovó? I don't see them," Xana asked.

"In heaven, playing their harps," our grandmother replied. "Sometimes their music wafts down to earth; some people hear it but most of them, if they hear it, don't know how to appreciate it."

"Oh, but I don't hear anything, Vovó. Even when I rise up into the clouds, all I hear is the roar of the plane tearing through the sky, cutting it into two slices. I don't see or hear angels."

"Of course not, Xana. It's still early, too early for you to see or hear them." Vovó stood up and left with that wide smile of hers that filled the whole house.

⚛

Xana grew more confused. Had Carolina not told her there were no such things as angels, no harps in heaven, and that the devil was in fact running around loose on earth looking to take up residence in anyone he could? He was always hunting for lost souls, worried that if numbers were not big enough, hell would go broke. That was the reason people looked for more and more of their friends and neighbors to send there, as many as possible, Carolina explained in triumph.

Xana sucked in her breath with difficulty and sweated out of fear. She did not in any way want to become part of those numbers. If it was true that she did not like earth's heat, then she would like hell's fires even less. There her lavish wings would disappear, melted away like a dying candle. So she would then lose the world she saw from the sky that, although uncertain, was a part of her, until Carolina and the village women stole from her the secrets of all that enchantment, of so many beautiful things from high above the clouds. She would feel them smoothing her face, the dew refreshing her brow on hot days, and her whole body dancing in leaping gestures of satiny blue. Xana was not just soaring, she was doing more than that: she was in fact walking on air, running, twirling in pirouettes, and feeling the fresh, moist sensation of damp silk. From above, she could see rising black basalt cupolas extending to the ends of the earth, and rows of houses with their roofs of bobbin lace—and below, she breathed in the mystique surrounding the bridges, arches, fresh rolling waters of the streams, reflections of bent branches under the diaphanous air of the lagoons, water rippling on windy days, and a solitary floating leaf waving farewell in a playful flutter.

Troubled, Xana compared that whole world lived under veil of night with photos in Vovó's album and saw no similarity between the two.

"Look, Vovó, the leaves on the trees are so different from those people in the pictures! What are the women hiding, Vovó? Always the same, always the same. The faces, a dead man; the bodies, a stick; and a scorched look."

"I don't know, Xana. I only know that your mother, out of everyone in our family, is very happy. She's as pretty as in her picture, and always has a golden laugh that echoes and wakens the whole world."

With a perplexed look Xana fell silent, disturbed by the possibility of that laugh, the music of a totally unknown voice. One could observe in her a certain uneasiness, a *je ne sais quoi.* She was accustomed to Vovó's smile, to her pensive deep expression, to the remoteness of all her shadows.

Come to think of it, my little sister was always turned inward on herself. She did not know how to have fun and would scarcely react to humor or other shenanigans she disliked. Xana would all of a sudden be rebellious, evenhandedly generous, unexpectedly joyous, sometimes mischievous—but only when she forgot herself. The rest of the time she was generally serious.

"Serious? So Vovó was like that, too?"

"No, Xana. Our grandmother has always been, shall we say, a sort of Mona Lisa with that enigmatic, haunting smile of hers, always serene, steady as a plumb line, or an anchor securing a married woman without a husband."

Xana turned around and looked for Vovó. She found her and asked, "What is it, Vovó? What is it that you are protecting in your smile? Your teeth?"

Her answer died in midair, with no echo, no reply.

❀

Moments later, Xana ran her hand ever so lightly over the velvet-covered album, which at that point was in the room. For some time she was held captive by all her senses, having the company of Vovó, who that afternoon was seated in a wicker easy chair knitting her stockings. Beside her sat a small basket with handles, also made of wicker, in which my grandmother stored her knitting; one magazine or another; old postcards with dual images, one on the left and the other on the right; and a stereopticon viewer that turned them into a single 3-D image. There were also photographs that arrived whenever we received letters from America.

"Hey, it's the postman, the postman—with a letter, a letter," our shouting shook the house. On such occasions we were like chickens pecking at corn kernels. The sensation felt good, and everything was warm like the down of baby chicks. The album cover was made of velvet, very warm, and in three colors: flame yellow, wine red, and chestnut brown. In the center was a cloverleaf-shaped mirror, which reflected like a photograph the face of the person gazing at it.

"Xana, come here," my grandmother called, raising her voice until she was heard.

"Coming."

"Where are you? You're always disappearing, daughter of my soul! Oh, my little silly," my grandmother said.

"Come out from under the bed. You never stop pulling that stunt of yours of hiding like someone who wants to retreat from life—but perhaps only by straddling a windowsill, half in and half out."

Vovó called my sister again and asked her to fetch the photo album. "No need to hide, Xana." And we all gathered around the album, an album that had already traveled the globe, having come from very, very far away: from Brazil to the island, from the island to America, and from the United States back to São Bento.

"You must guard it with all your might. One day when I'm no longer alive, one of you will go goodness knows where—likely America, or maybe mainland Portugal. But I would like it to stay on the island. Perhaps our little one will take care of it."

And Vovó mused to herself, "My girls, remember that it's not just an album, it's a genuine relic, an authentic chest full of balm—a trove of travels far and wide, of immeasurable memories, some buried, others on the tip of your tongue."

My little sister, restless and uneasy and not knowing how to gauge deathly silences, turned to Carolina, who was not at all so metaphysical and explained the gist of everything to her.

The answer came and fell unexpectedly.

"You know what, Xana? Vovó's like that because she has no teeth."

"But she has teeth. You're a liar, a liar!"

"No, I'm not lying. Real teeth like yours, mine, and Mamã's are for laughing; false ones like our grandmother's serve only for smiling."

Furious, and almost crying with rage, she flung herself at Carolina, stamping her foot on the ground. "Liar, liar!"

"Mana," Xana asked her sister, "isn't it true that Vovó's smile is full of tenderness, round like the sun, the moon, the stars? As sweet as sugar, as warm as blankets from America?"

Xana was right, with her air of pure innocence. Our grandmother was beautiful, elegant in manner, her face serene and shining. She was a woman of departures, a woman without fear. She crossed the oceans in times of both peace and war, walked across endless lands, many of them forgotten places in America's Far West—those lands on the other side of the Atlantic that had given her a husband and four children, only for her to see everything fall to pieces a few years later. They became islands, but never linked up into an archipelago. Generation after generation they went their own ways like meteorites streaking across the sky, my grandmother recalled in a moan at the depths of all the silences, in an incomprehensible tongue.

At those moments of direct or indirect references to America, I sensed in our grandmother signs of fatigue, slight yet so subtle and sequestered that they always left me in doubt as to whether they were real or imagined. As mysterious as the choppy waters of the sea. And my grandmother, always enigmatic, centered on her lap, her lap of wonders that was, like the Madonna's, so giving yet at the same time so withdrawn. But Carolina did not think so, becoming more daring and clever, and more grown up.

"You know," she told Xana, who understood nothing, "our grandmother ran away and left her husband alone in America. She came to the islands for her health, or so she claims. But in fact she came to São Bento because she was sick of our grandfather. He had lots of mistresses, lots of friends, and he forgot all about his family." Xana looked lost.

"Grandpa went to America when he was still very young, nine years old. He went to school and soon became a millionaire, with spinning mills and other businesses. Do you understand that, dead goat eyes? He was RICH. Do you hear me, Xana?"

"Let go of my hand, you liar. Go away! Go to hell!"

"Oh, you don't even know what it is to be rich. Rich means that no matter how many stupid things you do, you're always right. So

Vovó wasn't right to leave Grandpa, because when you're not rich you aren't entitled to anything. Get it, Xana? I know you don't understand squat about anything. But listen to what I'm saying: in the long run our grandmother was the one who was wrong," Carolina declared in triumph. "She stuck us in this bitch of a life, all split up from one another.

"Look, Xana, you don't know either Mamã or Papá, neither of us knows Grandpa, nor our cousins or uncles, and they don't know each other. What a bitch of a life, you hear? You're not old enough to understand yet. But it's what I'm telling you. A shitty life, that's what it is"— and rain fell silently on Xana's face. "And me, Xana," Carolina went on, "what do I know of you, and of our other sisters, let alone of Daniel? What do I know about Mamã and Papá, who raised me till I was six on this side of the ocean and left us together yet apart, me staying with Papá's mother and you since you were five months old with Mamã's, who treats you like a princess?

"Yes, a princess, because you, Xana, are like a daughter to her. I know that Papá's mother means nothing to you because you hardly know her. But the poor thing has dozens of other grandchildren, so she can't give me what Vovó gives you.

"And now let's see if you tell everyone what I told you, and what I heard from Daniel when he was reading our grandmother a letter—a letter that the postman just left under the door.

"Did you hear the racket she made? It sounded more like thunder, followed by a flash that shone so bright it covered the whole house in black. I myself don't understand, Xana, but I think we're nearing the end of the world. That's what Papá's mother said. Something's about to happen that will touch our family and tear us to bits."

✼

I went into the bedroom as usual and saw our dear grandmother cutting and cutting patchwork scraps, her entire face coming undone while Daniel read her the letter in a whisper. Shattered, my grandmother listened to it, and indicated that I should stay in the room. That whole deluge of words was totally incomprehensible to Vovó, all scrambled, without rhyme or reason.

The pain hurt, squeezing her, squeezing out of proportion at first, a kick to the stomach. Then her head throbbed like the galloping of a hundred horses. A handkerchief and alcohol were needed right away, pressed tight to her hot forehead before it could burst with the sound of popping balloons. There was a secret hurt hiding inside of her, seeping all through her body and into the recesses of her soul—an always-open wound, alternating between red and purple.

Our dear grandmother then planted her elbows on the edge of the bed, propping her face up in order to rest her head as it weighed more and more heavily, and remained in that position for a long time, an eternity, with a cold emptiness the color of a corpse. With difficulty Vovó gradually raised her head and looked around. Again, she let it fall limp onto the bed. "That cursed letter was the devil's handiwork," Vovó despaired.

That cursed letter seemed to oscillate between two or more meanings. "Was it or wasn't it true? Could it be untrue? Only gossip? Or just pure fantasy fabricated to occupy those who lead their lives behind closed doors?" our grandmother pondered, her mind wandering.

After a brief moment she set aside what seemed to her a temptation. She shooed it away and begged my brother Daniel never again to speak to her of the ill-fated letter, now reduced to ashes.

❀

One summer afternoon, when my grandmother set off under her parasol to go visit her closest friend, Xana once again got hold of the album stored in the bottom of the trunk, where it was buried deep under the sheets, towels, and doilies. It only saw the light of day on special occasions—like when we were sick, or relatives were visiting us, or Mamã's friends interrupted our household routine in search of news of those who had left, with an eye to seeing one more photo confirming that the people so far away in truth not only seemed healthier but had also acquired another trait, growing younger compared to those of the same age who had remained on this side of the ocean. Once many of those who on the island were regarded as poor, and others as "simpleminded," arrived in the land of miracles on the other side, they soon assumed a different demeanor, a different appearance, a different way of looking and speaking. And all that would intimidate those who stayed on this side. Hence a certain resentment, a natural envy, a jealousy. And then our visitors would comment, "So well dressed"—as their own sallow skin morphed into a clear, soft complexion, their arms and fingers dripping with jewels—ultimately insinuating that any Tom, Dick, or Harry who was not part of our family owned more and better possessions than we did.

Abundance there was measured by its weight in gold, even though a good deal of it might have been made of tin. Such was the understanding of the people who sought out not only us but also the other families with members who had emigrated.

Dona Maria, her voice slurring, stiffened and without losing her nerve, blurted out, "I don't know how, after so many years, your family still hasn't been able to accumulate some real wealth. Lots of fancy things, beautiful china and some silver, but nothing impressive." And having said that, she got up and left, with a bit of a twitch in the corner of her eye. Her genuine fur stole, reeking of money, slipped off her shoulders and fell to the floor. When she leaned over to pick it up, the pince-nez slipped off her nose and shattered to bits.

Vovó politely escorted Dona Maria to the door. She left in a fury, and her steps made the earth and everyone on it shake.

My grandmother was sick and tired of hearing so much senseless blather. Those long conversations did not interest her, much less move her. They sounded like afternoon-long litanies, rising near the island's lofty Pico da Vara and passing to the south until its dark shadow fell over the land, without my grandmother replying. Her expression, then scattered and forgotten, located somewhere else, pulled her back to reality.

She was profoundly irritated at those who came over not so much to find out news of the emigrated relatives as to gossip, and to turn her house inside out. "They ignored the obvious," my grandmother sighed. "The pain, the ugly hurt that waves carried in and out every day, every night, at every high tide, every low tide—some the color of emeralds, others gray under the island's leaden sky."

⊛

As time passed I began to understand better and better my baby sister's feelings toward my grandmother. Still a very young child, Xana at around three years old exhibited in her fragility a very special gift for perceiving that lady, our grandmother. They understood one another well in spirit, even though Xana still did not know how to express what she was feeling—but, as an older sister, it fell to me to convey what I myself thought I had found in that little head of hers—a sense of being where one is not. She viewed Vovó as different from all other women, even Tia Luísa. Thus, when Xana began grasping that difference, she would clutch Vovó close for a long, long time, so great was her fear of losing her.

My grandmother was not of this world. Her real self had evaporated years ago, so it was hard for her to readjust to an environment that had little to do with her. She was almost a stranger. And I would ask myself how my grandmother could subject herself to hurtful comments that wounded her very core, to the point of my sometimes hearing her voice tremble with indignation against that chatter devoid of noble feelings. They never inquired after her family's health, whether they were happy, or when they were returning. No, nothing of that sort. What the women who came to visit talked about was just what they saw in the photographs; what lay beyond them was of no interest. And it was the very stories behind the photographs that interested our grandmother—seeing if she could discern something that might again restore her hope for them to return.

And Vovó beseeched all the saints to reunite her family and bring them back as soon as possible. "It wouldn't take lots of money," she said. "Just enough, just enough," she prayed every day.

❀

After her visitors left, my grandmother would religiously put away our family album. And every time that happened—with Xana wide-eyed despite not knowing what was going on, although attentive to anything she did not understand, which made her even more curious—I would hear my grandmother croon a song so warm and soothing that I could only manage to understand the lyrics after several tries. Her soft voice was kind and filled the corners of the house with silences.

Her footsteps were soundless, and the words in her mouth fluid; for this reason they fell silent, sliding smoothly into an indecipherable murmur belonging to the realm of the unheard. She spoke more with her eyes always cast far off into the distance than with her vocal cords. The little she said came out in parables. It unfolded vertically, residing in the background, and belonged to another order of perception and understanding of things. Later I realized the lyrics were of her own composition, and that the tune was the same as one sung by the Romeiros, our Lenten pilgrims. "Nothing more appropriate for an eternally traveling family," I thought to myself:

> *Album, album, what can you tell me*
> *after a hundred years of collecting*
> *how many more photos do you desire*
> *to keep you satisfied?*
>
> *How your insatiable desire still horrifies me,*
> *how many more do you need . . . in order to be done?*

That tune sounded much like another that struck fear in our people, mainly in our children. It was sung only in the month of November, throughout the night and, of necessity, on the corner of the houses at the intersection of two streets. That song was called *"Lembrar das Almas"*— "Remembrance of Souls"—a ritual of long-ago traditions, of Our Fathers and Hail Marys intoned by multiple voices. First we would hear the shuffling of clog shoes along the pavement, dissolving into the darkness of night and echoing toward the ocean, bodies approaching the house's gable in a soft rumble. Then the flash of a match or lighter, the half-lit lantern, and the flickering flame would sometimes twist and almost go out, only to return to life anew. From under the covers the impression for us children, younger and older alike, was of lightning bolts illuminating the night, crashing down into mirrored reflections. Afterward, we could hear the breathing of voices seeking harmony. Then they cleared their throats and at last blended their voices. The church bell rang, and everyone raised their voices as one, singing prayers of undulating melodies like a cradle rocking young souls without any destiny. The songs came out like shooting stars streaking across the sky.

Those sounds were familiar to us, permeating the bedding and shaking us body and soul. The men stretched out the songs more and more, until they fell into the rivers and streams, in a noise of *ow-ow-ow*—just like the church bells ringing morning and evening, pealing merrily on days of christenings, and tolling mournfully on days of the dead. Their voices, like candles, would be extinguished one by one, until they faded away. And then the singers left, each of them racing off to the glowing embers of the hearth awaiting them at home.

The sounds abated furtively, thinning out, and finally trailed off into the night.

❀

During the warm afternoon on the next day, Xana surreptitiously removed the album from its hiding place and made a point of scrutinizing under the magnifying glass the cast of characters who populated it. Her tiny hands shook with a feverish anxiety, while careless language she had forgotten spilled out of her mouth. Her glazed eyes noticed something she did not recognize—perhaps spotting her grandmother's round face in the wedding portrait, perhaps the secret she had buried half in the corner of her heart, and the other half in a graft of the hardy rosebush beside the kitchen patio of the mansion where Vovó had once lived in New Bedford. And it was amid the haze of frayed thoughts and unknown people that Xana became upset by a particular photo, mysterious in its color, somewhat smoky and eaten away by mold, but at the same time shining in some dead eyes that stood out from the rest of the figure. Man or woman? It was hard to say. As for the clothing, from what little was visible it appeared to be something indefinable, without time or style, something bewildering in the family album. And while Xana was trying to unveil that creature's face, a warm sweet hand brushed against her hair, resting tremulously, lightly, lightly, on her shoulder. And her question could not wait.

"Who's that, Vovó?"

"No one!"

A lopsided smile, enigmatic as the photo was strange, spread across her face—Xana looked astonished, with an uncertain expression, her head buzzing. And with an uncontrolled impulse she escaped amid the riot of colors and aroma of the trees in the yard and burrowed herself into the hedgerow.

Later, when she tired of her hiding place, she carried back with her the scent of flowers.

❀

Pico da Vara loomed majestic that day, right in front of Vovó's house, clad all in deep mazarine blue. It resembled a father protecting his daughter. Its grandeur and magnitude soothed Xana. With the view of the mountain in her heart, my sister played alone until she wore herself out.

Afterward, she ran off, anxiously looking for Carolina. She had to tell her what was going on inside her head, and when Xana failed to find her, only her old refuge was left: she retreated to her lair, shut out the world and, once hidden under the bed, again took possession of the album, for something told her that secrets lay in those photos—perhaps restless eyes whispering the most ancient memories of other lands and peoples. But not only that. Besides everything that could not be glimpsed in those photos, the album could be regarded more as an omen than a gift—and while Xana continued to scrutinize it further from all different angles with the magnifying glass in order to see if she could spot something that might reveal to her the true image, the reality was one of inexorable surprise. What at first glance she had assumed, based on clothing, to be a person, although indistinct, in fact more resembled a face that was in no way part of the human kingdom, belonging at best to that of animals, or something in between, perhaps.

My sister was now left with her tongue hanging out, drooling unawares. She felt her heart pound, then begin to race. She did not know quite what to do. She searched again for her sister, who was raving in delirium with souls from the other world, with witches and other mysteries. But afterward she kept her secret all to herself. She did not want to tell crazy Carolina what she had found.

Xana had discovered that in the purity of my grandmother's gesture the previous afternoon, when the old woman had brushed ever so lightly against her shoulder, something had irritated Xana in such a way that, although sweet, was mixed with an unusual pain tearing a bit at her skin, leaving a slight blood blister—enough for Xana to have seen in Vovó's gaze a smile fade from her face. It was an annoying lesion, accompanied by a trembling of her lips in a slight flicker.

But that crying and crying? Only once, when Vovó fell and broke her nose. She tripped with a jug in her hands, and it shattered to smithereens. One by one she gathered up the shards covered with water that had spilled from the vessel, with a suffering expression on her face like the long tidal flats on windless days. In her gray eyes, huge tears began welling up. And Xana broke into a blood-curdling scream, raging against the ground and against the loss. She could not abide such an insult, such humiliation to her grandmother.

"Vovó can't fall, no! Vovó can't suffer!" Xana repeated, her eyes searing with pain.

❀

With Vovó's every tear, the ground shook beneath Xana's feet. It was cracking open, and the heat emanating from it burned her ankles, rose to her belly, and like a volcano came out in tongues of fire mixed with frogs. She felt her head bursting, and fainted.

Minutes later, having emerged from a welter of confusion, she returned to her old self and, in her initial effort to grasp what was going on, felt another sorrow return to her mind identical to the one caused by her brother's departure.

So for Xana there had been two types of crying: one that would come abruptly from within, sometimes in sobs; and another in a wheeze laden with bitterness, her face and body contracted. But now there was a third kind of weeping, one that as soon as it erupts and begins to leap about uncontrollably, like the still waters of the fountain, does not swirl about but falls silent, makes no noise but pours onto the chest, scalding. It generally results from a moment of grace, as if something inside us were crying.

In the first case the tears are bitter and salty, in the second case hot. It is perhaps excessive, a torrent that no one knows whether it comes from the soul, the river of life, or unknown memories.

Our little girl's face was tortured, damp like flowers in the morning dew. Her eyes were lost, disenchanted, not sobbing, in an eternal hope suspended in a deep nameless hurt, at last exhausted by a slow fatigue that transported her to a ballast of forgotten memories. And indeed the plane was coming—the plane that flew in circles playing hide-and-seek, the plane that would not touch down, the plane that would not let Mamã and Papá off.

❀

After that day of suffering, when pain transformed itself into a "person," nighttime brought cold harsh north winds. Hail fell on the roofs and filled the gutters. This was right at the time of the *matança*, our ritual pre-Christmas hog killing in harvest season.

Carolina really enjoyed stories—ones about the evil eye, witches, women with cloven goat's hooves—but my grandmother lacked patience. To occupy her, Vovó gave her old magazines, and sat playing cards with her. However, her granddaughter soon grew bored, so she would go out looking for her friends. Carolina would go off sad and dispirited, because her grandmother only told her things of no interest to her.

My grandmother was alone, feeling helpless. She sat in her bedroom rocking chair, breathing to the tick-tock rhythm of the wall clock.

She knitted her stockings and thought, "I don't know how I can manage Carolina. I don't know how to reach that girl."

Vovó sighed, "God help me!"

Carolina was a child of the streets, and that was what worried Vovó most. Carolina preferred her father's mother—the one who cured pigs of their evil eye; who filled the house with incense, invoking the saints and blessing every corner of the house; who made teas and other remedies to relieve the poor of their suffering; who would say a blessing over the occult Great Book of Saint Cyprian and announce the fates of all who consulted her.

Carolina thrilled at those incense-scented prayers, which seemed never-ending. She disliked school and did not care to study. But in these other matters she was an astute observer who retained everything. When playing house, her preference was to exercise such talents. She would go up to her piglet and sprinkle him with water, saying and doing what she had observed Papá's mother doing.

"St. Gregory of Montemor, deliver my piggie from all evil, all envy, all evil spells. Begone, evil spirits, beyond the hills, where you'll stay chained up, where you'll see neither sun nor moon."

Carolina would sprinkle her piglet again and continue, "St. Cyprian, help me combat all the evil that exists here in this sty, let it all run down to the deep dark sea, where hogs can't even grunt or snore, nor cattle low, cocks crow nor donkeys bray." And she never stopped until she got bored with the game.

Papá's mother was her great friend. Countless times the old lady filled a small altar in her bedroom with candles; at home she was more discreet. The services she rendered for townspeople normally took place in fields, in livestock pens, on street corners, and at thoroughfare intersections.

That day our grandmother knelt down in her bedroom and ordered Carolina, "Let us pray for the souls of the departed, for the spirits that roam the earth, for others lost on the fringes of the sea, without rest for centuries on end."

So far so good, but when Carolina realized the weight of forever and ever, never-ever, of the tick-tock of the clock, she broke into a cold sweat. She felt and knew she was in danger. Who would come save her if her grandmother did not even notice her? Her grandmother was praying, praying, always praying, and her candles flickered in the cold. Carolina wanted to go out into the street, already desperate from having been cooped up indoors for so long, wanting to escape from that house, and wishing she could die rather than be stuck there trembling in the cold. The clock struck the hour and never seemed to stop: Forever and ever, never-ever; forever and ever, never-ever.

Carolina had no idea of how to escape her grandmother. She was sure that time would never again release her, never again let her leave that cold place reeking of mildew. She was sure she would sooner or later be swallowed up. And how sad everything would be. A shiver descended over her, leaving her with a chill. It was the devil, come looking for her in order to heat her up in the furnaces of hell. It was then that a whole world of itching overtook her body. She scratched here, scratched there. A restlessness, a despair, and the terror of being caught in the devil's clutches. Carolina wriggled and writhed, moaning in pain—her wits were tangled and she did not know how to undo them. Sweat poured off her like waterfalls on winter days. And she thought of the sun while in that blackness, without her grandmother to open the window shutters even a crack. Next came stomach pains, cramps, and diarrhea. She stifled her screams and slipped away, taking every precaution so her grandmother would not see her leaving. All scrunched down, she made it out the door, scurrying to our other grandmother's house.

⊛

At Vovó's house, on nights when gales blew through the cracks in the windows and doors, we would play cards and entertain ourselves by looking through the magazines stored atop the china cabinet—a luxury at that time. There were magazines from England and the United States, already very old, of World War I vintage.

Uncle Joe was sweet as honey. From time to time he would show up all of a sudden, leaving America behind and walking through Vovó's door without warning. He would arrive from afar and bring the latest news, talk with his mother and open up the suitcases he brought on his trip. He would bring candy, gum, balloons of every hue, and a blue ball with the island's white clouds. Hair clips shaped like little boots or scissors, just imagine! It was all a fantasy that left us in total delirium, albeit to the detriment of Vovó and Tia Luísa, by then in their seventies and eighties, respectively. All that euphoria left their heads spinning, unable to bear so much fuss, so much joy, so much jumping around and elation. And the shouting continued, shattering like a mirrored reflection: there were dolls made of porcelain or of rubber, and other tiny ones of celluloid, and then a dollhouse equipped with furniture and everything else—a fascination for us all. Sometimes we played nicely, other times we got into huge fights. And our grandmother would step in, patiently calming the waters.

Just as suddenly, Uncle Joe—always dressed in straw tones, from his hat down to the hem of his trousers, and in warm weather even his shoes—would vanish. We called him our uncle-in-passing, quick as a breeze, like in fairy tales. Almost as soon as he had arrived, he was off again. For him, several days or a few weeks were enough, and then he was recharged for his next march through life. His absence, however, hovered in the air of the house, in the bamboo in the yard, on the cliff while hunting wild pigeons, on sea rocks when catching octopus, limpets or crabs, along with fish like *realengos,* bright multicolored *rainhas* and white sea bream caught on a line, to the delight of my grandmother and us all.

His absence cast us adrift in a sea of shipwrecks.

✵

"Come quick, girls. I'm going to tell you a story. This time it's a true story. Sit here beside me.

"You know what, my dears? In America," Vovó recounted, in a tone of voice that scraped just like a millstone grinding wheel against wheel, "people called princes, kings and queens have vanished; they have left for another world. In America, when I lived there, everyone addressed each other familiarly as *tu*—and here in Portugal, since the start of the Republic, we no longer have counts or dukes, either."

"No one's better than anybody else," Vovó told us. And a bored Tia Luísa interrupted and said, "As far I'm concerned, I don't know anyone who, no matter how distinguished they may be, doesn't wipe their ass just like everyone else."

My grandmother shuddered. She did not like her sister using crude expressions in front of the little girls. Tia Luísa apologized and headed to her room. It was time to go to bed.

"Now, on our island," my grandmother resumed telling her story, "in our villages, the old titles were being replaced by other more interesting stories, like those of mermaids, whales, shipwrecks, and many other tales that came from distant lands like Brazil, from which no one ever returned; of adventurers gone to the land of Tio Sam seeking gold—some who stayed and, only on the rarest occasions, others who returned to the island claiming fortunes and victories, sometimes true, other times full of fantasy; some who were lost forever without having ever sent word to their family; others who called for their relatives after a brief time; and still others postponing and postponing their return to the island, never coming back."

Xana and Carolina did not understand what Vovó had just told us, but we sat there for hours on end, our eyes riveted on the china cabinet, waiting for more.

With Vovó and Tia Luísa at our side we learned that life was a divine gift, a sharing, a quest—as the old ladies reminded us every day.

❀

At the doorway cooled by the long shadow of the roof, our grandmother imparted in the fullness of time all her wisdom and convinced us that above all else there was beauty in every hour of the day, every hour of the mild or cold nights—preferably cold ones, when bodies would nestle together in order to warm lost souls.

"Life was fascinating in its own right—always, always different in summer or winter, fall or spring," Vovó said hesitantly. "It was sublime in the singing waters of the streams, in the hiding places of the endless hills and canyons." She was also the one who taught us to listen to the mysteries hidden in the earth's bowels, in the oceans' depths, and in a sky that in Nordeste was far nearer to us than the sea down below at the foot of the steep cliff.

Anything that struck fear in us, if Vovó found out she soon dispelled it discreetly, reminding us that the spirit that illuminates people is the same one that abides in all things, in all persons—in the camellia bush in the yard, the chrysanthemums in the garden, the ice-cold foot of a child, or the purplish color of a poor woman.

We were closely connected to Vovó's secrets. And she always accompanied us on red-hot summer afternoons when all the villagers would journey from town to an orchard that seemed as far from our houses as New Bedford is from Boston—words that few uttered in the village and that were familiar to us, although we did not understand them well. They sounded good to the ear, redolent of garments from America.

The winding dirt path extended far out of view. It seemed, though, that the world ended there, that to set foot on that soil was to breach forbidden territory. Vovó marveled at, and was satisfied by, the vastness of those spaces, chasing moons out of the shadows. She would extend her gaze for the longest time, as we listened serenely to the fresh burbling of the waters in the stream that sliced between imposing cliffs; and afterward, the sweet aromatic drying herbs that were laid out under a hot humid sun were soon moistened with a drizzle that awakened them—and again dried them with the least little breath of wind, with the return of one last ray of sunshine beating down, flooding Vovó's face with moonlight.

We were scared of the shadows when they danced at the whim of the breezes within the dense forest. The interplay between light and dark created a dynamic of objects that went in and out—perhaps someone who moved about there on the prowl, who knew? And then there was our fear.

"Do you think that bogeymen go around stealing children to kill?"

And my grandmother would say nothing. Whenever we were afraid we looked at her face, and saw Vovó smiling and confident. Then we would choke back our repressed fear with a sob.

Frantic trilling at that hour seemed to rend the firmament. The racket made the whole earth tremble, and its echo resounded unto madness.

My grandmother remained silent. And Xana continued dreaming in her own way, until Vovó gave the signal to leave.

"No, Vovó. Let me look. Wow, there are so many old ladies with shawls on their heads!"

"They're not old ladies, Xana, they're birds perched on electrical wires."

"Let's go, Vovó. I'm afraid. It's all so dark."

"No, wait, my girl, be patient. Let me stay here a bit longer, till the sun nearly touches the water."

"Oh, Vovó, I'm so afraid. You're a very old lady, so you can't protect me. If bogeymen catch me, they'll roast me in the oven."

"That won't happen, Xana. Those are things they say to scare children like you."

"Come on, let's go, Vovó. Now look at the sun, it's already dropped into the sea."

"Let it set, because it will return tomorrow. It always returns every day, Xana."

"And now, Vovó, what's going to happen?"

"Nothing, Xana."

The sun set, but left us enough light to get home.

All of a sudden Vovó said, "Oh my God, your hand is so cold, Xana, and here you're walking beside me without saying anything to me. You have no reason to be afraid anymore, I'm right here with you, but forgive me if I forgot your fears, my little silly."

❁

Within minutes, night was descending upon the earth to extinguish the day. The *trindades* chimed at church. Our grandmother and Xana picked up the pace. Some men and women, to avoid being caught off guard by the night air, ran along a path that crossed three others—a magical space where anything could happen, although my grandmother did not believe in this. It was said that during the night, lost souls and beautiful ladies headed there dressed in costumes of other eras, even from as long ago as the time of ancient Egypt, in luxurious shades of the golden sun on a clear day, a purple the color of wine, and a blue never before seen that was so brilliant it could cast a spell. When men let their gaze slip down through their sumptuous robes, they felt a chill. Their feet were cloven like goats' hooves. They ran and ran, and pounded their soles so hard it startled the night.

The next day, those who had gone there to test their manhood stifled their voices, and choked back the fright they had felt.

❋

When we neared the house Xana broke into a run, and Vovó noticed that her dress was damp. She had not sat in any water, nor had rain fallen for many days. Then it dawned on Vovó. So she turned quickly to me and moved in close, terrified. "Now, my dear Isabel, don't you know what happened?"

"What was it, Vovó? Why are you so troubled?"

"Our little girl wet herself out of fright."

Once she calmed down Vovó told me what had happened with Xana in the orchard, and she swore never to forgive herself for being so selfish. Under a mantle of silent suffering, she forgot about her little girl.

❋

From time to time a murmur would spread through the village. My grandmother never wasted time on rumors or superstitions, nor did she even let herself comment on them whenever neighbors awoke on blue or gray mornings and came out gossiping, to turn the town upside down in a few minutes. After that, no one got along. Vovó maintained her silence, as usual. She turned her back and tried to find time to cultivate her own garden, now with great difficulty, sometimes falling. She would talk to her flowers, get angry with the weakest ones and exult in her asters, pansies, fuchsias, and her huge Van Gogh sunflowers the color of liquid autumn sun, like those on one of the old American calendars that hung in her kitchen for many years. Some of the other calendars showed beautiful suggestive young women on occasion displaying cool innocence, other times with smoldering looks on their faces. She had expired catalogs; they remained unchanged for a lifetime, just like the suspended time of those long, monotonous, endless eras.

❋

Off in the distance, under the enchantment of a rosy day's end, the church tower bell tolled—then, illuminated by a dense yellow-violet sunset, a fireball announcing a glorious tomorrow—or so she had been taught by her neighbor Altina Peixoto, one of the last preservers of traditional lore. She had explained, with those tiny sunken eyes of hers, how to read weather signs.

In a sibylline voice, Altina approached Xana and prophesied, "Look at the colors of the sunset, my girl. Whenever you see the sun sinking into the ocean, notice whether it lies in the shelter of a clear ring like the edge of a blade, or like a fan in an opaque sky. In the first case, a day of blazing sun is guaranteed; in the second, it's bad weather for certain, regardless of what the moon or the screeching of the *cagarras* may decree. Don't forget, my little girls."

❁

Weeks later, our good neighbor lay down forever, exposed to the sun's rays for one last sunset that she had, throughout her lifetime, regarded with consistency and fascination, and with the certainty of each day. Misty faces accompanied her, hunched over by the silence of death. The old woman's corpse took up the entire width of the street—she in the center, men and women flanking her. To the rear stood her dark, cold house. No more sunsets in our good neighbor's sight; instead, darkness even blacker than the tar on our new road. She would not get to see it, so she could not miss it. She was accustomed to packed dirt roads; wheeled rides were only in oxcarts. As for the city, she did not even know what one was.

The sun was fading on the cloudless horizon. A cricket chirped in the distance. Closer by, a bird swooped. And its presence was immense, because the secret contained in the sound of its tail was immense.

CHAPTER 2

Mother-of-pearl was the color of that autumn morning. I remember it as if it were today.

It was November. I am backtracking a few years to the moment when my sister was born under the fateful sign of the plane crash on Pico da Vara, which days earlier had intruded upon the serenity of the hamlets around here just as the trees were dropping their last leaves.

It was past three in the afternoon when everything turned overcast. Unfortunately, the sun had left the sky. In its place were earth tone clouds mixed with others of silver-gray—some broken ones the color of white buttercups, others as black as soot. It felt dismal, just like what we experience when caught by twenty-foot swells while plying between islands in small boats. Thunder clapped, and its endless echo resounded beyond the stream near my parents' house. Fiery lightning bolts came crashing down on all sides. One struck right in our backyard. Its brilliant downward flash charred the fig tree. In the pitch dark, ominous black birds passed overhead and a hawk's cries drowned out the pandemonium of the universe. The wind flew round and round in circles, insistently hovering over our house. It seemed to be preparing to devour our entire family.

The wind redoubled its strength. It kept shifting directions as night fell. The gates to the backyard, henhouse, and pigsty were all blown straight up into the sky by the gale. It seemed nothing remained on the ground, or else that the ground was up in the air, because more things could be seen taking off than landing. The rain intensified and intermittent hail fell. The drovers, bug-eyed with fatigue from battling wind, rain, and hail, rounded up the few oxen they owned in order to herd them home. And as the dim light faded, São Bento's streets stood deserted. The moon, although full, did not show its face. Then all of a sudden in the midst of dinner, a cavernous but imperceptible rumble rose to the clouds and filled the entire earth. Howls and bleating, grunts and incessant braying mingled with the sounds from the shifting winds. Without realizing what was happening, we all sensed at the same time that something was about to occur. At that precise moment when we all opened our mouths to warn everyone, our tongues shriveled up and terror overtook us. A hot, horrifying roar then erupted from the earth, rising to the skies and raining down upon us. Our house shook and its fragile walls wheezed like bagpipes. We suffered fear in absolute silence, and were afraid even to speak, lest it make matters worse. Then just when we thought we were out of danger, the jolting returned and the walls buckled, and part of our house's north-facing gable collapsed like a house of cards.

The earthquake's fury demolished a room in our house. It also precluded the possibility of adding on to it sometime around New Year's, as my parents had hoped.

❀

It was amid all this confusion—brought on by grief and despair, loss and bitterness—that another noise arose that was unidentifiable at first. At the very instant when the whole earth was shaking, we heard this other voice thrown into the mix, all shaken up in an unstoppable tumult. Its echo rent the air and rose up into everyone's bodies. Our heads were hardest hit. It sounded like canvas windmill sails vibrating against each other, driving us to the very brink of madness. Later, still dazed, it dawned on us that it was Mamã's voice shaking. The rain was also shaking in the garden, where one by one our hens were dying, drowned in a manure slurry. Relentless thick ropes of water shook our roof, seeping into the attic and pouring down the walls. Shaking too was that infinite boldness of Papá, who did not trust in anything or know where to begin. On one hand, he sought to subdue the panicked animals, while on the other, he wanted to come in to help Mamã, who was moaning and groaning out of her mind.

Hours later we realized Mamã was worsening. Syphilis and acute anemia would confine her to bed for a lengthy period, requiring every precaution because, besides her own life, another was gestating in her womb. Late in life, indeed; unexpected, to be sure. But the truth is that neither my father nor mother wanted to lose the being they had conceived. Mamã was entering her seventh month of pregnancy. The risk to her own life and that of the new being growing inside her was, according to the doctor, high. Every precaution was necessary, but her medications had their price, an unaffordable cost at a time when cash was simply scarce, even though our home provided well for day-to-day living.

And after all that effort to save mother and daughter, with contractual loans supplemented by the sale of two calves, just thinking that everything could from one moment to the next end in the worst way was too heavy a burden to bear.

⸙

At each of Mamã's screams we all recoiled. Without warning, a volcanic wave surged in my father's brain. He could not afford to lose everything. He dashed outside with a lantern in search of surviving animals caught in the rubble of the house's wall and the stones that enclosed the pigsties. The livestock were all disoriented, trampling over each other without knowing where they were going. Among our chickens, not one remained. But the horse, two hogs, three calves, and two kids escaped that unforgettable night's fury. They were brought in one by one, amid curses and epithets, to the upper courtyard under the opposite gable, where they would be better shielded from the wind during the torrential downpour with no letup in sight.

After much effort and exhaustion, Papá felt like a stray dog. With no great prospects for a better life, he leaned along the house's south gable and poured out all his bitterness in tears. He emitted a horrendous shout to the skies, curled up into a fetal position, and saw his life circling the drain all around him. He put his hands to his head and tugged at what little hair he had left. He solemnly tiptoed into the house, his face contorted, and headed to Mamã's room, where she continued emitting ghastly moans punctuated from time to time by excruciating howls.

⸙

Nighttime was already several hours old. Soon the clock would strike twelve, and no one wanted to sleep except Carolina, who was lying with our elderly aunt in one of the dry sections of the attic. All of us, consciously or otherwise, wanted to take care of our own bodies, lest they wind up under the house's rubble in the blink of an eye. We snuggled up against one another in the same bed with Daniel. None of us dared open our mouths to ask what was happening in that next room, just below the dry spot where Carolina was sleeping, that to us seemed so distant, even forbidden.

Then we heard something that startled us. Besides all the racket outside, there was someone opening the gate. And it was not the wind, because if it were, the gate would have continued slapping. Someone had closed it. And so we realized it could only be human, because soon afterward we heard the back door of our house, the servants' entrance, creak and then be closed with care.

Who would have been coming at that hour, and in these circumstances?

We could not imagine. Surprised, and as if moved by one and the same emotion, we looked at each other dumbfounded, but nobody spoke until Daniel decided to break the silence.

"Mamã's getting worse. Didn't you hear? Last night Senhor Padre was advising some of the villagers he met along the road during his customary rounds to his parishioners that mother and child were on the brink of death. And he warned, 'If by morning church bells are tolling, you'll know they're for the deaths of both mother and child.'"

A vast chasm opened between each of us. An infinite desert cast us far away, our frightened eyes anticipating the fear of that cold, dark loneliness.

A cry suddenly arose among us in unison, then descended to the pits of our bellies and drowned out all the exterior noises. Papá raced in like a wild man. In a short time his face wrinkled deeper than the furrows gouged by his plow. He was very nervous, so he paced back and forth, first in one direction and then the other, walking around in circles without comprehending a thing. We continued to shriek, and amid our screaming a louder shout resonated, shaking the entire house. We thought it was another earthquake. Then a deathly silence fell.

And all of a sudden we heard the loud noise of a crying that was nothing like ours.

It was a cry of *iéé, iéé,* the cry of a child filling the house with light.

We did not understand. We did not want to believe what was happening. And as we were pondering vacantly over what it could be, the clock struck twelve.

"It's a girl!" Papá said, with the look of rain and sun on his face.

"It's a girl, a midnight daughter."

"We want to see her, Papá," as we leapt out of bed.

"No no, not yet, my children," Papá decreed, and he said nothing further.

❁

We were crazed with eagerness to see the little girl, while Daniel displayed deep concern on his ever-sweet face. With his sensitive attentiveness to everything happening at home and in our family, he saw in this birth a coincidence that terrified him. He approached us all and confided, "Don't you remember it was on the same date and at the same hour that Tia Emília died last year?"

"How do you explain the birth of our baby girl occurring so unexpectedly far ahead of time? And why today, and why now, at midnight? Could the roar of that ill-fated plane have contributed to hastening our little girl's birth?"

Daniel persisted with curiosity, while we females quizzed one another—he, the only boy, full of shame; we girls, pretending not to understand a thing. Except for Carolina, we knew a bit about how children were born and how long they spent in their mother's womb; nine months, so far as we knew. What we knew nothing about was the possibility of babies being able to enter the world prematurely. Hence our terror and amazement, and soon thereafter our curiosity to see, to touch, to feel the body of that little girl who henceforth would be our baby sister—"the apple of our eye," as children were popularly characterized when maternal advanced age made the prospect of pregnancy remote.

❁

The constant clamor of the opening and closing of doors, to which we were unaccustomed, led us to believe there were complications. Mamā was fading away with what little blood she had left; her moaning was by now almost inaudible, her whole body sore as though torn by tractor wheels or butchered like whales. The impression we had was of a belly that had been distended down to her feet. Piercing sounds returned and from time to time became indistinguishable from those of the animals. Her room remained shut, as though sealed.

This was not the most auspicious moment to visit Mamā. Curiosity was gnawing at us all, but the door would not be opened.

Papá, by then calmer although with his face downcast, begged us for the love of God to go to sleep.

He snuffed out the oil lamp and went into the bedroom. Once the light was extinguished we realized that outside there was only silence, an oppressive silence that sent us off to the realm of dreams that almost always turned into nightmares. Could it be an ambush? Something worse, prepared to take with it whatever remained? The terror that fell upon us in the dark of night was immense. We prayed in whispers, sobbing, begging the angels and archangels to save Mamā and not take her away with them.

We huddled close to one another and began drifting off, slipping into the land of slumber where dream worlds would take over our lately shaken, wounded, orphaned hearts, sealed in a meaningless vacuum.

❀

The morning dawned sunny, like a negative image of the night before. But those looking toward the other half of the island noticed an unstable atmosphere more opaque than clear, and they were uncertain which way to turn. For the time being there was neither wind nor rain, nor quaking earth. The weather calmed down. It came to protect us, to settle in as night surrendered to day, leaving us with a dark infinite hole clearly audible to us, especially after having been exposed to the crazy racket of the night before. It seemed as though we were deaf to any noise on the entire face of the earth.

Filtered light streamed down onto the landscape, spilling between the leafless branches of the plane trees—and at the onset of cold weather the intricate ribs displayed their laciness as a perfect cutout in vivid relief against the light from the heavens. All this relieved people's faces, yet at the same time disquieted them. No one said anything, and the sensation that lingered was reduced to surprise and suspicion. The truth was that both up on Pico da Vara and down by the sea the results of the previous night's destruction were vividly present. The sea was all foamy—not the customary shade of American snowy-white foam that appeared on the island, but the color of mud, the sulfurous yellow shade found in caverns.

The sea was terrifying that day. Anyone who saw it once did not look again. A dense fog hung low over the water, spreading a light so eerie it scared even the bravest people. It was not like the ocean at São Bento. Goodness only knows who or what must have put another sea there that in no way resembled our usual one.

"How would it look without its white foam, an incandescent white full of silvery stars?" they asked one another. Some were annoyed, others embarrassed. They went home and closed their shutters, because anyone who looked out the window onto the murky waters, full of a light never before seen, stood there for a time seeing nothing, like when they observed a solar eclipse. Except in this case the ocean of our village's everyday life had been eclipsed; in its place reigned a monster with long clay-colored whiskers.

One could say that the Atlantic had been turned into land, all at the expense of whoever stole what little ground our island possessed—perhaps the biggest pirate ever, when compared to the corsairs and other bandits who assaulted our archipelago innumerable times. The ocean lapped the entire shoreline of our island, and in the lower-lying villages along the south coast its fury carried away houses, people, and animals.

And if no one believed our village had also been subjected to that night's storms, all they had to do was lift their eyes toward Pico da Vara in order to confirm that nature's awesome violence had far surpassed anything imaginable. The mighty peak was all but unrecognizable, its nobility wounded, utterly disemboweled, carved away, stripped of its forest, which was sliding down through existing canyons and opening up so many more, blocking rivers and streams by forming dams that with their colossal volume were dragging everything down to the sea. As for the earthquake, the damage it caused was not so bad, at least not in our village. All the same, many homes were cracked open, while others had their mouths agape, as was the case with ours. It was necessary and urgent to rebuild the lost room, our parents decided.

❀

After a few days things started falling back into place. Clothing was taken outdoors to dry in the sun, and all the windows were opened in order to let the warmth of early November's waning sun into the house.

The day had just dawned radiant and sunny, and there was not a cloud in the sky to discourage anyone at all. On Saturday in every season of the year, women made their way to the street without fail.

To clean house, back in those days before indoor plumbing, was to cleanse one's soul. Jug after jug of water had to be hauled, and then the women would wash the floor, which in the majority of homes were made of packed earth. Wooden floors, when they existed, were scrubbed with a stiff brush that left them squeaky clean, like new. And, amid all this bustle, children were squirting water and running in and out while their mothers, broom in hand, would "knock heads" until they stopped bothering those who were working. Glass windowpanes were difficult to wash. When one went heavy on the soap it was the worst chore of all, leaving a dull finish, and there was no other option but to wash them again. In order not to have to repeat the task, prudence was required in the expenditure of energy and the strength of one's hands. Women flung basin after basin of water against the windows until they shone like crystal. And even that did not satisfy them. It was still necessary to scrub the walls and perfume the house with rosemary and cryptomeria branches.

Barns, stables, and chicken coops were also cleaned to the same high standard. Then at the end of the afternoon came the cleaning of the trails, cart paths between the seedlings and flowers in the yard, and, last, the street. It was swept and swept until the ground was left smooth, practically glassy. And the pack of youngsters flew around screeching like hawks, playing tag or hopscotch, racing around among the women, running off again to hide—and the women's brooms would land on their shoulders, sometimes on their heads, other times on their legs. Carolina grew frenetic with her zigzag maneuvers, emitting nervous cries for fear of being caught. Once her heart calmed down, she would go back to playing hide-and-seek, laughing and squealing like crazy. Vovó smiled. Tia Luísa feigned anger.

"What kind of hour is this for you to be coming home? You're acting more like a baby goat, girl." Tia Luísa continued, "Now go wash your feet. It's time to eat, then head for bed."

The church bells chimed *clang-clang-clang-clang . . .*

At the ringing of *trindades,* Saturday's "fairies" ran home. Not a one remained on the street. The night air was dangerous. And they all knew it.

⁂

The entire gable on our house threatened to collapse. It was urgent to repair it.

A thousand winds would come, another thousand rains would fall, and nailing boards here and there was not going to solve the problem. Papá, lost in his thoughts, turned to Mamã.

"Our current life is not going at all well. We have to ask your mother for a small loan in order to buy building materials. We must shore up the gable soon, before it falls in on us. The worst part is that this all seems like witchcraft to me."

"No, no!" Mamã replied. "Don't even think about that. Negative thoughts are of no use; they must be tossed far away, into a bottomless pit.

"Forget it," Mamã insisted. "If things keep going on like this—if I can't get over this state of acute anemia that leaves me half-dead, and if the baby continues to need such expensive medications in order to survive—I'll just need to leave, to have a talk with my mother and tell her I'm heading to America, land of my birth, in order to earn money to rebuild our lives on the island."

Papá said nothing. He turned pale; he was a feckless man. And Mamã continued, "Don't eat yourself up, I'll get you a *Carta de Chamada,* an immigration visa, in no time flat, and after two or three years' work, we'll be back home with our children and have enough money to recoup our loss. Meantime, don't tell anyone a thing. Perhaps life will smile upon us," Mamã said with a trace of hope.

"No!" Papá replied. "What we have to do is sell some of our land."

"No, never," my mother pleaded.

"I see no other way out then, except America. You're the only one who can save us all," Papá countered, demoralized and swallowing hard. A dispirited expression was visible on his face.

❀

The morning following that end-of-the-world night, as a lost rooster crowed in the vicinity of our backyard, we were startled awake by strange voices. It was unusual for our house to be full of people so soon after daybreak, let alone in an agitated mad clamor. It was normal for that many women to gather only when someone was dying.

So while we were trying to understand what was going on, we heard Mamá's voice calling from the back of the bedroom. We wanted to go in, but there were so many people that Daniel realized the time was not right.

"Let's wait till all these people go away. We have to be alone with Mamá and the baby."

But friends and neighbors, gnawed by curiosity, thronged to see that little girl they were calling a midnight daughter. "A survivor," they commented, "weighing just a few ounces, only the size of a doll, but one no doubt with enough determination and daring to breach the darkness, and to pull back the curtain ahead of time on the world that awaited her." The women came out of the room one by one in a muffled, almost secret murmur.

We saw some of the women wrinkle their noses. The spriteliest one offered, "Oh, do you still think this child will survive? Do you think so? And as for the mother—alas!—only by some miracle!"

❀

Morning was already well underway when the last woman left. Then like birds escaping in flight from an open cage, we ran into the bedroom, and the surprise almost knocked us to the ground in a mixture of disgust and delight, doubt and even puzzlement.

"Oh, she looks like a mouse," Carolina said out loud—and then to herself, "What an ugly little thing!" Mamá was purple, purple as her sheet and quilt. And the crucifix faced her with its crown of thorns shedding blood, blood of the sort that our mother scarcely had left. Carolina recoiled, and instead of approaching began retreating, retreating, looking in any other direction than at the bed. She tripped over a chair and flinched in fright. She just wanted to disappear.

When Carolina would go no closer, we tried another feint to disguise a situation that was becoming a burden to us all. So we passed our tiny girl from hand to hand, nervous fingers touching her with gentle caresses, to serve as our seal proclaiming her the family princess. Our mother, although debilitated, still remained alert, very alert to our reactions. She said nothing. In her honey-colored eyes we could see a star shining with acceptance and comprehension. Mamã was certain that the child, despite her weak little body, would grow up to become strong—such a powerful force or mystery that Mamã recognized it in her at birth, compared to her other daughters, and even to Daniel.

We were leaving the room in order to let mother and child rest when we suddenly realized that Carolina was missing. She was not there.

Her absence spoke volumes.

The neighbor ladies said afterward that she had left the house at a run. We later came to find out that she had spread the news throughout the whole community so that, when she returned home, her face was distorted and swollen from crying so much. The baby was alive, and Carolina had been afraid to approach her. She entered the room without even looking at the cradle. She snuggled up next to Mamã and fell asleep with her.

The afternoon was still far from turning into night.

When Carolina awoke she saw that Mamã and the baby were still asleep, so she got up with great care in order not to disturb them. She tiptoed to the door so as to avoid making any noise, slipped away, and climbed up into the attic. She did not want to see anyone, much less hear the squeaks of that "mouse," ugly as the devil—and the women were saying, "What a beautiful girl, she looks like a doll, that little dear, with such a round little face."

The days passed slowly and were more or less calm.

Christmas was approaching. It was still a few weeks away, and Mamã remained weak, her face pale, her body stooped. Still, there was a slight air of festivity throughout the whole house. Despite her condition our mother began reclaiming the reins over household chores. She was responsible for the laborers. First thing in the morning she assigned field chores to the men and household tasks to the women. The latter already knew the routine: Luciana would go to the kitchen—while Felisberta, among other duties, took a midafternoon picnic in a heavy hamper that she balanced on her head, to carry to the men working the land. Every Friday our eldest maid, Senhora Ascensão, always came to fire up the wood-burning oven, knead and bake the wheat and cornmeal bread doughs, along with baking beans, sweet potatoes, pumpkin, winter squash seeds, and meats, usually goat, rabbit, or chicken—animals that were raised here at home.

⚙

My mother felt ill with all that racket going on around her, so she shut herself in her room.

She called out to Senhora Ascencão and wailed, "I'm fed up with all this, I just can't handle it anymore," her tears falling uncontrollably. "I wasn't cut out for this, my friend. This is not my calling."

"And what do you want to do?" Senhora Ascensão asked.

"I don't know. I only know that I have no strength, that I don't like this life, and God forgive my father for not having helped me. I could've been a teacher. I wanted to be a teacher. And I never got that dream out of my head. And then so many children, one every other year, with only one boy to boot. And now this unplanned child disrupting lives, mine and hers. May God keep her, my dear little girl.

"And my mother-in-law, my mother-in-law, Ascensão? How often she makes me cry! I know it's not out of malice. In fact, she's very generous, at times kind, but some of her ways are so different from mine."

We older girls all realized that our dear mother's voice was fading bit by bit, like a melting candle. She who used to sing so much when she was happy—and whose peals of laughter could be heard from afar—was tired, tired of everything. She no longer laughed, no longer embroidered. No longer sketched.

"Oh, so much despair, Ascensão. I don't even have milk to nurse my daughter, much less blood to sustain her. What a fine specimen of womanhood I am, my friend, ha-ha-ha . . . Let me laugh to keep from crying. My mother-in-law is so, so right."

"No!" said Ascensão. "What the devil has come over you? You're tired; you're not yourself. Sleep. Rest. When you wake up, you'll feel better. What you have to do is eat, for the love of God, if not for yourself then at least for your baby daughter."

Mamã wept. And she went to her bedroom.

❁

As the Christmas season approached, it was growing urgent to kill one of our two hogs that had escaped the storm. But in order to carry out the ritual slaughter, or *matança,* sustenance was needed to feed our closest relatives and the guests who would be lending a hand with the extra tasks on those three feasting days. After the creature's death we would not lack for food, but on the day before and the actual day of the *matança* how would we solve such a problem?

My parents went into the dining room. They spoke with the door half closed. They racked and racked their brains but could not find a solution. Papá even raised the possibility of selling the last calf as a means of covering part of our debts and still having enough to hold the *matança.*

"That's that," Papá said, by now totally discouraged. "In for a dime, in for a dollar, and let the devil take the hindmost."

❁

Papá's mother—stocky of build, with Minho-style gold hoop earrings, very round face, and a knotted kerchief on her head—was nearby and summoned me to join her. She winked at me and in a highly conspiratorial tone asked me to stay put while she went home, then returned. Minutes later she entered panting, with a happy expression on her face, carrying a huge basket in her arms, and in her apron a load of heavy items. She was a kind, generous old lady, but this time she outdid herself. Her offering was greater than ever before. She did not want to see either her son or grandchildren in embarrassed straits. In the basket she'd brought five hens, two rabbits, and, in her lap, two dozen eggs. Enough to lay a sumptuous table.

Two days after this gift she bestowed on us, final preparations for the *matança* were underway. Some relatives, mainly female, arrived after dinner, ready to collaborate on the chores for that evening and the following day. Senhora Ascensão spent all day and night baking loaves of bread including sweet egg-rich *massa sovada*, as well as cookies and meringues, while Luciana prepared the chicken soup, rabbit stew, rice pudding, and the coveted roses of Egypt pastries fried on rosette irons. Joana and Ana Lúcia, Mamã's favorite cousins, set the table in traditional formal style for the next morning. Most of the china came from the house of her mother, who was unable to help out with much more than that. Without land to cultivate she led a different lifestyle, similar to a city dweller's.

The house Vovó rented when she returned from America stood out from the rest in the village: richly furnished, decorated in cheerful although subdued colors, with beautiful curtains and bedspreads, knick-knacks everywhere, mattresses and bedsprings from America, and a huge enameled wood-burning stove in shades of yellow and green that heated the entire home. My grandmother had a little cash that she'd invested, as a result of the divorce settlement she signed with an X since she did not know how to read and write. But in spite of everything, with astute management of that nest egg she had learned to live with class to the end of her life. It was from her house, located down in the center of the village, that the platters, place settings, carafes, and glasses came up to my parents' home. All were hand-painted in soft shades of old rose, dusty green, and pale yellow, with such a lightness to their designs that they entranced children and adults alike.

No porcelain in the village could equal hers. My grandmother brought it from America when she returned to the island, along with the rest of the contents of her old New Bedford mansion. She was still young, in her forties, of average height with a fine figure and elegant posture. She would not wear a kerchief on her head and refused to dress in black widow's weeds. She walked with her head held high, although without arrogance or pridefulness. It was just the way she was, turned inward, with a slight smile; in her eyes, a fleeting nostalgia. She visited friends, who were few and chosen with care. She disliked gossip, and her highest imperative was, "Thou shalt not bear false witness."

Despite not knowing how to read, she would listen with pleasure to Portuguese translations of long novels like *Anna Karenina* that Daniel and I would read aloud in installments, without rushing. Our reading took over a year. And when the novel ended, Vovó asked that Daniel and I reread to her the scenes she enjoyed most.

The books came from Brazil, sent by relatives who over time were growing scarcer in number. My grandmother returned to the magazines religiously preserved in the china closet, along with a few other books of lesser importance. Even without knowing how to read she cherished them, would smell them and all but hug them, for they were her most loyal companions—her books, her foreign magazines, and her many, many photographs.

❀

Mamã's cousins Joana and Ana Lúcia took advantage of that special moment alone together in the dining room. They caressed every item they picked up and lost themselves in the tranquility of the hours. They lingered over the covered cheese caddy, which fascinated them not only for its interplay of colors but also its design.

"Some sort of promontory, or an elephant with no trunk," Ana Lúcia said. "To me it's a ship's keel," Joana rejoined. "Oh, look," she continued, "have you ever seen colors as lovely as these? Those that serve as the background spill out in a cascade of dark green, light green, and fade to the edge in a dull, almost faint yellow."

Here and there, scattered random flowers looked blown about by wind gusts, and like pigeon fantails they displayed the many shades of their palette. They appeared gossamer, as if a gauzy cambric veil covered them, and from the bottom of the petals a phosphorescent light emanated, warming the gray-green with chrysolite outlining the leaves—then the bordeaux, the sapphire, and at the tips a dusty pink and faint sky blue. And last, along the edges of the cheese caddy, a lilac next to the peach blossom.

Time passed, and the cousins lost track of time for hours on end—a time as gentle as a cloud blown by the night breeze. In the distance we heard ocean waves lapping, and the cousins were talking and talking, dreaming of buying everything and so much more. But only in America. And again that dream recurred, growing and growing, pointing their hearts to the shore opposite the rising sun.

❀

The following day at 8 a.m. sharp the first men began to arrive. The morning dawned with a clear blue sky touching the blue of the sea. Pico da Vara itself felt closer, close enough to touch. To the far side on its crown, and on this side overhead, wisps of white clouds scudded about; an ash-gray blot in front of the sun dimmed its brilliance. And in the vaulted remainder all was smooth, as calm as still water. Far out on the periphery of sea and sky, a boat pierced the horizons where they meet at sunset.

The whole crew, assembled at their posts, requested the cheery traditional pre-breakfast glass of brandy, *aguardente*. Then they quickly sat down, because winter days were so short that it was necessary to start in right away eating the fresh goat cheese, stewed fava beans, and *massa sovada*, and drinking coffee served in huge mugs.

After the hearty meal they proceeded fearlessly to the pigsty. And my mother, who was there for one final farewell to a creature she had grown fond of, left in order not to have to see him suffer, because the day before she had seen him crying, believe it or not. Then the men drank more *aguardente* to invigorate muscles that would be indispensable in restraining the hog.

Like the sweep of a scythe, his squeals sliced through the atmosphere. And then it was all over. The bonds were loosened on the pig, which fell flat on the ground where it would be singed. But when they threw flaming straw on his back, to the surprise of the heavens themselves the pig stood up and lurched forward a few steps before keeling over dead. Everyone shouted at the same time, expecting the world to end. The sky darkened, and a thunderstorm rolled in. Ana Lúcia, who was carrying a pitcher of wine plus glasses in order to quench the thirsts of the most parched men, dropped the glassware instantly. The pitcher as well as glasses shattered, and the *festa* adopted another tone, that of gray obscured by shame—a stain to darken forever the days of my uncle, the hog slayer.

Rain began to pour. Some of the men retreated to the house, others took shelter in the barn. The butcher stood there, petrified, sopping wet, weeping from the agony of his wounded pride. "What went wrong?" he wondered. "My brother's house must be truly cursed!"

My terrified mother heard him and nodded her head up and down pathetically in agreement. She knew deep down that something was coming to an end. However, she remained silent.

She now had another daughter to raise, and even then nothing could assure her that the little girl would survive. She closed her mouth, and there was no way she could eat, or even drink a light flour broth. Where was their money? And her medications? Then we heard a deep wail: "Oh, my America."

Someone heard her in that soft endless sigh, namely Papá's brother the hog butcher.

So numerous were Mamā's uncertainties that she grew more frail and insecure. Her brow furrowed deeper, while the timbre of her vibrant laughter thinned from one day to the next.

The house stood once again intact, cleaned up and provisioned for the entire winter and spring. We prepared for our little girl's baptism the following week. However, Mamā awoke that morning soaked in a cold sweat. Her baby girl was not in the cradle, nor anywhere to be found. Mamā ran into the street and searched for her everywhere. In desperation she ran through backyards, cut across ravines and headed straight toward the source of a horrendous clamor coming from far away that sounded to her like a stream near the next village over. She crossed to the other side and climbed up the cliff, behind which stood a secluded pool where young people used to bathe.

All of a sudden she saw her little girl bobbing by herself, being pulled head over heels, first rolling on pebbles, then tumbling from boulder to boulder. Farther below, she was in another pool, her little body atop the water's surface that was clogged with wilted white camellias. Out of her mind, Mamā dove in to save her dead daughter, and grabbed her. At that moment when she was clutching the baby to her breast, the whole world came undone. The puddle of water vanished. Her little girl disappeared. A peal of laughter echoed, and stars scattered across the fabric that draped the celestial dome. "Would my little girl lose her soul?"—Mamā asked herself, helpless and full of remorse—"and why didn't we get her baptized sooner?" she wondered, crazed.

"Of course I couldn't have exposed our little girl to the early winter chill air," my mother rationalized, out of breath.

Everyone knew that the child had been born prematurely, so needed to stay indoors longer. "And now what will become of me? What will become of my daughter who because of this is condemned to eternal limbo, the place where unbaptized children are sent?"

Tormented, she moaned and writhed in bed. In a raucous crescendo she blamed herself for having lost her daughter.

In the bedroom, swathed in a white cloud, the cradle stood empty.

Papá had just awakened, disoriented, so still did not grasp what had happened. Then he heard a sudden chilling cry of anguish, a distress call from someone gasping for lack of air. And in an instant he realized what it was. Mamã was trapped in a nightmare from which she could find no escape.

"Calm down, woman," our father pleaded.

"It's nothing, just a dream that's over now."

Mamã was still sobbing, half-awake, understanding nothing, not knowing where she was. Caught between sleep and reality and unable to distinguish one from the other, she opened her half-shut eyes with difficulty, closed them, opened them again and turned her head, looking at everything around her. At last she realized what was happening.

Then, like a bird on the wing, Mamã leapt out of bed, heading straight for the baby. She clutched her against her body and held onto her for a long time. She wept and wept, and continued weeping ceaselessly, so deep was her sorrow.

Hours later at the crack of dawn Mamã implored Papá, "We have to baptize our little girl this very day, before it's too late. Ease my mind and broken heart, for the sake of your father's soul. Go get Senhor Padre right now and ask my cousins Laura and João to be our child's godparents."

By the end of the afternoon of that very day my sister would be baptized. Urgency was the watchword on that gloomy Saturday. We all proceeded to the church except for Mamã, who continued weeping and feeling more debilitated. She believed this dream was a premonition, and felt she lacked the courage to go down to the village.

When we arrived at the church, Papá and the godparents headed straight for the altar while we, including Carolina, who was normally restless but at that moment a bit fearful, remained seated in the front pew. The priest approached. He greeted us one by one, offered his prayer, and called the sponsors with their respective candles to draw closer. Then came the customary question.

"What name do you give your little girl?" There ensued a long, long silence.

A deathly silence. The silence of a dead person who had not had a wake. Who had no one.

You could have heard a pin drop. Glances crossed the void, and soon everyone realized that no one knew. Papá had relied on the godmother, and she on my father.

"What are we to do?"

"It's simple, Senhor Padre," my father retorted, standing next to me. "As far as I'm concerned, give the child her mother's name, since the accursed blackbird stalks her with death every day," he said with a long-suffering air, and a huge sense of shame for what was happening in that pure act so important in his little girl's life.

"Nameless—my daughter! Nameless, my God!" Papá twisted like the flickering, melting candles, weeping on the inside, feeling guilty and swallowing the pain he choked down his throat with difficulty.

The water was already trickling over my baby sister's head during a "Father, Son, and Holy Ghost" when Daniel realized something, but he was so nervous he did not know what it was.

"Our little girl's name, not that; it can't be the same as Mamã's, no-no-no," he shouted in distress, beside himself.

In desperation he raised his voice in a shout that shook the church walls.

And he decreed, disrespecting his elders, "Not that name, no!"

The priest snorted in derision and began losing patience. Had he not been a great friend of my Mamã's mother, he would just as soon have exercised his power, finger pointed toward the street, with a temporary excommunication.

Papá, puzzled and frantic, soothed my brother.

"Everything will work out," he cautioned. "The girl's name is already registered. There's nothing more to do. Of course, at home we can find a name more to your liking. Then you can choose, if your mother and sisters are in agreement. I don't want to hear any more about it," my father replied, drenched in a cold sweat.

Outside the church a ray of sunshine awaited us, its kaleidoscopic motion softly scattering itself during a light drizzle like tiny pearls, twinkling on the edge of the celestial vault. According to popular superstition, it was a sign that witches were getting married, performing their finest bridal dances.

With no need for umbrellas, we hiked up Rua da Canada from Eira-Velha, home of Mamã's mother, who that day had stayed at my parents' house. We crossed all of Mangana, and then the long road that led us to Burguete to my parents' house, very close to Pico da Vara, which that afternoon loomed over us visibly.

Once we reached Burguete, Papá sidled up to Mamã, and in a whisper told her what had happened in the church. We heard her soft, almost silent sobbing. Then, resolutely, a shout.

"My name, never."

Daniel intervened in the disagreement and asked, "Mamã, why not call her 'Xana'?"

"Now where did you find that name, my son?"

"Why, in one of Vovó's magazines, the ones she stores in the china cabinet."

Mamã was persuaded and encouraged, but the rest of the family, in particular Papá's mother, considered it total madness, an inexcusable whim if not an actual sin. Mamã's mother remained silent. To her, it all boiled down to the question of liking the name or not. From her calm and serene demeanor, we deduced that this idea suited her very well.

Daniel, pleased with Mamã and her mother's muted reaction, vigorously insisted that this should be the name. And he was prepared to explain to our parents and the rest of the family the significance of that initial [ʃ] ("sh") sound in the name *Xana*. "It was also the [ʃ] for the "ch" in *achada,* the godsend that was the little girl who had been unexpected; the [ʃ] for the "ch" in *sacho,* a shovel to dig the earth; the [ʃ] for the "x" in *xarope,* the syrup for easing a cough; the [ʃ] in *xaile,* for the shawl that warms Tia Luísa's shoulders. Oh, and the [ʃ] in *xilofone,* for my xylophone."

And if they had not ordered him to shut up, my brother never would have ended his litany. Always stubborn as a mule, and willful in excess.

My mother was headstrong, too. She let herself be swayed by her son and displayed self-confidence. Daniel was right, she thought. So, ignoring her mother-in-law's opinion, she shot looks in just one direction: toward all of us girls. Mamã perceived our complicit silence, and turned toward us with a joy never before seen. She pulled Daniel toward her and thanked him for the idea of that name.

In a spiteful tone, Mamã announced to the whole family, "We must rebaptize our little girl, with 'Xana' as her name."

Papá's mother did not speak to us for days. She summoned my father to her house and in tears told him she was disillusioned with him as her son.

How could he have agreed to a name that was unfit for a human being? She accused him of weakness, of being henpecked. And, moreover, of ruining his life.

"A hothouse flower, that's what your wife is. She doesn't even help you with field chores."

"No, mother, don't say that."

"Yes, I mean it! Besides, she's forever sick. A talented girl, to be sure. An excellent embroiderer and seamstress. But very stubborn. She always gets the last word; there's nothing more that anyone can say. A pushy thing, ruling your life and trying to rule mine," she continued in exasperation.

"Did you see the way she disrespected me when I appealed to her good sense to cross out the name 'Xana'—or 'Cana,' sugarcane, or 'Gana,' bravado, or whatever the devil it is—and instead to accept her name just as recorded in the church, which is in fact a Christian one, unlike the other, which is more like a name for things and animals than people?

"And now, look around at your luck.

"So many girls and only one boy child, who is, worse yet, a good-for-nothing. A weakling, inclined to the arts, like his mother—with his artist's nose, broad forehead, eyes full of light, bearing a strong resemblance to his mother in his honey coloring, from hair to eyes and skin—not one to help his father in the fields. Some sissy you've got there. And now, this unexpected misfortune weighing heavier on the scales, this one they call 'Xana,' my God! Poor creature, with a name like that pinned to her back for the rest of her life.

"A curse has befallen you, my son. Be careful."

For Papá's part, had a pin dropped at that moment, he would not have heard it. He got up and went home, his head slightly bowed and with a circumspect air.

❀

Mamã did not know what had transpired between her mother-in-law and her husband. In order to get more rest, she asked us all to go to her mother's house to help arrange the *presépio,* our Nativity crèche, and to set up the Christmas tree in order to maintain the American tradition. We had permission to remain overnight, spend the next day and, that year, stay at Vovó's house until the Feast of Kings on Twelfth Night. Mamã seemed to be suffering from chronic fatigue and had lost interest in life and everything, hanging on to secrets in the decay of languishing days.

We remained apprehensive. Daniel and I rounded up our sisters.

However, if the girls realized anything was amiss, none of them let on. Their interests at that time centered on what they could not even remotely believe. They were astonished, almost startled, by Mamã's surrender. A Christmas just for us at Vovó's house, where little Xana was living with our grandmother right there in the center of town, very close to the church.

❀

The *presépio* occupied a large portion of the house. It was a replica of the village, with its various streets, houses, the church in the background, and on the left a beautiful fountain where the women went carrying trays piled high with laundry on their hips—and all the parts made by my brother Daniel over the years. The materials were clay for the figures, cardboard for the rest, in some cases wood; and greenery, brought in from the forest and orchard to build the mountains, ravines, canals, the mills, and the regional road with its magnificent plane trees. All the village trades were reproduced there: the shoemaker; the plasterer climbing his ladder; some women in conversation, others doing laundry in the public washtubs; men together at the taverns; a dog passing by; cattle being herded to their stalls; a *matança* with all its attendant ritual; the grape harvest, the grain threshing; processions at Divine Holy Spirit *festas* with their patrons, the tasseled banner, the priest and parishioners. In short, everything was gathered together there, so that a great part of the excitement in the village of São Bento could be viewed at a single glance.

In the center the Christmas tree was set up in a place of honor. It was hung with postcards sent from America that had accumulated over time. Between them, tangerines were strewn all over the tree, which overflowed with dried figs, carob fruits, and candies.

From that abundance an infinite magic emanated. Children and adults came to see the *presépio* and Christmas tree, all moved by the same sentiment—their fascination with little things, and how they identified with it all. The divine in its inscrutable expression.

❀

"It's suppertime," our grandmother announced, starry-eyed.

We went into the kitchen, where a veritable bounty was spread out for us on the table. A white linen tablecloth and rich dishes awaited us. Cabbage soup with pork and beans; for dessert, sweet *massa sovada* bread and rice pudding. We ate in silence because, if we made noise, my grandmother warned, we ran the risk of having Satan wrap himself around our feet. None of us dared challenge whether what she was saying was true or mere intimidation. Not even Carolina, who was adept at dealing with Beelzebub at our other grandmother's house, was likely to break this rule. At this house everything was different, so she could not get her bearings; it seemed the world was pulling the rug out from under her feet. She found it strange territory indeed, and Carolina would not take that risk because she wanted to stay with us alongside the *presépio,* the Christmas tree, and all the treats Vovó had set aside during the year: blackberry and guava preserves, quince marmalade and peanut butter to serve during the festive seasons, in particular around Christmas and Easter.

After supper my grandmother allowed us a few minutes to laugh and play, then shooed us off to bed.

And the soft light of the lamp flickered out.

❀

Once the days that Mamã had let us spend at Vovó's ended, we hiked back home up to Burguete. "The family has to be together," Papá observed, almost beardless, with thinning very fine hair and dark glowing eyes.

Little did he know that, in the absence of farmhands, my mother had released us from household chores so that at our request we could go be with her mother. On the slightest pretext we would run down the paths to her house below before Mamã could change her mind. We would arrive soaked with sweat. On rainy days we played in the storeroom; on sunny days, in the yard under the shade of the fruit trees.

At Vovó's house no one bothered us. Each of us played in our own way, and if by chance we did not get along, we were promptly sent back to Burguete. The old ladies' heads could not stand our shouting, much less our misunderstandings. Moreover, as the chiming of *trindades* approached, the men returned from the field and it would be time to go inside. At night it was a party, joyful, everyone talking all at once: daughter Maria Isabel would help Mamã, while Angelina, the quietest, would smile with pleasure. As for me, I would laugh out loud at mischievous Carolina, who pulled the cat's tail, subjecting him to various tortures in secret, until Papá restored order—not in the style of his mother, who invoked Satan, but his own way, with a reprimanding manner that might take the form of a couple of swats to the head, a tug on the ears, or a harsher punishment commensurate with the misbehavior. And all this in order to give us a proper upbringing, lest we forget good table manners.

Days passed, and Xana was gaining a little weight. She was no longer a "mouse," or even a "cat." She was a normal, although still frail, little girl—with a very round face—and eyes as clear as glass, so alert and transparent. It was difficult to feed her. She would close her mouth, and no one could pry it open. The only way to feed her was to make her cry, in order to create time enough to slide a spoonful of gruel into her mouth.

❀

With spring inexorably emerging, bird life was awakening in a convulsed throbbing that seemed to explode from the sky to slip the bonds of earth in a hallelujah of life and death. It was the season for pruning trees, trimming hedges, tying up vines. Time to plow, harrow, and sow seeds on the land: wheat, fava and *tremoço*, or lupin, beans, potatoes. Along the roadsides grew rows of flowers: lilies, azaleas, daisies, and calla lilies. Blackberry brambles climbed the backyard fence, and no one tore them out; they were pruned with the same care as shrubs and trees, just as Mamã wanted. Blackberries were prized for desserts and jam. Huge garlands of a shrub known as *primavera* climbed the fence, arching down in clusters to the ground.

The men spread manure, broke up clods, and smoothed the soil's surface with hoes. The land sat for a few days to rest. Afterward it was sown, planted, and watered as needed.

❀

Maria Isabel's birthday was the first day of spring, March 21 to be precise. Back in those days few people celebrated birthdays, but at our house there was always some sort of treat. This time it was traditional *canja* chicken soup, and a stew made with wild rabbit that Papá had hunted. We were so happy.

Mamã was giving Xana a bath, while singing a beautiful sweet, tender song; tender, too, were her eyes. Then, when we least expected it, a raucous noise swept through the house's porous walls. What was that horrendous shouting? Had there been snakes on the island, no one would have tried to find out. We would have been certain it was a snakebite. But no. Our mother was breaking down in tears.

"Xana's dying," she shouted, crying.

"My darling daughter's tiny body is puffing up, puffing up like a pumpkin. Her little eyes are swollen shut. I tried to lift her eyelids in order to look into her eyes, and what I saw was a dense, dense fog."

Papá's mother, who was close by, crossed herself and hurried to exorcise the evil eye that had been cast on her granddaughter.

"I'm sure someone wants to kill her," she said. "Good heavens, good heavens! I already know what's happening: sometimes witches leave a dagger in the cradle"—there were so many such cases that my own grandmother had handled. Sometimes they left needles all over the mattress.

She hastened to instruct, "We've got to catch a grasshopper and pin it up behind the door."

She added, "Run, Felisberta. Go fetch a horseshoe, and if you can't find one, go to Senhora Clementina's house so she can give you a sprig of rosemary. I'll anoint Xana's body with oil and rub a pinch of salt on the roof of her mouth in the sign of the cross. The devil will not enter my family's home," my grandmother, known far and wide throughout the village for her boldness, declared in defiance.

But then Mamã, on an uncontrollable impulse, lost her temper and let out a cry that terrified us all.

"I don't want to hear old wives' tales," Mamã said, flames shooting from her head.

"I want the doctor to come right now, Daniel. Run, run quickly; go summon your father, he's in Fontainhas."

❀

When Papá arrived, he was silent. He harnessed the mare right away and rode at a furious gallop to the village where the doctor lived, about six miles away.

Our little girl continued to puff up more and more. Sometimes she resembled the sea, all blue, other times she was gray in color, swelling up like the high tide. My mother was wide-eyed, lamenting the fate of her little one who was still holding her own—a real fighter, that little girl of hers. In a flash, without anyone noticing, Xana turned into low tide, the sea receded, and she returned to her natural state.

She was robed in foothills of foam as white as the full moon, white like sheets bleached with lye and laid out under the sun. The white of that foam was milky, full of light, a fluorescent luminosity that removed far from their minds any indication of a final breath.

❀

Six hours later the doctor arrived at our house. Xana was smiling in her cradle as if nothing had happened. Her little body was back to normal. A divine grace? No one knew. But the doctor decided to stay a few hours to see if any symptoms would yield clues for a diagnosis. But after much waiting, no signs appeared.

Scarcely had the doctor left when Papá's mother began cursing her son's bad luck, piqued by the fact that her daughter-in-law had rejected her folk ways in favor of medical science. Unlike my father, who had raced to save the little girl, his mother complained and insulted her daughter-in-law for spending so much, "for wasting all that money," she lamented. "And why save something that has always been doomed to die? An inconsequential little thing, all eyes and not much else.

"After all, there was nothing to lose," Papá's mother said, bitter and offended, in total certainty that her granddaughter's savior had not been the doctor. "The proof was plain to see: he had not cured any disease," she gloated triumphantly, yet hurt.

Mamã, nervous from having thought she was about to lose Xana, was unable to contain herself upon hearing this; she could not believe it. For this lady, despite her outbursts, was at heart a good person, above all generous. But now what was happening with her?

I had already run out of patience.

For a few minutes Mamã remained impassive and slack-jawed and immobile, hearing but not comprehending anything—perhaps poking holes in clouds, perhaps gazing off in the distance, glassy-eyed without seeing. Then, when she was herself again, she looked at us all up close, with a clear, starry expression, and proclaimed in a loud voice, "Sooner or later I'll be able to forgive your Papá's mother, but never again will I subject myself to anyone's poison."

Never, ever again.

❀

Mamã left the house, slamming the door. She needed to unwind, to escape an environment so charged it left her listless and pensive. She sat on a rock down by the stream and stayed there for hours on end. When she returned, she deemed it best to go over to her mother-in-law's house and speak everything on her mind, once and for all.

"Look here, my fine girl! What kind of face is that? What do you want from me?"

"Oh, I don't want anything! What's more, I am not as 'fine' as you suspect. What I want is for you to leave me alone and not misunderstand me, for God's sake. There's no blame here on either side. We're just different, that's all."

"Different?" our father's mother seethed. "Different because you had a mother who didn't straighten you out, much less prepare you to raise a family?"

"Oh, that's one more insult. I'm very, very sorry, but the truth is I'd never trade my mother for you, Senhora, although I recognize some virtues in you, like generosity and even kindness. I'm not that ungrateful. If it's envy that's upsetting you, then eat your heart out. And if not, well then, continue doing good in your own way and leave me alone. In peace, forever."

Soon after that scene, my mother ceased to be the same person.

A lightning bolt struck her that dark night. She entered a long, deep depression, and thereafter locked herself in her room in the dark with Xana, refusing to speak to or see anyone. Whenever she came out to eat and prepare her little girl's bottle, she would move like a sleepwalker, as if unable to see, hear, or feel. She lost interest in housework and turned into a near stranger. For a long time she neither laughed nor sang. Her voice was dwindling away like a trickle of water, and the light in her sad eyes was going out. She felt the need to retreat to the old silences of her faraway secrets.

And whatever she was carrying around locked up in her wounded mind, no one could any longer decipher.

It was the middle of the night, and everyone was sound asleep. Around the time the clock struck twelve, while the house was covered in darkness, our family, young and old alike, awoke to strange noises— the sounds of chairs being flung about and furniture that someone was moving from one side to the other in the middle of the house. A terrifying hell. Outside, the animals were out of control, all howling and braying wildly at the same time—and the strangest thing was that one of them, penned in a stall right below my parents' bedroom, was bucking against the walls and floor with volcanic force. Brilliant flames shot up out of the ocean, only to be extinguished and returned anew to their primordial state. The volcano eruption was so explosive that people were running in every direction in order to get far away from it. It kept ebbing and flowing, and no one wanted to stay.

To leave was the destiny of all our people, fleeing the mold and tuberculosis that were claiming lives every day, fleeing dismal places with no future. The island was hemorrhaging due to a failure to provide any sustenance for its children. Meanwhile, the mare kept dealing insistent mortal blows on her stall, without pity or mercy.

Upon reflection, how could that be, when the stall where the mare slept was almost ten feet high? The situation was hideous.

Papá was spewing fiery epithets, foaming at the corners of his mouth with rage. He had to put an end to that. He climbed out of bed and raced into the darkness of the house, his arms slashing like swords through the dense, impenetrable air. He was under siege all around. At last he located the back door to our yard.

He opened it all the way, crossed the porch, went down the stairs, and shouted in defiance, "If you're the devil, come and get me!"

The noise of hooves shooting flames was heard next. And the reply was a hollow and endless silence.

Early the next morning, it was whispered that even the mermaids had turned tail and left.

❁

The events of that night recurred twice more. Mamã, who had been raised not to believe in otherworldly occurrences, went down to the village without saying a word to her husband, much less to her mother. In the morning she headed to the priest's rectory, and no one ever learned what was said there.

After that she began to ponder what her life would bring. Countless times the notion of abandoning everything and moving overseas had crossed her mind, although not because she was all that fond of America, where she was born and raised. She had a different reason—to turn her back on things she was not cut out to face: the anemia always sapping her strength; the gossip and demands of others; and a workload so heavy that, despite domestic help, Mamã was obliged to rise before the crack of dawn and could not go to bed until after daylight had faded.

She would have traded all of that for a piano, which her wealthy father had refused to give her. She was an artist at embroidery, reading, drawing, writing poems in private, only to tear some of them up so no one could see what was in her heart.

America was fermenting inside her body, seething in her mind—the routes to an uncertain fate, and her escape. Who could know?

❁

Around nightfall the following day, Mamã announced that she was going to leave. She had already talked with Papá and then with her mother. She would be leaving Xana with the old ladies, placing the trust of a lifetime in them. As for us—the older girls and Daniel—we would continue to live in Burguete, with the aid of our domestics Luciana and Felisberta, and assisted by Papá.

We were happy, not because we were going to be parted from Mamá, but because it made us feel even closer to the America that sat with us at the table by way of our closest relatives, all of them real only in photographs, in our imagination, yet at the same time so present in the smells and the things that Mamã and Vovó told us about them. In that respect they were very close to us, certainly much more so than was the city. After all, where did good things and our fascination with the new come from?

All of it, every bit, had come from New Bedford. So when Mamã announced she was leaving, nothing seemed at all strange to us. We began making plans, inviting all of America into our house. We did not cry. We jumped for joy. Everyone's eyes were smiling.

Mamã apprised us that she would be returning home in a short while; it would be almost like going to the city and back. Our existence had always been divided between here and there, and life there was as familiar to us as the island ground we trod every day.

Mamã promised us once more that she would not be gone any longer than it would take to afford to transform the gloom of our house into light and color.

One morning several weeks later Mamã left, brimming with confidence. She held her head high. In the outline of a drained expression she was hiding a secret that had come from afar, that she herself did not know. She did not say goodbye to anyone. If she wept, she did so only on the inside. She was going alone, cutting through the morning's dense milky fog, from which a man of indeterminate age emerged, coming out of nowhere—dressed in shabby clothes, moth-eaten over countless years. He was there to join the pilgrimage, and bearing on his lips English words that few could understand: *shut up, all right, sure, come on, son of a bitch, son of a gun.* He muttered the same words over and over, perhaps the only ones he knew. He was someone who must have left many, many years ago for the New World. Someone who had gotten lost in the infinite network of American byways without sending word to his family. Someone who was now returning only to find an emptiness from all his absences. Someone with a squalid countenance and sunken eyes, dirty and cold. With a beard to hide his face and ward off miseries.

He wore no shoes or sandals, relying instead on the callused soles of his feet. And, like a scruffy dog, he took off by himself, fleeing toward the row of windmills in the direction of the rising sun. And they never saw him again. All that remained of the man was his litany repeated endlessly day and night, night and day: *son of a bitch, son of a bitch, son of a bitch.* A litany that wafted up among the boulders in the streams around there, grinding and grinding away in the wheel of the mill, which never again stopped humming it.

⊛

That ditty delighted some and dismayed others. But from this day on, no one who went to the pharmacy in the neighboring village could pass by without feeling tormented—whether by demons screeching like banshees, bursting, oscillating wildly, sinking, and pounding out a drumbeat along the banks of the stream with an echo unfolding forever; or by mermaids that had come from the ocean to bathe in the satin-smooth waters of our serene babbling brooks, without waves or wind, in scenes from an island of love.

A few days later, it was said, after the man with no name or age had disappeared into the fog, a flock of doves alit on my mother. Others claimed it had been a shower of magnolias, such was the fragrance she exuded with every step, firm and confident. She seemed as light as a bird on the wing, declared those who saw her that morning when she left, heading in the direction of the setting sun.

⊛

Around nine that same morning, as soon as we awoke, the truth hit us like a bucket of ice water.

Luciana announced that Mamã had already left. Then she hastily laid out the details: first by bus to the city, then by boat to the island of Santa Maria—and from there spirited away on the wings of an airplane. "That's how it was; that's all there is to say. Now, don't bother me; I have a lot to do."

We were silent, at a loss for words, as if our world had been turned inside out.

We suddenly felt orphaned, and replied in unison, "But why didn't Mamã say goodbye to us, the way everyone else does?"

"That wasn't right, Luciana, the way we were left hanging on the edge the abyss," said Daniel, who had landed in a bottomless pit as black as a moonless night.

But the truth is that it was not quite like that. She had informed us of her plans and even tried to explain, and to suggest to Daniel and to each one of us that her departure day was nearing. What she failed to do was to prepare herself to say goodbye to her children and the old ladies who were left to raise Xana, born early and five months later separated prematurely from her mother.

We felt something in the air that resembled a betrayal, an emptiness of a person who suddenly finds herself barefoot in the mud during the chill winds of April.

CHAPTER 3

October!

Six months had passed since Mamã's departure that spring morning. We were living through a lull between storms. But we couldn't escape the fact that a mudhole was miring us deeper and deeper. We could tell that the truth was no longer being spoken, and that things were ceasing to be transparent and silences were weighing heavily, opening up caverns of darkness. All around us, life was being changed and transformed, while we failed to grasp the scope of what was to come—until the day when everything became crystal clear.

Papá was getting ready to leave our island too, to cross the vast ocean beyond which his wife was struggling alone. His bags were packed. Xana was nearly a year old. Just as Mamã had done, Papá assured us he would be back very soon. He was leaving, he explained with a tear in the corner of his eye, solely to bring her back as soon as possible.

He bade us all goodbye—his mother, nieces and nephews, brothers and sisters, and neighbors.

Papá went down to the village to Vovó's house, opened the door, greeted her, and headed for Xana's room, from which satiny petals floated toward him and perched in the warmth of his timid expression, landing one by one on his long dark lashes, dark as his dark eyes. Papá did not notice anything, and if he sensed something he kept it to himself. He did not speak. He leaned over the rail of the crib where Xana emitted sounds that made no sense, except for *maammãã, maammãã, maammãã* . . .

My sister was left behind, in an echo without a return.

❄

Soap-like bubbles blew through her half-closed lips, rose skyward, and refracted onto her chest, multiplying in variegated hues. A rainbow hung overhead. Xana babbled on and on, expressing herself more with body language than with her uncoordinated lips, having no way to convey her message except by saying *maammāā*. Her hands, likewise tentative, fluttered to the rhythm of the sounds in a choreography of reds, yellows, and blues. Her eyes shone with curiosity. Her mouth quivered. She tried to touch, to grasp, to trap the sounds in her hands with great force; to feel them in her perfume, in the flavors of pablum, grapes and blackberries. And her drool spilled out in excitement, in every shade of a thousand colors, a thousand aromas, in a relentless struggle to name them: she wanted to show off in front of Papá, she who perhaps spoke a different language.

And so it was that, without realizing it, Papá found himself caught off guard in front of his little girl. He saw very clearly bouncing toward him between her little teeth the most beautiful tongue of damp orchids. Restless and somewhat drained, he stayed there thinking for a few seconds.

All of a sudden, as if the Holy Spirit had descended upon him, a light came on over everything. And so he understood his little girl's efforts and told her of the secret contained in the language of flowers.

"With daisies I love you, my dear; with belladonna I offer you dreams of adventure; with sunflowers, the warmth of affection; with blossoms from the incense tree, the search for a new world; roses I won't give you, my child, because I don't want you to get hurt."

Papá went on that way for some time, his eyes riveted on his little girl, enumerating the flowers Mamā adored that covered the island's roadsides. Their stalks of lacy leaves were fragile; their minuscule petals resilient, dainty, embroidered in the shape of a miniature daisy. They gave off no scent. They danced at the slightest breeze and carpeted the roadsides from early spring until the end of summer with their shades of pink, white, lilac, pale violet, and jasper red.

The hours passed and passed . . . and now he had to leave.

He came even closer, moving in to make contact with Xana. He placed a wreath on her head and bestowed a damp kiss on her forehead.

He licked and licked her, as a mother animal does her offspring. Then he closed his lips and exhaled a slow, lingering breath over her. Xana stirred and tried to raise her body. That was her way of speaking.

Soon thereafter he heard a cry that sounded the way I imagined a wounded hyena would, howling at the sun as it faded behind dense leaden clouds, from which burst an ancient hysterical laughter coming from afar, from infinite trackless deserts.

Papá felt uncomfortable, out of sorts. He grabbed his felt hat, waved it aimlessly, and, when he turned back for one final farewell, shot a look of pity at his mother-in-law. And again there was that facetious laughter pursuing him.

Once Papá turned the corner, my grandmother went to be with Xana. Vovó, warm yet so sad, brought along with her a figurative shower of sharp needles. She dressed the little girl, pulled her booties on her, and picked her up with difficulty. She crossed the room in the middle of the house. She needed to glance around the backyard, with Xana nearby taking her still tentative first steps. Xana was slow to walk and talk.

My grandmother fed Xana her pablum, while marveling at the soaring Pico da Vara across the way, and to her left the always roiling and ever saltier ocean. This sea of memories, this living water of dreams, in varying shades of blue, gave rise to other adventures; that space of joy and death, life and pain. And my astute grandmother in that sea of patience of hers, teaching Xana to listen to the earth's belly, the whispering of the stars—such as the pecking she had just heard coming from the basket where the hen was brooding on her eggs inside the kitchen.

"Hear the peck-peck, Xana?" insisted Vovó, fascinated by the crescent moon. "Peck-peck. Listen, my girl."

After a while, as day was breaking, the egg appeared to break. Peck-peck . . . And then they heard an endless cheeping. Xana clapped her clumsy palms together and squealed with joy; she went so wild with joy that in the process she nearly killed the poor chicks, since her first steps were every bit as ungainly as theirs.

With the drizzle subsiding, my grandmother picked up our little one and headed for the wall separating the house from the yard. A dry

breeze stirred up the hot, hot summer dust, which brought along memories of the old days: a whiff of silences, of emptiness, of losses.

Vovó, however, harbored distant memories in her pained eyes. She
was beautiful, of medium height, with eyes that shone like stars and a
soft pale complexion. That morning she was wearing a dress the color
of the sea, her hair pulled back and caught in a fine silver hairnet. Her
expression filled her entire face. From it emanated a slight movement
of her lips, like a flower blooming, in a soft smile of fresh spring water.

Vovó looked in the direction where the wind was kicking up. It
was blowing from Nordeste, the northeast. Golden leaves began to fall.
A narrow ray of light filtered through the threads of a large cobweb
entangled in the dry branches of our old peach tree.

✺

Years passed, and in the spring when Maria Isabel turned eighteen, it
was time for her to leave for the other side of the Atlantic. In a letter she
had already apprised our parents that she did not wish to continue her
schooling. Mamã's response was despairing: "Since you don't want to
study, you need to book your ticket as soon as possible so you can leave
and start working here." Maria Isabel set aside those and other words
to which she was accustomed. She was happy, feeling like the richest
girl on earth. Soon she would be over on the other shore, which she
somehow already knew from photographs and dreams—that other side
of the ocean, from which came good things: candies in the widest range
of varieties and colors, sacks of sugar so fine it looked like white flour,
fancy clothing entirely unknown on our island, and everything else that
would be hers from then on. The America of our fathers, aunts, uncles,
and cousins who were scattered to the four winds. Maria Isabel feared
nothing; she was always ready to work. She was strong and dedicated
to her household chores. She left nothing for Mamã, who was always
weak and anemic, to do; on the contrary, she had the same fiber as Papá.
She already had it in her head that she would work very, very hard in
order to fulfill Mamã's ambitions: to accumulate enough money so
when they returned to São Bento they could build a palatial home that
would be admired by all. Mamã was eager to rival her wealthy father,
who had forgotten his children, in order to show him that she too could

make a fortune. "I would give my all to attain that," Mamã repeated in all her letters.

❀

At the end of the following year, it was Angelina's turn to follow in Maria Isabel's footsteps—one more daughter contributing to the growth of the family nest egg, another one coming along who did not wish to pursue her studies. And her punishment was to pack her bags immediately, Mamã retorted in a fury, seeing her dreams circling the drain.

Angelina was, however, very different from Maria Isabel. True, like her she also did not wish to continue her schooling, but leaving the island was not what Angelina wanted, not for anything. Nonetheless, Mamã's response was a slap in the face. "Daughter, you either study or hit the road and work hard like the rest of the family."

Angelina's reluctant departure was for that very reason far more keenly felt, far more painful. Her forcible absence left a deep scar on us, a mark difficult to forget. Moreover, she was esteemed by all. She had always been a reserved girl, exceedingly obedient, tender in her gestures and extremely affectionate. She was so cautious that people were scarcely aware of her presence. Up until Angelina was about age twelve, when Mamã decided to leave, none of us girls remembered her having ever been scolded, much less punished. She used to hold Tia Luísa's hand while accompanying her on walks through the village on her morning rounds, gracing the weakest with a kind word, a chunk of bread, or firewood to heat their stoves.

My grandmother also harbored a very, very special affection for that granddaughter, with her milk-white face and sweet, loving expression. Despite this, Vovó no longer wept. Her tears had dried up, like long-parched earth.

Tia Luísa did not follow her sister's lead this time; there was no way she could resign herself. She wept over the loss of her niece, her faithful companion. She wept over the misfortune of her family, increasingly separated, increasingly "falling apart at the seams."

"And there goes another girl off to those lands at the end of the earth," mourned our great-aunt, in a closed-coffin sadness.

Tia Luísa—just as she had predicted first to Mamã and Papá, and then to Maria Isabel—foresaw that Angelina would weep "tears of blood," enough to break your heart and pierce your soul, "tears of oil" to set the pitch-black night ablaze. Thus my grandmother's sister mourned with an inconsolable grief, feeling the ground slipping away from under her feet, thrown into a free fall.

Unlike Vovó, Tia Luísa never let her hair show, keeping it hidden beneath a kerchief tied under her chin. Her face was wizened; her totality was a sea of affection.

She never slowed down at home. From morning to night she was on the go, tending to the neediest. Her clothes were somber and threadbare. She continued wearing long skirts of the old-fashioned style, and her colors of choice were gray and black with white stripes. As for her figure, it did not exist.

❋

Daniel still remained on the island. And while he was of an age to depart, he stayed. He was continuing his studies, per Mamã's wishes. It did not cross his mind to drop out of high school, despite health problems: he was prone to bleeding—anemic, like Xana. He was therefore unsuited for America. Mother told him in a letter, "You must stay at our island *liceu*, so you can earn a degree later in Lisbon."

❋

Our family was dwindling year by year. Daniel, Carolina, and I remained at my parents' house in Burguete. Xana was still living with Vovó in the center of town. We younger ones wanted only to visit Vovó's house but not live there, and later in adolescence we became ever more estranged from Xana. In Burguete we enjoyed another kind of freedom. And besides, that was where our friends were.

But to our surprise, one day we received a letter with orders from my parents to move to Vovó's house. "There's no way to support two households," Mamã proclaimed, incisive and desperate.

We wept.

We promptly broke down weeping, crushed. We were deeply attached to Luciana, our governess. All of us, from our eldest sister on down to Carolina, with Daniel and me in between. Our baby sister was the only exception.

Luciana was much younger than Mamã; perhaps that was why she had become best friends with Daniel and the rest of us. Luciana's leaving in such a way, in that sea of losses on which we shipwrecked, was like losing a leg or having a pebble stuck in one's stomach.

Weeping and lost in bitterness, we vomited putrefaction that day.

❋

It was a drizzly afternoon soaked with tears over our dear Luciana when we left my parents' house back in Burguete. The walls were already cold, and Carolina and I were shattered; Daniel was less bereft. He had always been closer to Vovó. He was delicate, pale of face, and he needed the type of care that could not be found at his parents' home. There was no way he could do without Luciana's friendship. He wanted us to continue staying together. But under Mamã's orders that was out of question. Felisberta would have to take Luciana's place in Vovó's home.

In a soft voice, Daniel continued reading the letter, stunned. All of a sudden he lashed out furiously in a loud voice.

"It's always like this. They always take the easy way out. They're always ready, ready to separate what could stay joined forever and ever. Like the tick-tock of the clock turning its tempo into a life sentence.

"All this," Daniel repeated in desperation, "just to harpoon and haul in that white whale dream of hers of being a grand lady, outshining all who visit our house.

"Mamã is always halving and quartering, cutting up and dividing, without realizing the tragedy into which her family is sinking day by day."

"It's all for our own good," Mamã insisted in every letter. Daniel laughed and laughed, as his tears fell with bitter irony.

We had never seen my brother so angry or furious as he was that morning. He suspected that out of those who had departed, not one would ever return: neither Mamã nor Papá, nor our sisters. The America that was made entirely of riches would not come to our island home after all; we were the ones who would have to go meet it. The land of bounty required our physical presence. And that said it all. "Sooner or later, America," Daniel thought to himself. Those still remaining behind would be caught by surprise. And once again more separations, fissures, nausea, and another earth tremor.

Our expectations were crumbling, and Mamã was like a millstone, her bags always packed, always packed, yet she never returned.

❁

That same day, when we descended the steep, winding street from Burguete on the way to town to Vovó's house, I lagged behind to brood—while Daniel, farther ahead, led the still sobbing Carolina by the hand. To amuse her, my brother decided to race her down the hill. He was hoping to extinguish the pain that was stuck in her throat, to make her forget. They ran and ran, all the while making a racket loud enough to cast out demons and afford surcease to the pain that persisted in her throat.

It was at this moment, during a hike that for me seemed endless in separation and departure, that for the first time I saw the village below with comprehending eyes. I stopped to look for a while, and everything became clear to me, clear as when fog breaks and splits its milky gray cloak in half to send down a funnel-shaped light that illuminates the entire earth.

Ever more alert to all I perceived, I heard Carolina at play with Daniel, heaving a deep sigh that could not have come from one so young—so deep it made me stumble over other memories, some good, some bad. At that precise moment we felt as sour as vinegar from so much acrimony.

I stood there watching everything around me again. The mountains, some rounded, others like nipples pointing skyward; the wet and dry thousand and one shades of green; one little church above us to the west, and another on the other side of the village, a bit more humble. Our church was almost obscured, with only the crown of its steeple showing.

Flowing in that direction, the three arterials of the community branched, with their tile-roofed houses like bobbin lace, whitewashed, with some stripes of indigo and others of ocher.

All the homes there hovered over the Lord's house, so those who approached São Bento from the east or west on the regional road would of necessity have to look down to the sea. The village, except for the tiny settlement where my parents' house was located, spread out toward that area, all of it overlooking the waters closest to what people saw, yet at the same time far away.

The entire seaside coast of the county of Nordeste was elevated.

❀

Along the road, plane trees were leafing out and fencerows were filling with blue taros.

Now back in those days, crossing the cemetery along the side of the road between Burguete and the village below always entailed great effort—a macabre adventure for both children and youths. A phosphorescent light emitted by fireflies was proof of the danger in which anyone could be caught. Before they reached the high, high walls with a wrought iron gate of stanchions through which they could see the graves of those who rested there, the children and young people would be shaking like leaves and rehearsing a long ritual that resembled an airplane takeoff.

They stopped, crossed themselves, drew some deep breaths, and prayed, "Feet, don't fail me now!"—lest the souls awaken and pull them into the graves. Their sweat poured down like rain. When at last out of danger, the children and youths realized how much their hearts had been racing and sought to calm them right then, so their hearts would not jump out of their chests.

And I was thinking . . . and watching and laughing and crying over this new world of mine.

❀

At the entrance to the center of our village, I heard the clamor of children's voices, their effusive joy after school let out. Some were playing ball, others tag, or spinning a top while their mothers, who had finished fixing dinner, leaned out windows waiting for their husbands and children.

Carolina was beginning to show off more, daring her girlfriends whom she encountered along the road. That afternoon, other than her brother, no amusement struck her fancy. She seemed self-confident. Daniel's hand was firm, and from it emanated a whiff of hot air. In her throat there was no longer even a trace of pain.

And I, somewhat disoriented, was falling farther behind—and feeling myself grow up, thinking of the obligations involved in looking after a grandmother who needed more from me than I did from her. Vovó's diabetes and heart disease were shortening her life, and day-to-day worries were becoming more difficult, beyond our control.

Xana, for her part, constituted a responsibility that haunted my grandmother day and night. Carolina's showing off was an even greater burden. Besides being difficult to handle and rebellious, she disliked school. She was in third grade, and from time to time would disappear, not returning home until nightfall, to everyone's alarm. And that was exactly what she wanted—to attract attention.

Doubtless she persisted in her mischief in order to annoy Vovó and Tia Luísa. And I feared for the worst. Feared indeed, for I had never assumed the role of protector, much less teacher. That role had until then been assigned to Luciana. And I did not know what to do or how to act. I already felt somewhat adrift.

Inside I felt like a leavened *massa sovada* dough that was rising, an immense anxiety casting a pall over my vanishing youth—a responsibility that made me shiver with goose bumps.

I found myself drowning in troubled waters.

Daniel, in turn, being a young man, could wind up having better luck, I thought. According to the custom of the time, he did not need to worry about household chores. But then again, he was different from many other young men. He accepted his feminine side without complexes or prejudice, and like a responsible youth was always inclined to take care of the old ladies and us—Carolina and me, and later on, our little girl Xana.

He was the most conscientious of all us siblings, from Maria Isabel on down to our little sister. He had great sympathy for Vovó and took responsibility for raising us, accompanying us, and helping the old ladies.

Every letter sent pertaining to my brother said the same thing: Mamã insisted that Daniel continue his studies, a requirement she never forgot. She just wanted more than anything else to have a university graduate in the family, so she could fling back into her ungrateful father's face what he had done to her when she was visiting the island for an extended period as a ten-year-old and had begged in a letter to him in America to be able to continue her studies and soon thereafter received this sentence spewing venom.

"Work on the land, like the other girls your age."

Poor Mamã!

It was at perhaps that exact moment when she shut her dream inside a coffin.

So while I kept thinking about this mistake of our entire lifetime, we were arriving at our grandmother's house in the center of the village, where from then on we would stay for as long as God (or Mamã) wished.

⊛

We never would have thought our grandmother would mark that date with so much joy and elegance. In fact, she insisted on making the day into a celebration. She wore a dress I didn't recognize, in blue-flecked emerald green fabric, with an oval neckline, ending in a bow of the same fabric. In the doorway she waited for us with a smile on her face. Her words were few, but her touch generous.

The waning afternoon blew cold air that cut like a razor. Vovó walked quickly over to the gramophone: it had a beautiful honey-colored varnished oak cabinet, two doors below for the largest disks and two above for smaller ones. She took the curios off the lid, raised it, put a disk on the turntable, grasped the handle, and gave it a crank.

Music burst forth, enchanting and nasal, sweeping away lost absences while evoking with a certain nostalgia the golden era when that same gramophone was humming nonstop on the other side of the ocean. It was the Roaring Twenties again, back when swarms of people would head out to their mansion on weekends, invited or not by her then-husband, a distinguished businessman and political figure.

Years later my grandfather announced his candidacy for mayor of New Bedford, but he was soon thereafter removed from the slate when upon investigation it was found out that he was divorced—making an example of him in a society that demanded "purity." Vovó, however, never understood nor accepted this decision that made no sense to her. "Hadn't my ex-husband risen in the world on his own merits?" she mused. "And as to his private life," she added, "what the devil did his marital status have to do with other people?" When they were still married, Vovó would rise to his defense: her then-husband was always an able man, a hard worker, respected according to many standards. Already successful while still in his twenties and thirties. Thus he deserved further consideration, she repeated, perplexed.

❋

When Vovó turned her back to put an end to that thought and flip the record so it would continue to fill the house with joy, a veil suddenly dropped down and covered her face with a long, shallow silence. She remained that way for what seemed an eternity. I noticed, however, that the spark in her eyes was still alive. She was leaning slightly toward the portraits—some of them hanging on the wall, others sitting atop dressers—of her American wedding and our grandfather's factories.

We saw no expression of emotion. However, a serene look clearly appeared on her face, free from hatred, free from blame or wounds of any sort.

The freshly washed curtains were rehung in the windows, and the most beautiful comforters came out of the chests to brighten her house. There were only a few flowers: chrysanthemums in the kitchen table vase, and an early white camellia beside the glass dome over Baby Jesus, inherited from my great-grandmother. In the corner of every bedroom, a branch of fragrant cryptomeria.

❋

In those first days at our new home, I felt somewhat deserted. The old ladies, as always, redoubled their efforts to make us comfortable.

Our grandmother's house, unlike my parents', was large but dark, with few windows and walls oozing moisture. The two bedrooms at the front were relatively sunny. Between them was the enormous mid house room. Behind that was the spacious kitchen, with a rectangular oak table standing on four sturdy legs, flanked by two benches on the sides and two chairs at the head, and along the wall a huge cabinet. Two adjacent rooms were isolated from the rest of the house: one was for the maid, the other stored sacks of wheat, dried beans, *tremoço* beans, and boxes of clothing sent from America. In chests, put away under better protected conditions, were lengths of fabric, bedspreads, blankets, curtains of various colors and patterns. And that aroma, that aroma of American clothes. Xana was always right beside Vovó, shying away from us as if we were strangers.

She was a scaredy-cat, fearful, filled with chasms that gaped open infinitely. One foot always slipping, the other clinging to life and to colors, which were music to her.

She stared again and again at the warm colors of the American colonial chandelier, standing there for a long time. When she walked away, she carried the whole light fixture with her. She also took the colors: honeycomb yellow, deep Bordeaux red, the blue of the Flemish paintings hanging on Vovó's bedroom walls, and the bright green of the island's fields.

❊

In every part of our grandmother's house, thin silences slid through the outer walls. All you could hear was the buzzing of one or two flies, the busy click-click of Tia Luísa's shoes, or tapping coming from the roof to waken sleepers. The clock's pendulum was more audible, especially as morning dawned. Outside, a vague murmur arose, and then the commotion of women waiting for fish, in order to lay out the midday meal. They wore shawls on their heads, not so much to bundle up as to conceal the secrets of the night, so numerous were the incidents that would unfold in the dark, some real, others invented.

Throughout the afternoon the farmhands would arrive. From time to time you could hear the creaking of an oxcart with wood for the oven.

Xana would run to the door, chase the cart down to the end of the street, and follow the "music" that emanated from its wheels, a music that bore no resemblance to the light, graceful sounds, almost always in a waltz time, from the gramophone.

The noise from the carts was creaky and whiny; whining and creaking, the plodding oxen proceeded. Xana returned home panting like a puppy, her tongue hanging out, and brought with her the scent of magnolias.

Outside, the children's shouting faded away, and the world paused.

By then it was suppertime. Vovó called us to a well-laid table with a white tablecloth of smooth, satiny fabric. The plates were lovely, the soup delicious, and the stuffed capon a delicacy rare for that time of year. *Massa sovada,* sweet rice pudding, and conserves topped off the meal.

Bedtime that night was unusually early. And everyone was wakened around five in the morning—a time convenient for the priest, who was barely able to drag his feet, and whose sermons were scarcely audible.

Around five, Carolina and Xana awoke to a racket that drowned out the *cagarras'* shrieks. Under the Christmas tree sat little baskets filled with carob beans, earthenware and enamelware. We all dressed quickly. Vovó took great care with the clothes she wore. She donned a turquoise and white polka-dot dress; pinned a brooch on her bodice, a gift from her ex-husband; pulled her silver hair up in a bun; and put on a gray felt coat, a three-quarters-length style from the 1940s—a time when, during World War II, she had ventured to visit America again. Memories of Christmas trees festooned with lights of a thousand colors came flooding back to her, to a time when Vovó's house was merry. And afterward came her divorce signed with an *X.*

❀

Daniel went on ahead carrying the lantern, and we all clustered together following his route on a night when the moon was asleep. We arrived in time. The pre-dawn *Missa do Galo* Christmas mass was just starting. Toward its end, seasonal carols filled the air, drifting through the nave of the church. An orderly line moved forward to kiss Baby Jesus. In exchange, each person left a *serrilha,* a sixpence or, in rare instances, a silver coin. The value was always meager, even from the wealthiest parishioners.

We left the church as early morning rushed toward the new day.

Roosters were crowing and dogs barked.

❀

Time was passing, and the dancing shadows persisted. I noticed almost everything, so it was starting to dawn on me that my adjustment was not going to be easy. Xana in those early days embarrassed me. We were

odd in a certain way. Eyes too big for the head, seemingly lost in a nebu
lous eddy of water. Like animals, we would size one another up without
speaking. So I tried this approach:

"Come, Xana, let me give you a kiss.

"Come here, I won't bite. Don't run away, no one will harm you.

"Come here."

She pulled back, shrinking from me and at the same time wanting
to approach, to ask for something she could not name, submerged in a
sea of innocence. I persisted in trying to win her over, to embrace her
once and for all, without fear. But she proved shy; she refused to speak.
I wondered if perhaps she felt confused.

She was accustomed to comings and goings so fleeting that one could
not identify a single thing. She liked her brother very, very much, but
whenever she wanted to express herself she would turn her back and
disappear. And while I was racking my brain I sensed that Xana was—I
don't really know how to put this—perhaps more of an invention than a
reality to me. An indefinable something I could not make out, no matter
how hard I tried—maybe keeping my feet on island soil and its incomprehensible emptiness, if they turned toward the ocean's distant shores.

Suddenly I noticed her running off. And then from a distance, feeling safer, she flashed me a weak, cautious smile. After that she went
back into hiding, probably fearing my presence would take the place of
our grandmother's.

I understood her, but it was difficult to cope with her behavior. I
tried.

◎

Of course the closeness between my sisters Xana and Carolina was
almost spontaneous. This came as no surprise, since their ages were not
as far apart. Xana simply did not like it when Carolina hit her or hid her
toys or said bad words to which Xana was unaccustomed. But it was not
long before Xana and Carolina had a falling-out—one moment the best
of friends, the next fighting like cats and dogs. The differences between
them were irreconcilable, starting with the way the two had been
raised. Xana was introverted, like someone who feels cold and needs to
be wrapped in a blanket; Carolina was extroverted and manipulative,

more a girl of the streets than a homebody, and with a jealous nature that irritated us all.

But I was used to Carolina; with Xana, everything was exceedingly alien to me. I thought to myself, however, that perhaps Carolina was suffering even more than her little sister because, being six years Xana's senior, she was old enough to remember Mamã's tenderness. And the worst part was that since Mamã's departure, Carolina found herself shuttled among Luciana, Tio António, and both of our grandmothers.

In that situation what mattered most to her was finding ways to scrape together some loose change for chocolates, to sneak a few spoonfuls of jam, and, to Vovó's dismay, to swipe the beautiful porcelain miniatures kept in the china cabinet. They sat there as a reminder of times when Mamã played with them in the New Bedford mansion as a child.

Carolina wore the old ladies out. She would insist on taking one item or another—especially a glass dome suitable for covering (just as we did in real life) the Holy Spirit crown, except this headpiece was woven of arrow leaf. And it was not for lack of toys. Mamã sent many from America, but the ones behind the glass were what Carolina longed for, far more than chocolates. It was an obsession. As if by magic, she could open the china cabinet without difficulty and leave not so much as a trace. She would run off, and for a while no one would know where she had gone.

She was a Cinderella heading off in every direction. Vovó despaired. "She seems like a wild child," Vovó murmured in distraction, with a deeply wounded expression. "Yes, a child of nature—sometimes belonging to everyone, other times to no one, this granddaughter of mine," Vovó continued, indignant and worried. "How can we raise her in such a situation, Luísa? What can be done, my God, when each person raises her their own way?"

"Patience, sister! Let's take things a bit slower. You know full well that a nest is not built overnight. It's a matter of time."

❋

In truth, the old ladies—Vovó as well as Tia Luísa—were exhausted from worry. They could offer only their love, of which they still had plenty, but they could not do more. So that was how Carolina was growing up, ever more mischievous, more jealous of everything and everyone. And the person who most paid the price was Xana, her greatest "enemy." However, she quickly changed moods, then would lend her sister toys she owned, only to demand them back soon thereafter, thus stealing the pleasure of a moment that, once interrupted, left Xana beside herself.

One day Xana foamed with rage.

"No, no, I don't need your toys," and then she kicked them all.

Carolina lunged at Xana and pulled her hair.

Xana screamed, "I'm going to tell Vovó on you, and pray for the devil to take you." And, seizing the moment, she shoved Carolina, and her glass tumbler broke into tiny shards, clink-clink-clink.

Scared to death, Carolina wept like rain running down the windowpane. She saw Vovó coming in from outside and went straight to her, "It's not my fault, it was Xana's, for pushing me."

"Now, let's all calm down. I don't want to see anyone crying, so let's close this sad chapter and say no more about it. Whichever one of you opens your mouth first will get smacked twice. End of discussion."

It was obvious that Vovó was upset, but not wanting to show it. Yet there was nothing to do besides forget about it, although the loss of that antique gold-colored glassware pained her.

After a few seconds, Vovó noticed Xana's fury and then remembered that the worst thing you could do to this girl was to deceive her. She had never forgotten the fake "birdie" during that click-click of the camera shutter, when nothing ever appeared. Being deceived was what irritated Xana most.

Hours later, Carolina very quietly returned the toys and kissed her sister's damp, silent face.

The sun was setting here, in order to go illuminate other lands and peoples. Wintry nighttime was falling. Layers of frost covered the town. Vovó hurried to fetch her beautiful American blankets out from the chests, but Tia Luísa insisted we not use them. Although no one knew why, she preferred the older comforters that our great-grandmother—Mamã's father's mother—had brought back from Brazil when her in-laws and husband for some unknown reason decided to return to Portugal. However, her time on our island was brief. She had lost her husband, stricken by a heart attack at just age thirty. With no head of the family, plus three children, she had to embark on a new adventure by heading for the Promised Land. Unlike the old blankets from those long-ago times in Brazilian lands, the American ones my grandmother brought us, with pride and a glint in her eyes, were new. Their texture was unique, fluffy and soft, their colorful warmth the shade of light. It was so appealing to curl up in them that it seemed we were sleeping on cloud castles, surrounded by a perfume that filled the house.

Those were gloomy times indeed. The oil lamps' soothing light flickered intermittent elongated shadows, climbing and dancing around the four walls up to the ceiling. At each unidentifiable noise our hearts leapt in fright. Silence reigned, especially in the houses. We would whisper. We spoke so low that not even the devil could hear. Throughout the night it was good to hear a soft voice fall on empty spaces. We would stay near the table after supper, listening for the voices to disappear softly, lulling us with their endless echo.

Tia Luísa and Vovó also recalled the olden days in America, taking difficult paths, as well as other times like those of childhood, where tenderness found its place in the home. Daniel in turn remained attentive and thoughtful, sending the smoke from his pipe twirling into the air, perhaps imagining a new painting, sculpture, or even a gardening project.

❊

Amid memories intersecting with reality, the old ladies would map out each next day, which in general would be identical to the one before, while Vovó in her rocking chair wiped away her worries and prayed some Hail Marys that soon transported her to dreamland. Then it was time for Daniel to wake them and send old and young alike off to bed. Sometimes he would stay up reading or writing, other times drawing sketches for pictures he was going to paint.

Rosary beads could then be heard sliding, sliding—rustling until they quieted the conscience. Each day was for him another day of perfecting, of devotion to a higher cause that he himself had chosen for his life, a life he had constructed like a spider weaving its web. He knew just what he wanted. Hence the stubbornness they attributed to him, when it was in the end only a matter of conviction. A little too much puritanism to suit the tastes of Vovó who, with no expectation of dissuading her grandson or influencing him in any way, opened up to her sister.

※

As day dawned, Pico da Vara awoke robed in a white bridal gown covering half of one side of her body. The sun shone outside, and the wind was blowing back the waves. That morning the sea was the color of emeralds. Next to the dark stones lay a fine silvery dust. In the trenches, hail piled up like stars fallen to earth. And happy children dashed madly into the street. It was a feast day, so ephemeral. The cold sliced like sharp blades. People lusted after the snow's whiteness and wanted to eat it—and even could, crunching it pearl by pearl as their hands turned purple, the color of the dead.

※

It was Sunday.

The bells were tolling.

All Souls' Day.

This was the year's longest mass, most of the children and young adults thought. Everyone in the village dressed all in dark colors. The sky was tinged with heavy shadows, but once in a while a narrow ray of sunshine broke through.

The church stood nearby.

In the streets, not a living soul.

Everyone was inside. Desolation. Deep darkness and so much black everywhere. Long, endless sighs. And nimble fingers running through each rosary bead at a dizzying pace, in order to work off sins. Closed lips in unison made a buzzing that filled the air with the sound of swarming bees. And how icy cold it was. It stuck to the flesh, and one's whole body trembled. Our grandmother moved along, unnoticed by others. She would not wear black, even when someone had died. Her blue-gray coat, flattering to her figure and alabaster face, lent the air a luminescence that could be scarcely seen, scarcely noticed. She trailed behind us; Daniel moved away to take his place among the men. Reserved seats were waiting for us up front near the main altar. I was next to Vovó, standing. Xana and Carolina sat on the step next to the railing that separated the faithful from the altar.

The mass commenced. The stench of death predominated, mixed with mold, naphthalene mothballs, and burning candles. Endless hymns were offered in an incomprehensible language. They dragged on and on, amid sighs and the dead light that filtered through the windows. There was one prayer that ran on for as long as a miller grinding flour for hours on end.

Carolina squirmed, then squirmed some more, and did not last very long before she went over to Vovó with a stony look on her face and asked to leave. "I gotta pee-pee," she pleaded, with huge tears in her eyes. She exited, but never returned. Xana, sitting with the other children, entertained herself with a handkerchief she used as a doll. She was seated facing our grandmother and peered into her eyes. Xana wanted to tell her that she could bear no more, that her little body could not endure being stuck in the same position without moving—nor so many people dressed all in black, like the coffin at the funeral for Uncle Félix of Rua Mangana in Achadinha, "and I'm afraid of him."

She was about to say something to Vovó when all of a sudden we heard a frightful noise. The priest was preparing to ascend the pulpit, a kind of crow's nest embedded in the column of one of the naves, to the right below the altar. It felt as though a deathly fear was falling heavily on the faithful.

❀

His sermon began.

Xana looked up and instead of a priest saw a blackbird with a black-and-orange hooked beak, jumping like crazy from side to side. He hopped forward, then to the right and to the left, all crazed, his hair resembling barbed wire. It seemed certain that none of his flock would escape without having a stone cast at their heads for the evil of their sins.

The initial whispering of the faithful before the start of the mass gave way bit by bit to an unaccustomed shouting that cracked open and crumbled the church walls like cornbread. And when the blackbird fell silent for a brief moment, in search of a stone with which to pelt a sinner once again, what we heard was a roll call of laments and sighs, hollow coughs and blowing of noses, with which there converged a cascade of tears of guilt.

"Forgive us. Do not forsake us, O Lord our God," they all said in unison.

Like so many gray reptiles, they kept shedding tears and whispering endless Hail Marys. And the stones did not stop coming. They were leveled with such violence that they seemed to come out of the belly of a volcano that from time to time would go dormant, only to resume with redoubled bursts in an overwhelming explosion. At first they resembled fireworks; some thought it must be another plane crashing onto Pico da Vara. And with each fury and screech from the blackbird, the sun hid behind clouds, shivering.

I glanced over at Xana. There she was again, as happened every Sunday, with her head stuck through the balustrade of the railing, transporting her over to the other side, that favorite place of hers. From there she could see everything and feel safe. But something was upsetting her: it was that soot-colored blackbird. Intrigued, she searched Vovó's face. The smile that blossomed from Vovó belied what the priest was saying. Our God might be the one of that priest, of that pulpit, but Vovó's God was different—the God of flowers, tolerance, and joy.

Her head held high, Vovó assumed a facial expression that gave Xana a warm feeling and a promise of not abandoning her granddaughter to that blackbird. Vovó again gave her a broad smile, as if to say, "Believe in the God who alights every day on the flowers in our backyard."

From that moment on, my sister started viewing everything in a different light. I noticed that her contorted face was gradually relaxing, as her eyes looked away from the pulpit in the opposite direction, toward the Infant Jesus of Prague, her companion in fantasies. She believed that saints spoke, opened their eyes, and on their lips danced a smile the color of the sun. Sometimes they were sad, but at that moment they were already starting to warm. Then Xana closed her eyes tight, in order to forget everything to the point of oblivion, and to recall the Hallelujah Saturday when men went into the street with wooden rattles to announce the season of celebration: Easter Sunday and then the feasts of the Divine Holy Spirit, when the church would be adorned with flowers, its snow-white walls whitewashed in the spring. Light, light everywhere, that was what Xana saw.

And fireworks exploding outside, and girls being crowned next to the altar, dressed in white organdy with matching bows fluttering, as the church filled with a rainbow, with voices singing the *Te Deum*. And the smell of incense wafting out the wide-open front doors. More and more fireworks soaring into the sky, announcing the time for Hallelujah. And that's the way it was, back when God was a nightingale.

❈

After a momentary pause, a brief commotion was heard once again. It was the blackbird climbing down from his pulpit. He was drenched. We noticed a slight shiver, then his body began to tremble. He headed for the sacristy. Everything was finished. A purple mantle then fell over the church; a thick dust blinded everyone.

Beneath the debris of the darkened church, jam-packed with rocks, all the rats arrived from miles around: rats that gnawed shawls, linens, the wood of the altars. Everything all chewed up, and those people there, amid the rot, stuck to women's menstrual blood. And the priest, without telling anyone, begged God to send more rats to frighten the sinners. Men and women shouted in hysteria, terrified, hiding and crawling beneath a dust thick enough to cut with a knife. They were afraid to raise their heads, to feel the curse that would consign them to hell. It was a sentence nobody wanted to hear. Some fled in one direction, some in another, elbowing each other and falling on rats, creeping and yelling, terror stricken.

That day there was no man who did not behave like a woman; they were crying and shaking with fear.

The dust was settling, settling. And the rats, themselves scared, returned to their subterranean hiding places, primarily back to where the corn was stored.

God's people began to disperse, ashamed: their faces the color of wax; the color of corpses; heavy bodies; fallen heads, stricken with fear.

They were weighted down by a world made of lead. They shuffled their shoes, sandals or clogs, or in some cases the soles of their feet, through the church. And their steps were slow.

They left "humiliated and offended."

❈

Xana grew so shaken, so nervous—while in the churchyard, people were timidly commenting on what had transpired inside—that she began to speak incoherently, trying to say everything at the same time, like a fireworks explosion on a feast day. Her words all seemed to want to rush out of her mouth, run together in an unstoppable garble. And, since that was impossible, Xana wept nonstop out of anger and rebellion; she simply did not want anybody to come near her. Whereupon Daniel, from a safe distance, idly began to play with words—*una duna tena catuna, paia papaia pica não pica releque: makes ten!*—a nonsense counting rhyme based on the numbers one to ten that students learn in first grade.

Xana liked it and grew ecstatic. A broad smile crossed her face in no time. Her eyes widened in amazement. That was just what she wanted, without realizing it: the smell, the color, the smooth skin of a petal. "One petal, two petals, ten petals," Xana said in delight, squealing with so much pleasure.

❁

People around her stopped, slack-jawed, their eyes riveted on her. And they all proclaimed, "It's a miracle, a miracle," while my grandmother remained calm. But her joy was immeasurable; for the first time, she heard from her granddaughter's lips the sweet word "Vovó." Xana seemed crazed; she was in fact beside herself, dazzled, throwing around words like someone pulling clothes out of a bag that had just arrived from America and tossing them about. They came in all colors, in the language she was mastering. Since childhood she knew how to eat and smell them, to roll them on Vovó's fingers and feel the sun on the china cabinet.

"Oooh, yellow!" she exulted, warm as a wagtail's throat, pearly, forever soft, between silk and velvet; fleur-de-lis, passion flowers.

❁

While Daniel was playing with Xana on the way home, he caught a distant glimpse of Carolina in the backyard climbing the fig tree in search of birds' nests. My brother left Xana behind and started running. He entered the house and headed straight through to the backyard. When he saw Carolina, he was so angry he slapped her twice. Their shouting was loud enough to fill the river banks and echo like thunder throughout the whole village. My grandmother, who had just gone into the house, went to help. She called Carolina in and promised her several spoonfuls of whatever kind of preserves she desired, but the girl was unable to hear her. She continued to sob, muttering incoherent phrases. She was hurt, deeply offended, with a deep-seated pain, although she did not even know where.

She did not want to see Daniel anymore, yet she did not wish to lose him. It was best to leave. At that moment she just wanted Felisberta the maid, so they could both play in the old orchard. She was a clumsy maid. She did not like being in the house. When she was done with her assigned chores, she would join the men in the fields, helping them to prune, sow, and even dig. To feel good, she needed to be in the countryside, and Carolina was the same way. They were good friends, and it was Felisberta who had taught her the pleasures of going barefoot, of running free, not only in the orchard but with greater joy through the nearly impenetrable dense woods while playing hide-and-seek, shrieking and squawking louder than *cagarras*—and at the same time, both of them frightened but neither one falling into a bramble thicket then emerging all scratched up.

But nothing happened. Felisberta and Carolina remained in a world of total freedom. They roared and roared with laughter, enjoying the way their mouths were sweetened with the aroma of the ginger lily flower, which absorbed essences of the entire earth. It was a comfort one could eat and drink, so strong was its concrete, palpable intensity. And everything was damp, and ever more aromatic. The smell was so strong that Carolina was about to faint—just as had happened in the opposite way to Tia Luísa the previous Sunday when, surrounded by people wearing cheap cologne on their unwashed bodies, she felt very unwell and seemed delirious, talking out of her head.

Felisberta was free as a bird in flight, so oblivious to everything around her, even to her friend Carolina.

"It's time for us to start back," Carolina shouted, all the while chewing on her fingers, aware that they had wandered too far.

The drizzle started off light, then began getting heavier. In just a few minutes it turned into a torrential downpour falling with a vengeance. They were drenched.

"Cursed rain," Carolina wailed, afraid of being berated by Vovó and Tia Luísa. They ran and ran, terror stricken, but it was too late. They were blinded by flashes of flaming light; boulders rolled with a window-shattering echo. Carolina grew impatient and frightened. She was nervous and bit her fingernails.

"Let's get outta here, dummy! You wanna stay out, exposed to the elements all night?"

"Shut up, Carolina, and get a move on!" Felisberta prodded. "Quick, before a lightning bolt splits us in two."

They stepped up their pace. Flowers were falling one after another onto the dirt paths.

✦

By now it was late afternoon and the rain had let up, suspended in mid-air. The evening tolling of *trindades* approached, and neither Carolina nor Felisberta was anywhere to be seen. A few minutes later, after what seemed an eternity, they came in the door sopping wet. After shaking off the rain, they headed straight for the wood stove to warm up. Tia Luísa hobbled over to her old chest to see if she could find dry clothing to fit Felisberta. "Go change clothes, you scruffs, before your grandmother loses patience," she remarked in a brusque tone.

The kitchen was toasty warm, and there were roasted chestnuts on the table, ready to eat. As usual, here and there lay photographs and postcards with which the old ladies amused themselves. We devoured the chestnuts as voraciously as the postcards.

Carolina lacked the nerve to go approach Vovó, who did not budge. She was far above all that. If it was necessary to take measures, as it should have been, only an appropriate punishment could be meted out. At the very least, giving her granddaughter a vigorous tug on the ear, and sending Felisberta packing, never to return. But that, Vovó mused, would only create difficulties. It wouldn't be worth it. The household needed peace and quiet. She thought to herself, "Oh, if it weren't for Daniel, I don't know what my life would be like. I'm tired, so tired, Luísa. What a great burden my daughter has dropped in my lap. And I always pray to God that nothing happens to this child. No, it's not worth it, Luísa. Not worth it."

Annoyed, she left the kitchen and headed for the parlor, where Daniel was.

✦

Vovó entered the living room in silence. She sat down at the side opposite the table where, by lamplight, Daniel was starting to paint a picture he'd been planning for some time. Vovó swelled with pride watching those outlines, which bore little rhyme or reason to her at first. It was just a formless mass that took shape little by little. All of a sudden something happened that Vovó did not understand. "It was a miracle in her grandson's hands," she told herself.

"What is that, Daniel?"

"Oh Vovó, pay attention. It's a house in ruins, with some door jambs unhinged by winds overpowering the trees till they're all bent over, touching the ground, which is strewn with dead leaves; a pitch-black overcast sky, and in the background, a clearing of bright blue."

Daniel applied his final brush strokes, leaning laboriously over the picture of that creeping shadow he was dissolving—contorting the movements of his fingers in order to add one brush stroke, then another, trying to impart form without definition. At this my grandmother's eyes flashed.

In an instant, Vovó saw in the painting something to which she could not put a name but nonetheless sensed. Something that comforted her, stirring up old emotions again and again with a mixture of tears and song.

❁

Ever since that day when Xana, like tongues of fire, strove in confusion to utter the words for smells, colors, and tastes, she never left Daniel's side. Every morning she climbed into his bed. And that aroma had a name: warmth. Xana was as light as a bird on the wing.

Everything that for three years had been pent up inside my sister now poured forth like water running from all directions. Words came not only from her mouth but over distant routes on a pilgrimage through the centuries, sometimes in sandals on highways, other times barefoot via backroads. They came too from a home where words were mixed in a new pidgin language—*soela* for sweater, *alvarozes* for overalls, *coxim* for couch, *pana* for pan, *jumpa* for jumper, *boques* for box—with no equivalent in island vocabulary. The words came from a home where English and American magazines piled up in the china closet—and also a bit from everywhere mixed with photographs, of which the most prominent were those containing Uncle Joe, who could appear or vanish overnight. The photos that accumulated in the empty spaces of the dresser and living room table were numerous, beyond the most privileged ones that found a prominent place in the family album, as well as loose ones that were either on the kitchen table or in the old ladies' laps, mainly Vovó's. And she always had her magnifying glass at hand. But it so happened that others existed that were quite extraordinary.

These in no way resembled the aforementioned photographs that stayed in a box stored with care by Tia Luísa. They were glass plates covered with a photosensitive solution that contained images of World War I, all of naval battles. Handling them required extreme caution. To view the images, it was necessary to use backlighting. The least carelessness could cause them to shatter to bits, Tia Luísa warned. They were relics, keepsakes that only came out when someone was sick. In bed, everything was safer; if by some chance one of the photo plates slipped out of your hands, it would fall onto a soft surface, on the bed, the sheets, or the cotton blankets.

❄

One time, Carolina was sick with mumps. Tia Luísa would not leave her bedside—not that the disease was life-threatening, but because it was impossible to trust that light-footed little sneak who at any moment might escape out the door, and then we would have a hard time catching her. So Tia Luísa stayed right nearby, pacing back and forth keeping watch while Carolina slept. And when she would wake up, our Titia entertained her with stories: tales she enjoyed so much, of witches, wandering souls, and goat-footed women, that when told by her aunt acquired a force that captivated all who heard them. They were accounts that, in a soft voice in the bedroom's half-light, resembled litanies, dragging on into the dark of night, where slumber awaited.

It was suppertime. Tia Luísa got out of her chair. She straightened the bedding, pulled up the blankets in order to cover Carolina's shoulders, set her head on the pillow, and softly kissed her on the cheek, as only she knew how to do. She was our goddess of the hearth, of the temple, all white, and thus known as Luísa Branca. Her face was white; her hair as white as fine snow, something she had seen on several occasions when she went to America back when her sister was having a baby every year.

All her life Tia Luísa had never done anything for own sake, but always for others'. She was down-to-earth, plain, and possessed a sense of humor that was pleasing to her neighbors, and to people in general. She would wear any old thing, and whenever she wore shoes she would almost always put them on the wrong feet. She wore a scarf and shawl. Gray and white were her colors of choice, but she wore whatever clothing was at hand. She was now in her eighties; no one knew her exact age. Her lips had shriveled and turned inward in the shape of a bun, with her sweet look of kindness and serenity, that infinite kindness of hers.

She crossed the center room of the house in silence and headed for the kitchen. My grandmother, who was expecting her for dinner, was startled by what she saw. Luísa held within her a light incomparable to any other. It was from there that her sweet kindness emanated, her devotion to those in need. "And from her sunny face," my grandmother mused, in view of what she felt but did not know how to name.

She stopped talking and stood there with nothing further to add.

And the clock continued its incessant tick-tock, tick-tock, tick-tock. Evermore, nevermore.

⊛

A few days after Xana's voice debuted, fresh as a newly opening flower, the house was filled with names of things. As Daniel went about teaching Xana her ABCs, he feared his sister's bold curiosity. It seemed as if she were on a sinking ship, pleading for help. There was nothing in that house, the street, or anywhere else that did not have something to do with the letters she was hopefully inscribing on the ground, while the following morning seemed as if it would never, ever arrive.

Whenever Daniel called her, she ran with so much eagerness that she would trip and fall flat on the ground. At a slow but steady pace, my brother was teaching her to read and write the alphabet: first her capital letters, then lowercase ones. Xana derived such pleasure from the letters' shapes. Each was created with fascinating movements, serpentining like a caterpillar among cabbage plants, veering in one direction, then the other. The shape of each letter suggested to her languages that only she could decipher. She disliked the letter *A*, she remarked to Daniel, for it had the shape of an airplane, which never brought what she asked for. The letter *C* stood for the word "céu," the sky, heaven, a crescent moon lying in her hand; *M* was for the mother she did not have. And, to Daniel's bewilderment, Xana had nothing further to add.

"Oh, but there's a letter that's very sweet. Do you know what it is, Daniel?"

"No, I don't," my brother replied with irony.

"Yes, you do. It smells like fennel. It's the *V* of '*Vovó*' and '*vento,*' the wind.

"Now look at you, Daniel, with the *X* of Christ's cross that you wear around your neck."

"Oh, and what about the *X* of your name, Xana. Had you forgotten?"

"No, I didn't. My *X* is just about to fall out of the alphabet, Daniel."

"About to fall out of the alphabet, Xana? What do you mean?"

"Oh, if the next letter, *Z*, didn't act like a bracket, *X* would fall out, and then I wouldn't have a name."

And off she ran jumping for joy, in search of her playmates.

My brother stayed there thinking, and muttered to himself with a hint of irony.

"Yes, Xana . . . that very same *X* that altered the fate of Vovó and the rest of the family in the American courtroom, when she sealed her own fate, and donned her own shroud."

❁

Xana liked to take the letters and mix them all up, then delve into each one in order to hear its white music filled with the light of the full moon. Some were soothing like Vovó's American blankets woven in soft, beautiful colors of the rainbow on a day that is both sunny and rainy. Guttural consonants irritated her. They were harsh and angular, abrasive like cats in heat at night. Worse yet, they made her imagine Mamã's gales of laughter, which Xana knew only from what Vovó and Tia Luísa had told her.

Unlike those consonants, the sibilants were the friendliest sounds, dancing over the piano keys, above the delicate whisper of a windblown spring over little round pebbles in the short summertime creeks. So she caressed them with the breath of a warm, soft smile that had always given birth to Vovó's velvety countenance.

❀

Xana ran to Vovó, very happy.

"Vovó! Vovó! I've finished my English lesson using the letter *V*. I'll read it to you: *É inverno, duro inverno. Neva tanto. O monte e o tecto têm neve. É um nevão. O vento varre a neve. Avô, Avó, vê a névoa. É um nevoeiro.* ("It is winter, a hard winter. So much snow. The mountain and the roof have snow. It is a heavy snow. The wind blows the snow. Grandfather, grandfather, see the fog. It is a thick fog.")

"I didn't make a single mistake, Vovó."

"Wonderful, Xana. I'm proud of you. Keep up your studies, my girl."

At that moment memories came flooding back to Vovó of times when Xana was still a baby and used to point her little body straight into the wind, seeking it with the voracity of a nursing infant in search of its mother's breast. But the wind was not a breast, let alone Mamã, my grandmother would think. Indeed, it was the *V* of *vento*, the wind that shook our islands with their tempestuous tides for days on end. It was also, and above all, the *V* of *Vovó*, whom Xana confused with Mamã.

"Listen, Xana," Vovó continued, "I can't read or write, my dear, but I know that not everything you're saying is necessarily just about letters. It also has to do with my skin and yours, the warmth and cold of the many flowers in the backyard, and the aroma that connects and attracts tenderness and affections. It passes through a heart that knows how to 'read,' and the window of our glances.

"I watch you, always at a distance, and gradually I'm starting to be able to read you. I descend into your dovelike heart, where your body's frailty is palpable to me—and at the same time it has the brutal force of a flaming ember."

❀

As a reward for her first lessons, which Xana learned quickly, my brother brought her a storybook from the city, which contained tales she had never heard. She was surprised and did not understand.

So Daniel explained, "I hadn't told them to you before because these stories I'm telling you now are new, and come from books. The problem was that I didn't have any tales to tell you besides those that circulate in the village," he insisted, talking only to himself.

Xana did not comprehend, her eyes lost and adrift in a look of amazement. Then suddenly it hit her like a ton of bricks. Daniel was seeking a way to convey that the old ladies could not read, and that long ago when he and his sisters were still living with their parents in Burguete they did not come to their grandmother's house to read but rather to play. "Back then you were a very small child, so we and our friends paid you hardly any attention.

"We liked you a lot, but we liked to play with kids more our own age. Do you understand, Xana?" She looked at Daniel, and he could see that she did not.

It would be better to look for the airplane. She hopped out of his bed and disappeared.

❋

They searched for her. The church bells were tolling *trindades,* and no one could find her. She had gone to the room of Tia Luísa, who was accustomed to going to bed early, like the hens.

On that late afternoon, Xana did not want to know where Daniel was. Clouds of gray doubts crossed her vacant face.

Exhausted, she went to bed listening to the chirps of a bird nesting on Vovó's bedroom windowsill. It was so tiny, and Xana gradually began falling sleep. The next morning she got up very early and, to everyone's surprise, did not go climb into Daniel's bed. She refused to eat or see anyone. Not her girlfriends, nor even Vovó at all, either. She remained stock-still, staring without seeing or hearing a thing almost the entire day.

❋

The day dawned radiant. Droplets of water hung like rosary beads, forming an asymmetric lacework on the fresh early morning leaves. Some of them grew full and began to fall drop by drop between the furrows of light and shadow. The day, enveloped in the air that had grown humid and vaporous the night before, slowly woke her. At that hour Xana was surprisingly not with Daniel, nor was she anywhere to be found. Carolina, who was cunning and knew her sister's habits, located her with ease and ran off. She was frightened to see those eyes burning as they peered from between the wall partitions. They were as huge as those of the ox in our neighbor's corral next door. Xana clutched Vovó's conch shell in her hand, and her skinny little body fit into the confined space inside the wall. Her eyes were not moving, nor could they see.

"Omigod-omigod, Vovó! Xana's bewitched. Omigod," Carolina bellowed over and over, terror stricken. Then she began running through the village, warning all her girlfriends in a soft voice that Xana was possessed and about to die, and that all that was left of her were the eyes bulging out of her head.

✦

Unlike the rest of us, Carolina knew full well what she had done to Xana, leaving her in a state of shock. We did not discover this until much, much later.

The day before, after having been offended by Daniel, Xana had hidden under Felisberta's bed, which was low to the ground so she felt safe there, because nobody could find where she was. Carolina, blessed with an infallible nose for detection, was able to locate her sister in short order. When Xana saw Carolina, she panicked and started to cry for help, but her sister stopped her by covering her mouth. "Shut up, Xana, or I'll kill you!"

"Don't cry. I just want to tell you a story, one that's much better than any found in books. Okay?"

"No, no, no, I don't want to hear your stories. Go away!" Xana shouted.

But Carolina insisted.

"Listen to what I tell you. Here's what happened. Back when Mamã and Papá went to America, it was because the witches wouldn't leave our house or let anybody sleep all night. They smashed our chairs and beat up Papá. And they were the ones who damaged the gable on our house and made it almost fall down. They're also the ones who killed the animals and cast a spell on you when you were born."

Xana recoiled and reached for the wall, in order to brace herself. She almost fainted.

She regained her composure and shot back, "You liar! You're a big fat liar, that's what you are! Let go of my hand!"

"No lie. You're so stupid, and if you don't shut up, I'll slap you. I saw everything, Xana. That terrible night I slept with Tia Luísa in the space above Mamã's bedroom. There were lots of strange noises, and the house was dark. Through the floorboards a faint light seeped up that was barely visible. I slipped out of bed in order not to wake Tia Luísa, and tiptoed over to see what was happening downstairs. Through cracks in the floorboards I could see Mamã lying on the bed with her legs apart, shouting. Some large thing was coming out from between them. And all I wanted to do was to disappear, run away from what I didn't understand. I couldn't do a thing. I saw so much blood that I thought they must have been cutting off her leg. I shook like a leaf. I wanted to go back to sleep and forget everything. But, my God, that huge thing was killing Mamã. And I was crying out of fear, unable to open my mouth, unable to understand a thing. A little later I realized that what I'd seen wasn't some object or a severed leg, but a little girl. Perhaps Mamã and Papá wanted to surprise us by ordering a little girl sent from France, and they placed the baby between our mother's legs in order to make it look like hers. And it was you, Xana."

"Me? You're nuts. Let go of my hand. Go away."

"Listen. For a long time, I thought babies came from France, but it's not true, Xana."

Xana held her breath. She opened her mouth and suddenly shot back.

"Of course they come from France. Every mother says the same thing. You're the only one who says they don't. You're the only one because you're a sackful of bigger lies than the ones that come from America."

Carolina refused to stop and pressed on.

"I'll tell you how babies are born, you ninny, but you can't tell anybody else, you hear? If you let any of this out of your big mouth, I'll turn you into an onion, understand? Or do you want to go to hell?"

Xana didn't let out a peep. She sweated buckets, swallowing her fear and just wanting to disappear. At that moment she wished she were a piece of paper someone had wadded up so tight that nobody knew where it was.

"Do you really want to know where babies come from?" Xana covered her ears and froze stiff as a board. She did not reply. She looked perplexed and her eyes seemed lost, spinning like a carousel.

Carolina again insisted. She laughed and laughed to the point of nausea.

"Look, listen closely. Babies really do come out of their mothers' bellies from between their legs, through the little hole they pee out of. And presto, that's all there is to it."

Xana shivered from the cold, all twisted up, horrified by what she had heard.

A cloud darkened her eyes, and Carolina's voice droned on, sinking into the thick fog in the distance.

Xana could no longer hear nor speak.

Once she felt like her old self, sad and hurt, she left that hiding place, exchanging it for another, and concealed herself inside the wall. She wanted to die. What upset her so much at that moment was the lying, always the lying. More than anything else it was her fear of the truth, her anxiety of one day waking up with a baby between her legs. And whenever she thought of that, she asked God just to take her away with Him.

Day by day, Xana languished, as her eyes became ever more prominent and her body smaller.

❀

Word flew faster than those chariots of fire from America, Vovó remarked to herself when she saw so many people flocking to her house, panting as they came through the door to find out what was going on, as if it were any of their business. Grandmother kept quiet, and nothing could dislodge her serenity. She was strong and, in such cases, ready for whatever came her way. She was very familiar with Xana's habits. Almost all of them involved seeking out a hiding place, whether inside the wall, in the hedge, under the bed, or in so many other places. "A different hiding place for each sorrow, according to its degree of pain," my grandmother explained to Daniel and me.

"Xana's always been that way, so there's no reason for you two to worry. During her first few years, while you were living with Luciana up in Burguete, unaware of anything, she had already gone through that wall of silences and mysteries five or six times. At first I experienced fears that left thorns in my heart—but later I got used to it, and at some point realized that each of those hideaways had its own meaning, which

I began to digest and later came to understand. And that's what you need to know so we can avoid panic in this household. For instance, in the case of the hedge, what Xana means is, "Don't deceive me. Let me wait for Mamã, who never arrives." When she goes inside the wall she's saying, 'I'm closing my eyes and hope to die.'"

As she had done so many other times, Xana reentered her wall, thrust into a long sleep of interminable absences.

⊛

She would not eat a thing. She was hiding in a cranny with her eyebrow cocked, hoping the angles of the walls would swallow her up. Neighbor ladies and relatives in league with one another would come over and fill the center room of the house. They declared that things could not keep on this way, that someone needed to notify her parents in America, that the old ladies lacked the guts to stand up to Xana's stubbornness, that she had to eat even if they had to slap her in order to make her do so.

My angelic grandmother, although not wishing to be discourteous, stepped forward and boldly shouted, "Out, out, you insolent creatures! So I'm not capable of taking care of my granddaughter because of my age? Get out and don't come back! Leave my house in peace!"

As for the accusations, none of them fazed our dear grandmother. She knew Xana better than anyone else did. And, regarding the issue of witchcraft, she had never believed in such foolishness. Instead, she relied on science, on what the doctor had explained to her concerning Xana's biological rhythms.

⊛

For my grandmother, the experiences of her time in America had been the best education. She was certain that the body possessed its own rhythms, which should not be disrupted.

She looked at Daniel and me and continued, "Actually, it's always necessary to insist, to try and make her eat and drink, yet without ever violating her dignity. I don't, nor will I ever, let anyone get in her way or mine. Only under dire circumstances. When she started hiding in those places, I consoled myself with the proverb, 'Those who don't eat will drink, and those who drink won't die.' And that's the way it was.

When she closed her mouth and wouldn't even take liquids, that's when I sprang into action, full speed ahead."

Turning to Xana, "Come on, drink your flour broth, and your chocolate milk," my grandmother insisted, letting Xana know that if she persisted that way, her little head might explode from exhaustion and lack of nutrition.

"Your head, my little one, holds inside it the source of life, for it retains your vision to see and recreate the world, depicting it with the most varied tones and tastes. Your nose is there for you to breathe and to absorb the smells and colors of the lovely butterflies, your butterflies, Xana! Your ears, I know that you keep them in another world, my dear. They hear voices I'm unfamiliar with, voices that leave your eyes bloodshot.

"But Xana, why do you limit yourself to being so distant?" Vovó asked, in desperation.

"Why don't you say something? Tell me, girl. Cat got your tongue, Xana? Where did you leave it? You must find it. What is this all about?

"Come on, come on. Look, you can't survive. If you keep this up, I'm sure we'll be separated from one another forever. Is that what you want?"

In a flash Xana grasped the meaning of "sadness." With a cry of terror she clung to Vovó and in a sheepish tone asked her for an orangeade filled with "tears." She did not want to, but she drank it. She felt a lump in her throat.

❀

When my grandmother was preparing to go into the kitchen to get her the orangeade, she looked back and noticed that Xana was holding the conch shell up to her ear.

"Why, this is the first sign of recovery in her giant, mysterious leap from darkness into the light," my grandmother exulted.

Her little girl could hear the ocean. And the smell of the tide whetted her appetite. Vovó flashed a half-moon smile. The worst of the crisis was over, she thought in jubilation.

Xana was just skin and bones, and her teary eyes continued "crying in the wilderness." But now she was playing with her conch shell, trying to rock it to sleep. And when the conch shell "woke up," it emitted distant voices, calming voices, nourishing voices. In the distance she heard the motion of the sea, the waves rolling onto the shore. And that was how she got to know Vovó's ocean, the one that washed her away and brought her back, alternating between high and low tides. A sea that spoke to her and deposited as many secrets as Xana wished to hear.

Now that she all of a sudden possessed the gift of speech, Xana asked Vovó a direct question.

"When are they coming?"

The answer was conspicuous by its absence.

Xana waited . . .

And waited and waited, but received no reply, and blocked out the noise of an invisible wing that was passing by. Still, she lingered another moment. Slowly and silently, she was beginning to wean herself from the wall, touching things around her, looking, staring, freeing herself until she left that dead spell behind.

And then, lo and behold, there she was full of joy. The entire house was white. So was the backyard. And the sky. So too was the start of spring.

❀

First thing the next morning, my sister woke up the whole household. No one could hold her back, so great was her energy, her eagerness and her desire to absorb life in a single day. Frailty was her strength. She liked challenging the older boys to race her around the house and most of the time beat them. At times she felt out of breath. But give up? Never! She adored competition, the feeling of life in the palm of her hand.

When there were no older girls or boys to play with, because they were all busy helping their parents, she occupied herself in the backyard. Sometimes she chased butterflies or played in the dirt; other times she would lie on the ground in order to listen to the hidden noise emanating from below. She was scared of earthworms, but liked listening to the marching of busy ants at work. She would press her ear close to the ground. Suddenly the volcanic hot springs would come to mind, and she shuddered in fear.

❀

She looked up and saw Daniel. He was gardening, pulling weeds, digging in the dirt, and planting flowers.

She left everything behind and went over to him. She asked him if calderas, with their boiling waters, existed all over the island. Some could not be seen because they were underground. Others rose to the surface to gush hot water like fountains.

She cozied up to my brother and asked, "Oh Daniel, isn't hell located right here beneath our feet, with devils kindling fires to burn those dead who are 'lost'?

"Are we all going to hell, Daniel?"

"No, no, that's not how it works," my brother replied unconcernedly. "It's not our bodies that do or don't go to hell or heaven. It's our souls, perhaps."

"What's a soul?" she asked, wrinkling her nose.

"Oh, I don't know. Carolina's the expert on such things. But she didn't want to tell me what it was.

"There's nothing for you to know, Xana. Now, shoo, shoo! Go away and let me work."

She would not be dissuaded.

"What if I do know?" she countered. "I think it's like this: Bad people fall out of their graves, go down to hell, and drop into the calderas. Good people rise from the ground and ascend into the clouds."

"Yes, Xana," Daniel replied, filled with patience, "that's more or less how it is. Now shoo, girl!"

She persisted, "That's not what Vovó says, Daniel."

"Oh no? Then what does she say?"

"She says heaven and hell aren't real places; they're inside everybody."

"Okay. And what do think that means, Miss Smarty Pants?"

"I don't know. But it's what Vovó tells me, and what she says is always true. Look, Daniel, when Vovó leaves for the clouds, don't forget to let me know so I won't get lost along the way. I want to go along with her inside her belly."

Daniel felt somewhat taken aback. Of all the things to say!

He turned around and headed back to the garden to finish his chores. He still needed to sweep the footpaths and clean everything up.

But Xana did not let him out of her sight. She needed him later to help with her backyard games. At three in the afternoon was to be the burial of her "daughter," so she wanted Daniel to play the priest and gravedigger.

"OK, Xana, let's get going," my brother condescended, a bit irked.

He dug the "grave," placed the porcelain doll inside, and covered her with yam stems and leaves so she would not get damaged. On top of that he packed dirt, mounded up a bit above ground level, as was done in the São Bento graveyard. Xana supplied the weeping for her "daughter," wailing like the hired female mourners of olden times. Daniel arranged the flowers on the grave, expressing sincere condolences and taking advantage of an oversight on Xana's part to sneak away as soon as possible, since he had experienced enough of children's games for one day.

Although still a child, Daniel would be conscripted to play a teacher or sometimes a priest. In the latter case he wore a dark skirt of Tia Luísa's that, since it came down to his ankles, served as a cassock. He would ascend the pulpit, which was the backyard wall. There he would softly recite his prayers and from on high preach lengthy sermons. He was accustomed to such games, so acceded to my little sister's wishes. But it was time to put an end to all that, for his friends were expecting him at the wooden-shoe maker's stall in the open-air market, where they gathered to chat, play cards, and talk about their latest flirtations.

❊

After several weeks elapsed, it was clear that the spring air had come to stay. There were signs everywhere. Birds flocked to the backyard, hopping from branch to branch in an incessant clamor. First leaves were starting to unfold, and swollen buds slowly began to bloom. Some flowers were ahead of schedule. The island's roadsides were covered with azaleas. Gardens were filled with daisies, fuchsias, blue taro, and, bordering the footpaths, several types of roses, all well pruned and cultivated.

The quality of the luminosity had also changed. Up in the hills, lights of much warmer tones spilled forth. The slopes were suffused in red, orange, and yellow flowing in silence toward the riverbanks below, covering the leafy tops of the incense trees with mysteries under the changing glass sky that delighted creatures and humans alike.

❀

An intermittent downpour fell in early April. Sunbeams in a kaleido-scopic cadence slipped through the clouds, which sometimes piled up, then dispersed, leaving nature swept of shadows and gradations of light, inscribed from time to time by a rainbow of distinct colors. That day the wind on the island seemed in repose. There was instead a gentle breeze that rose from the earth and impregnated the heavens. Suddenly, everyone turned around toward the rain and the farmers gave thanks. The rain began turning into fine drops and falling more slowly. At that point it was "gold" right on top of the planted fields. Men rubbed their hands in satisfaction, hoping for a good harvest.

Xana ran to the storeroom window, pulled up a chair, hopped up onto it, and stayed there for hours on end watching the water come down from the eaves, drip-dripping into the gutter below. Sometimes it fell with a gentle rhythm; other times it came down harder. Bubbles would appear, one after the other in an incessant interplay that drove her wild with amazement and delight.

Suddenly, the rain began to taper off slowly. It was now just a fine drizzle.

❀

Three loud raps on the door were the unmistakable sign of a long-awaited letter. It so happened that everybody headed for the door at the same time, including Vovó and Tia Luísa. Euphoria spread like a contagion, infecting all who were around. The news was good. Uncle Joe announced that he would be on our island very soon. He was leaving New York on the transatlantic liner *Leonardo da Vinci* and would be arriving in the city at the end of April.

Vovó went outside on tiptoe. She looked like a soaring ballerina. Her eyes beheld the celestial vault and opened to an array of light, which seemed to announce for some time the beginning of new life.

Right away Vovó began giving Felisberta orders. She wanted every-thing very clean. The mattress and blankets had to be aired for several days, weather permitting, to rid them of the annoying smell of mold and mothballs. He would require our finest sheets, a good quilt, a chamber pot, a towel hanging on the wash stand, and magnolia petals to freshen the bedroom air.

Carolina was entranced and ecstatic. She already knew what her uncle from America would be bringing: many things that were hard to find in the village.

Xana was experiencing the same enthusiasm as Carolina, except by osmosis. The last time Uncle Joe had come to the island she must have been about two years old, since she was already walking on steady legs. Carolina, then eight, had vivid memories of the gentleman, her adored uncle, who was different from other men she knew, above all in his bearing and scent. In those moments Xana retreated and tried to find a corner of the house all to herself and could only say "sweet, sweet," "my, my," and "Vovó." And she would stand there staring, inhaling the aroma of his clothes in order to get a preview of him. She was still somewhat frail, and introverted. Sometimes happy, other times cut off. And she used to say that she was a big girl, like Carolina. She would lean on her uncle, with her arms clutching one of his legs so tight that she confused the smell of flowers in the backyard with that of his American clothing. The year before, she still called Joe her "unca, unca," and said things like "unca, *balloon,* unca." And Uncle would laugh and laugh until tears came to his eyes.

As announced, Uncle Joe arrived in São Bento at the end of April and brought the sun with him. Candies of all colors and shapes, and chewing gum wrapped in waxed paper with a cartoon strip drawn on it, caused Xana to melt and made her delirious with joy. The gum mattered little to her; she did not care for it. But she religiously saved the wrappers, which had lettering and cartoons of people on them without rhyme or reason, and asked Daniel what those strange words she could not figure out meant. She'd thought she knew everything. Daniel explained to her that just as there are other peoples, there are other languages, as could be seen in Vovó's magazines, and one of them is spoken by Mamã and Uncle Joe. "Notice," Daniel continued, "that the very name you're saying, 'Uncle Joe,' isn't Portuguese, but American. Just like 'Boston,' 'New Bedford,' and all the words in Vovó's magazines. You didn't realize that since you were still very young."

The better to satisfy Xana's curiosity, Daniel pulled out the English textbook from his freshman year of high school and showed her other words. Unlike magazines, this book taught how to pronounce them. Xana was itching to learn everything all at once. Daniel calmed her with kind words. "Just as you learned the names of everything in Portuguese, I'll teach you how to say them in English, too.

"Tomorrow, I'll give you your first lesson so you can write letters to Mamã."

Xana leaned against the wall as always, but this time did not go inside. She did not know what to say. She was bursting with happiness, beside herself with joy.

"Letters to Mamã?" she heard, dumbfounded, as if they were keys of a piano striking over and over.

"Letters to Mamã? Letters to Mamã?" she kept repeating and repeating, like a mill wheel.

The following morning when Vovó opened the door, a festive air spilled out into the street, smelling of clothes from America and intoxicating the entire atmosphere. It was sweet. Nothing remained of the musty mold. One thousand one eager eyes looked in that direction. Some expectations hovered uncertainly on the part of one or another individual, chiefly a cousin, friends, neighbors, and hunting companions. Whatever memories came from those bountiful lands were not only appreciated but also viewed as a commercial promotion: Camel cigarettes, candies, jawbreakers of various sizes, fishing rods with a full complement of tackle, raincoats, rubber boots—all rare commodities, largely unknown to us.

Uncle Joe was still in bed, sound asleep. He had come to the island for the purpose of resting up, to forget. He had left the U.S. Army just as World War II was spreading its tentacles into a considerable number of European countries. In the hot Arizona desert he was struck during training by shrapnel from a grenade. His right arm was crushed and paralyzed. Uncle was discharged from military service, but not from the burden of being an invalid. The trade he pursued before enlisting had demanded a high degree of precision and concentration, like the parts he'd needed to measure and weigh with no possible margin for error.

They were airplane parts. The U.S. government's compensation for his suffering translated into a small pension. It was his good fortune to have inherited from his mother, with whom he had lived for but a short time, her ability to get by on limited resources. He relied on performing odd jobs, as his nerves allowed. His psychological imbalance derived most from the loss of a livelihood stolen from him and that he never again could pursue. Our uncle was changed and never again the same, Vovó thought, drowning in her tears.

My uncle stayed shut in his dim bedroom. Some old newspapers on the little table at the head of the bed lay waiting for his better days.

"I don't want to see anyone for a while," he beseeched Vovó.

But one moonlit night he decided to go out onto the patio. The moon was rising behind Pico da Vara, and he remained there watching that mystery of silences.

Vovó heard footsteps outside. She got up and saw her son, his back to her, wearing a bathrobe, looking at the mountain's contours in the dark, illuminated by the moon.

"Son," Vovó called out, "don't expose yourself to the night air. It's bad for your health. Come inside, lie down and rest."

"Don't worry, mother. I'm okay. I like the clean night air. Every so often I like to hear the barking of a dog in the distance, the crickets chirping, and the rooster outside the chicken coop, lost and alone in the garden. Let me stay here. Let me daydream, mother."

Starting the following night, Uncle Joe would get up from time to time, then go back to bed. However, we could also note a certain excitement in him, an uneasiness, a constant restlessness. He would go in and out, get up and lie down, take aimless walks and more walks, like a nonstop carousel.

Bit by bit, thanks to the old ladies' care, good weather, and friends, my uncle was purging himself of anxieties of body and soul.

❋

The days passed, and he became more and more alive, healthier and happier.

One morning he went to talk to my grandmother.

"I'm feeling so good, mother. It's been a long time, perhaps years since I've experienced this lighthearted feeling of something making me smile from head to toe.

"It's a gorgeous day, mother. The ocean is so peaceful, like a lake with no breeze. See how it is. It really seems dead."

"It's like a mirror in which that peninsula is reflected," my grandmother said with pride and a warm, gentle smile.

"Well, I've got to get going, mother. I'm joining some friends to go fishing. The coast is steep. Getting down there takes a long time. But I'd like to bring Xana along. Do you think I could take her with me, mother?"

"Oh, go ahead and take her, son. You're the one who knows best whether you want that responsibility. As far as I'm concerned, I trust you to make that decision."

Xana, who was nearby, upon hearing this conversation ran around turning the house upside down, so great was her excitement, her anxiety, and the earthquake that had emerged inside her.

❀

Off my uncle went with his friends and Xana, wearing his hunting gear and a vest stuffed with bullets, his army boots and island-style straw hat. He took along a fishing rod, and a rifle to hunt rock doves. His friends were humble men who made their living from the sea; that was in large part how they supported their families.

Uncle Joe never imposed on anyone during his brief visits. He long since had adapted to the ways of rural life—oil lamps, outhouses, and the limited variety of foods—and even felt an obligation to go to church in order to bond closer with the community to which he belonged, however indirectly. For that reason he did not complain, nor find anything strange. He felt at ease. He was treated by these people with warmth, not the coldness and alienation to which he was accustomed in his native America.

As they climbed down the steep slope, Xana slipped here and there. Laughing, Uncle Joe grabbed her hand so she would not fall and hurt herself.

When they reached the bottom of the cliff Xana was startled, not out of fear but in amazement, and stood there mouth agape and speechless.

All of a sudden she recoiled at something she did not know how to name. "Rocks, huge rocks everywhere. A mountain of rocks," she whispered in terror into Uncle Joe's ear.

"Never fear. I'll carry you on piggyback to a safe place near the cliff, where the rocks are pebbles the size of grains of corn and you can play all you want. So he left her in that safe place, quite nearby yet somewhat removed from where he would be, so he would not need to worry about her while he fished.

About an hour later our uncle returned to where he had left Xana, to check on her and see how she was doing.

"So, Xana, are you having a good time?"

"Yes, but I'm scared of the thunder. There's a lot of thunder here."

"That's not thunder, Xana. It's the rocks, the boulders that roll around roiling the deep waters."

"No, Uncle, it's not the rocks. It's the mermaids. They're washing clothes. Don't you see the soap suds? Wait a little longer, Uncle. I know they'll appear. In a little while they'll have to come get the white sheets, and then we can see how pretty they are."

"I don't think so, Xana. Mermaids don't like to be seen, and they save their singing for nighttime. Only very, very rarely do they come out during the day.

"Leave them be, Xana," Uncle Joe replied, slightly annoyed. "They're very, very pretty, and there are bad men who might try to kill them."

"Uncle, I don't want the mermaids to die. Not ever!"

The afternoon sun was setting fast, and tall shadows were beginning to appear, so they all started back up the steep slope of the cliff. They were returning refreshed and cheerful. They had enjoyed excellent fishing; Xana shared their happiness. Uncle Joe had shot three rock doves and could almost taste the rich *canja* broth made from them (one of his favorite dishes) that they would eat.

The men conversed while they smoked cigarettes. Xana did not understand what they were saying, for they were talking of things she did not know about. With a stick she began sketching pictures in the dirt. With great effort she drew a fish, then a heart. She amused herself by splashing her feet in the millrace, and afterward went foraging for watercress as a surprise for Vovó, who was very fond of it.

❀

The men climbed up one by one. Uncle had some difficulty, so performed a few movements in order to shake off the numbness in his legs. Xana kept climbing up the slope. Her little legs were like toothpicks that looked as though they would snap in two. Then it occurred to one of the men, "Why don't we lay your niece down on top of the big canvas bag with its drawstring, and she can hold on to the opening?"

My uncle's reply came in the form of a huge, huge guffaw. "Ah-ha! Why, that's a good idea, *son-of-a-gun, son-of-a-gun!*" he continued, as if at that moment he were still a boy. He dragged the sack along by the drawstring, as Xana nearly died laughing. She was going out of her mind, laughing and laughing and laughing. She squealed like a rock bird, and her shouts lingered behind, spreading out over the whole ocean. When she got up from the makeshift canvas "sled," Mamã and Papá popped into her head, without her knowing why. She asked for Uncle Joe's hand and clung tightly to it, whispering in his ear.

"When are they coming?"

"I don't know, my dear. I only know that they talk about you every day."

"Oh, I'm not so sure. I can't hear their footsteps, and they don't take me to the beach. And they don't take me hunting wild doves, the way you do."

Uncle Joe did not wish to pursue the matter any further, so he began joking with her, pretending he was unable to catch up with her when they ran, or to find her in hide-and-seek, whether at the bends in footpaths or in the middle of cornfields.

When they got home, they were sunburned. Uncle Joe carried a hearty laugh in his throat, shining like daisies on a sunny day.

His face was fiery yet relaxed, and he walked with a jaunty elegance.

❀

The green fields were carpeted in warm golden yellow. The island was blanketed in a thousand hues speckled with shades of brown. The wind blew through the wheat and cornfields, making them undulate like the sea. Out in the backyard Xana was playing with girlfriends, showing off new toys that had just arrived from America: another two-story celluloid house, fully furnished. It lacked for nothing.

Uncle Joe hung back at a distance, savoring his niece's delirious joy. He approached and joined in the fun. He took a couple steps toward the canebrake, which served as a hedge to protect the fruit trees from the north winds, and grabbed a dozen or so green stalks, lashing them together with twine made of arrow leaf. On top he set a big canvas bag while Xana and her girlfriends marveled in awe, unaware of what was happening. The children's eyes spun like a roulette wheel as their curiosity grew.

"Xana, come here," her uncle called.

He grabbed her and set her on top of the bundle of green stalks covered by the canvas bags. Uncle Joe steadied himself with one hand, while with the other he bent the stalks into a bundle, pulling them up and down, like a real swing. It was fascinating for the children, who ran to ask their parents to do just like the American *senhor* had done. When playtime was at last over, the stalks were scraggly and battered, as though a hurricane had just blown through.

The commotion going on outside prompted Tia Luísa to want to know what was going on. She was dumbstruck; not a word came out of her mouth. That was something that simply was not done. "To destroy the hedge that had been so much trouble for the caretaker to tend," she mused. Luísa wound up not saying anything. Her sister had forbidden her to antagonize her son.

"The 'poor boy' had already suffered a bit of rotten luck," thought my grandmother, who had never forgotten the letter buried for so many years in a bottomless hole in the house's center room.

❋

Carolina felt like a queen during those days; her body was all aquiver. She was a grown-up young lady, delighted by all the lovely age-appropriate dresses Mamã had bought her. She went to see her girlfriends in order to show off and share what she had received from her mother via her uncle from America.

The sailor coats for Xana and Carolina were a perfect gift. The latter's was peach-blossom in color, while Xana's was pastel blue, and they came with matching hats and shoulder bags. The 1950s saddle shoes of the season, black and white with laces, were not in fashion on the island.

Uncle Joe, who during his last visit had promised Carolina a present beyond her wildest imagination, brought her a surprise so grand she almost collapsed, as she felt the house spinning around her. "It couldn't be. Impossible. A bicycle! A bicycle, Uncle Joe?" Carolina wept with happiness. She jumped and jumped for joy, from a euphoria that left her stupefied, not knowing what to say. She ran to her uncle and hugged him tight, her arms hanging around his neck.

But there was a snag. At that time girls were not allowed such frivolity. What an inappropriate gift. Only an American would do something like that. "Bicycles were only for boys," the neighbor ladies whispered, behind the hands half-covering their mouths.

However, my grandmother felt it worthwhile, without wishing to provoke the locals, to approve Carolina's learning how to ride the bicycle without delay, as was her uncle's wish. Uncle Joe mustered all the patience he possessed and for several days continued accompanying her until she mastered the yellow bike of her dreams.

❋

That day, to everyone's surprise, Uncle Joe awoke early. He prepared to take photographs of the house, the backyard, and the road to Pico da Vara. He'd already scheduled his return trip to New York but said nothing about it to anyone. Only later did he tell two or three people he could rely upon to keep his secret. Once more he called to the old ladies, with feigned enthusiasm.

"Let's go take some pictures. Come on, Mamã. Come on, Tia Luísa. And now everybody. But where's Xana?" Uncle Joe asked.

Nobody knew where she was. They searched and called for her but were unable to find her anywhere until Daniel, after searching high and low, found her hiding in the neighbor's hedge. But she refused to come out. My brother lost his temper and dragged her out by force, such was the resistance Xana offered. For the first time, he gave her a good swat, then ordered her to pose for the picture. But Xana did not shed a single tear. At that moment she hated Daniel and bit her lip. She didn't want to be in any photograph, she stubbornly reiterated.

Daniel slapped her again, but no one could make her obey—not Uncle Joe nor Tia Luísa, nor even my grandmother. At that instant the only thing Xana could think of was the street photographer with the tripod on his back, that liar who had tricked everyone, who told the children to pay attention because a little bird was going to pop out of the black box, the loveliest one ever—and then there was nothing.

Daniel kept pinching her gently and pushing her forward. But she would have none of it, scraping along the ground, shouting, her vocal cords swelling until they turned blue and seemed to want to jump out of her mouth.

✦

Xana had never forgotten that day of lies. Not even Uncle Joe's camera could persuade her. His American camera was beautiful, very light-weight, and looked like a toy. But not even that was enough.

Daniel no longer knew what to do. In her last letter, Mamã had asked her brother not to forget to bring back pictures of the children. She wanted to stay updated on Xana, Carolina, and Daniel's growth. She wanted to show their pictures to her relatives in America. But Xana continued being stubborn as a mule and nothing fazed her. She just wanted to get far away.

Given this, her attitude created a hard-to-resolve situation. Her stubbornness was contributing to the quashing of our parents' expectations. Without Xana in the photo, Daniel worried, that little girl was depriving our parents of their right to see her. And this was something they did not deserve. She could not persist with her arms crossed: her obstinacy could not prevail over the entire family's wishes. They had to insist until she surrendered.

Daniel, whose patience had run out, threatened Xana, "Come get in the photo, or else I'll stop being your brother. The joking is over, you little brat."

In any event, Xana was no longer even fit to be photographed. Her puffy eyes, swollen red face, and disheveled damp hair made her a sorry sight. "Better dispense with picture taking," Tia Luísa interjected.

"What the devil! If she doesn't want to, she doesn't want to. It'll have to wait till another time, when she's calmed down."

A shadow fell over Uncle Joe. He was tense and troubled. He had been charged with taking pictures to bring back to his sister. So he felt as if he were stuck in a blind alley, caught in a thankless situation, between a rock and a hard place. On the one hand he felt obligated to fulfill his sister's request; on the other, bachelor that he was, he did not know how to weaken his niece's will, much less to persuade her.

However, something that occasionally emerged from his subconscious popped into his head. He recalled that on his last trip to the island, when Xana was just two years old, he had already glimpsed her tendency to hide from things, to flee the lens and never face the camera head-on. She would swallow her little eyes inside her, and the picture would come out shaky, with a zigzag pattern. My parents would see Xana's body, but never her eyes.

Uncle kept snapping photos in rapid-fire succession—one, then another, and another, and on and on—to see if he could capture just one candid shot of her.

Nothing doing.

Having exhausted all his options and still not knowing what to do, Daniel looked into Vovó's face, pleading for help, but to his surprise and incomprehension he noted no reaction from her. Without Vovó's complicity, Daniel thought to himself that he could not try anything else. So my brother at long last gave up.

The fact is that the photo taken that morning with a lush daisy plant as its backdrop was forever of just the three of us: Carolina, Daniel, and me.

As for Xana, she was nowhere to be found.

❁

Following that unpleasant scene, Uncle Joe took his niece by the hand and they both sat down on the low backyard wall. Little by little Xana began drawing closer to the camera and looked at it countless times to see if she could spot the cursed birdie that never seemed to appear. Her uncle took advantage of the opportunity to prepare once more to snap another photograph.

"No, Uncle Joe," Xana squealed, ready to bolt again.

But since she was very fond of her uncle, she lay her head in his lap and, without looking up at him, said, "When you come back to São Bento, why don't you buy me a camera that's a lot better than the one with the birdies? Instead of that lying camera, what I'd like is one that's able to photograph people's hearts outside their bodies. If you bring me one of those, I'll let you take as many pictures of me as you wish. Not just one or two, but as many as you want, okay?"

Uncle Joe stood up. There was nothing anyone could do with that little girl, he thought in disappointment. It was impossible to fulfill his sister's request. So she would not have the pleasure of seeing her Xana.

They sat back down and stayed a little while. Xana watched his movements. She drew even nearer to him and squeezed his hand, which was burning with a cold sweat. She squeezed and squeezed it to see if the two of them stuck together. Two tears could be seen falling from her eyes.

All of a sudden my uncle made a tender, unexpected gesture, brushing his hand over his niece's face, as if to photograph the feelings of a strong little girl housed inside a body of porcelain.

CHAPTER 4

Few knew it.

But among them was my grandmother, for certain.

The next morning his bedroom door was pulled back; pulled back too was his bedding. His body was already on its way back to the other side of the water, gone from the island, having left without farewells. Through the rays of a pale sun, a vague sigh of nostalgia shone into the house.

There was an emptiness, a dull pain, not the sort capable of making a person cry, but one that could be felt. And we all were in suspended animation, almost deaf, almost mute, like at *festas* when the noise falls silent.

The people of São Bento missed him, too. The *amaricano* had embarked, and it seemed that even at low tide the island lacked a sky.

❁

From across the street the madwoman's screams could reach Vovó's house, depending on the direction of the wind. Maria da Estrela had lost her mind one bitter cold morning when, after lighting the oven, she had gone out into the backyard. Since that time she had never again been the ruler of her own body, of her own will. The piercing shrieks of a caged beast that she emitted sent cats, dogs, and children fleeing in fright, their hearts pounding. Poor Maria da Estrela, chained up indoors, would not sit down. She wanted to stand by the window—a window that was never opened in either winter or summer. Only her eyes could go for a walk, wandering through the window, traveling through other expanses across from Pico da Vara to planted or fallow fields, depending on the time of year. Most of the time the light was gone from her eyes and they were cloudy, like those of someone who looks without seeing. Her world began and ended there.

Continued years of captivity had turned her into a wild beast, so dangerous was her fury. Behind the glass, a greenish drool issued from her mouth, mixed with mice and locusts, a thick foam of suffering and terror. Seeing her like that was enough to make anyone want to cut ties, leave, run, flee, flee forever.

Xana had just come back from playing tag outside. She was terrified. She raced straight into the house. She was unable to speak; she was panting, panting for breath, and she nearly vomited from exhaustion. She raised her hands and stuck her fingers in her ears. She was afraid of those insistent, never-ending cries, so took refuge in the remotest room in the house, where the opaque darkness of that endless, tearful clamor expanding into roars of an incessant *rrrrrrrrr* could not reach. And that racket kept going and going, penetrating her bones and the walls of the house. Her beastly wailing stuck to the skin like suction cups, leaving marks on young and old alike.

For those who lived on my grandmother's street there was a widespread fear every time the west wind blew, carrying into the night a howl that scattered the stars in the heavens, frightening souls and startling sleepers.

Throughout the morning, women would appear at their windows as usual. But that morning no one believed what was happening. The poor wild beast was at last silent. Maria da Estrela had entered her other phase—that of lulling her doll, her little girl, to sleep. She slept in silence, in peace. A flock of doves that had been cooing on the ground alit on the windowsill. The bright blue sky descended onto her lap, giving respite to a weary, defeated mind until a battalion again started encroaching upon her body, slashing her bowels—and into her head, which was stunned by mutilated bodies and swords at the ready, an incessant galloping of a thousand stampeding horses.

※

As weeks turned into months, Xana continued her English lessons. She would write short notes and hide them in holes in the barn and in the walls. She did not want anyone to see them, not even Daniel. Most of them disappeared, torn up by Carolina, who was uninterested in such childish silliness. Jealous as always, she would play the victim, moaning and groaning, declaring that nobody liked her. "What I truly am is a Cinderella," she would say in spite.

Of course none of that came close to the truth. Yet to please Daniel, she decided to surprise him with one of Xana's letters that had been stashed in a secret spot. Carolina knew the hiding place quite well. For that reason she decided to wait nearby for another letter to be placed there. Hours passed . . . and nothing . . . until nightfall, when Carolina spied Xana in the act. She waited for her sister to return to the house, and after making sure Xana was no longer around, ran to the barn and straight for the hole in the wall. She moved the rock and saw a letter there. After removing it, she replaced the rock in the hole.

Letter in hand, Carolina marched triumphantly up to Daniel, who was in the living room reading by the light of an oil lamp. My brother set aside his reading matter and, brimming with curiosity, unfolded the grimy slip of paper.

The letter read,

To day mom leave my dad cry and cry and cry
every day my dad cry I wish every day I call mom
she not say a word to me

Her words, although in the wrong places and at times incorrect, made sense. Xana closed her letter by drawing a heart, which she partitioned from top to bottom. On the left half she wrote *Mom,* on the right, *Dad.* Just below the heart, as a caption, she added *you live fried from me,* although she had meant to say *far* instead of *fried.*

Daniel cracked one of the bitterest smiles of his life, such was the irony he found in that mistake.

"*Fried,* indeed," my brother mused. "Perhaps the fittest word to describe Xana and our whole family's predicament. *Fried,* indeed," Daniel reflected, emitting a bilious laugh like a crazy person. It was time,

Daniel continued absorbed, to warn Papá and Mamã, to make them realize Xana was growing not only in body but also in awareness, bit by bit every day, as she learned more things, more names of the objects around her. And our parents still had not returned.

With that modicum of knowledge derived from a growing awareness, Xana felt herself gradually slipping away somewhere, perhaps into a well of dark cold water that she herself did not know how to explain. And if by chance she did know, she was not saying. Xana thought, for example, that a grandmother would always be a grandmother, a mother would always remain a mother, and she herself would always stay a granddaughter. And when she tried to delve deeper into her inescapable fog of confusion, she persevered unawares, but insistent that it was so. The person who was her mother would stay the same age forever, as would Vovó and Papá. And all of that was disturbing to her, however, without her being able to discern or understand the mystery of things in the least. She did not fully grasp what it was but now realized that she did not know if our mother was the same age as all other mothers. Perhaps they were just mothers. Mothers of forever the same age.

And that was how Xana perceived them, just like the time that was stuck on the clock's pendulum, thus frozen in a still distant past when there was no electricity in Nordeste's villages. Nor did she know if Mamã was tall or short, good or bad, or whether she would like her or not. She was a mother-in-photograph only. In the album that she leafed through countless times, Xana tried to find memories of the Mamã and Papá she did not know. Her eyes pored dizzily over the photos, ripping away the cobwebs.

That would have been when she began writing letters to our parents, hiding them in holes in the barn, not wanting to show them to anyone.

❄

When Daniel learned of her hidden letters, he deemed the practice innocuous. He wondered why she had not told him about it. He was such a friend to Xana, always sharing everything with her. Indeed, he had been the one who introduced her to the magic of letters and words.

"Why is everything with you always so hidden, Xana? Why? What did I ever do to you?"

She replied like someone suddenly caught naked. A furrow deepened just above her right eye, rendering her almost unable to see. It was a lazy eye that was unfocused, while her left one remained attentive, observing Daniel surreptitiously.

My brother was just now overcome with pity, and his heart melted. She seemed so tiny, so fragile to him, and he regretted having subjected her to an interrogation that seemed more like a sentence against a hapless defendant.

Daniel then raised his hands to his head and asked himself, "Oh my God, what a disgrace! What madness of mine blindly led me unseeing to this stupid behavior?" For a few minutes he remained apprehensive, crestfallen, shaking his head back and forth like that.

Feeling defeated, he sensed that Xana was moving further from him as she grew up. Suddenly he fetched paper, pen and ink, then sat down at the table and paused to think a while, not knowing what to write. He racked his brain, then made up his mind.

No, he thought, things cannot continue this way. I must write.

"Mamã and Papá, either you return to São Bento—because I'm so fed up with this life and have run out of patience—or else I'll quit school, pack my bags, and leave. It's time for you two to come back. Sad to say, Mamã, you still refuse to recognize this general reality, it seems to me. And I say this only for your sake, Papá and Mamã, since Carolina is now a grown woman, Mamã; sooner or later Xana will of course follow down the same path. And if you don't believe me, I can guarantee you'll live to regret it.

"Xana will then be a mere ghost-child to you both. I guarantee that only in this sense will she become yours."

Dejected, my brother kept thinking, his face etched with worry. All of a sudden, he picked up the letter he had just written and reread it. He found it bitter so ripped it up.

He confided aloud to the walls, "So far as I can tell, my parents must be afraid to face reality. Alas, they don't seem to want to accept it."

A stream of huge tears of powerlessness ran down my brother's face in a blend of anger and pain. Mamã and Papá did not understand the first thing about anything. And Daniel could find no way to awaken them to reality. My brother no longer knew what else to do but drop his arms and look for ways not to hurt them. He shook his head, lost and humiliated, and slumped over.

Suddenly he stood up, picked up the chair and flung it into the air, causing it to crash to the floor—shattering to pieces like our family, Daniel mused with irony and sadness.

But as for Xana, she was more than "broken into pieces," Daniel thought with detachment. The poor child was still in a state of exile. Not that such a situation was intentional, but the truth was that she had always been an outsider. Once again my brother was indignant, defeated. Defeated just like on the day when Xana clung to the daisy bush, stubbornly refusing to join us in the photograph.

And there we stood, without her.

❀

When we got home and failed to see Vovó, Tia Luísa, or Xana there, we realized right away where to find them. All we had to do was head west toward the main street or south along the footpaths, and soon we would know where they were. There would be the tracks from Vovó's American shoes, which could never be confused with any other footprints. The soles of my grandmother's shoes were rippled like accordion pleats, which protected her from slipping on rainy days and allowed her to tread sure-footedly on dusty ground. Carolina and I followed her trail. Xana was no doubt with Vovó.

The two of us then started running after them, calling out "Vovó, Vovó," with the river echoing "ah-AH, ah-AH . . ."

And as we ran faster and faster, clouds of locusts hopped around between us, scaring us with their low, unexpected jumping. The afternoon was warmed by the noonday sun, emitting the sweet and dense scents of hay stubble, tiny crab pears, satiny fennel, and blackberries plucked warm from the vine.

Near the orchard we had to cross a small bog formed by water from the public reservoirs, water that rose to the surface resulting in huge bubbles of a thousand colors that burst one after the other, to the local children's delight. Beside it, a fresh water source flowed along its gentle course in silence.

A couple steps from there and we were in the orchard next to the gate. At the entrance to the property a blackbird sang proud and strident, distinct from other birds. A flutter of wings dispersing the crowns of pittosporums, cryptomerias, and acacias ripped through the sky in search of other areas, causing a black spot that blended in with the heavy clouds.

❋

The threat of rain always left our grandmother distressed. I knew why, but never said a thing to anyone.

In those days, curvaceous legs were considered one of a woman's most desirable body parts. However, Vovó's looked more like a chicken's. For that reason, in winter and summer alike she wore two pairs of stockings: sheer outer ones and a thick hand-knit woolen inner pair. When they got wet, it made for the worst problem. They produced blazing heat and soon thereafter caused an unbearable itching. Therefore, at the least little bit of rainfall we would go on our way, picking up our pace as we sought shelter under tree branches. Xana's instinct was to run to Vovó for protection, clinging to her as she recalled that day when Vovó had fallen and broken her nose. Vovó should not suffer; she must not suffer, never ever again, she recalled, in that moment of pain.

Xana, despite the fact that she was still a child—and to my surprise—never spilled the beans about Vovó's faux leg curves. She knew that if by chance she opened her mouth, Carolina was sure to tell everyone Vovó's secret, and then everything would be very sad, as sad as the Day of the Dead.

On our return home, busy bees—a few on all sides, coming out of the orchard and also in the vicinity of the woods—with their articulated torsos in alternate stripes of yellow and dark brown, hurried with their harvest of nectar from multiple flowers. Scattered raindrops fell on the dry summer's-end clods.

The ground was steaming, and a mist descended over the tall slopes with streams flowing at the bottom, transmitting silences of fresh foliage. From among them there came music, singing. It was the cows' bells clanking around their necks, lofting skyward a sound like church bells ringing *trindades*.

The stars were stripped from the sky.

Men and animals headed into the dark of night.

Come morning, with the unfolding of dawn's fan, peasants began emerging from the barns with the cattle. And everything was moving in just one direction, away from the village and up toward the communal open land where there was pasture. The fields nearest the houses were reserved for growing food from seed, and afterwards for corn, wheat, and bean crops.

A few hours after the men's departure for field chores, the women got to work as usual. They rolled up their sleeves to clean house, light fires, and prepare dinners. It was around noontime that some of them noticed that their salt pork was missing.

Then they began counting the chickens.

The thief was back.

❋

One by one the women came out into the street and whispered, cupping their hands over their mouths to hide what they were saying. Suddenly a thousand frenzied voices arose in an endless clamor. There were faces pale with fear, staring without focus, others red in despair, and still others lost within themselves, for the ones hit the worst were those of the most modest means. The voices of these women coalesced and mingled with other sounds, their bodies shook in spasms of pain, and from them emanated a buzzing like that of disoriented bees. They were living in a continuous earthquake. No one found peace, and death itself lurked at every moment around every corner as well. It even seemed as though the Earth might be rent asunder from top to bottom in such a way that people could see what was on the other side of the planet.

He was broad shouldered, and everybody feared him. He resembled a bull. The chicken thief was called Arregalado on account of his bulging eyes. He had gone to jail countless times. This time, tubs full of brined pork were emptied. No one was spared.

The monster's bloodshot eyes threatened to fall out of their sockets, and his mouth was a fiery furnace spewing flames from the hatred he brandished. A knife stuck in his belt was a clear sign of his menace. He was not there to play, much less to make friends. The children took shelter at home, not understanding what was happening. However, they sensed that there was danger in sight, that the world was about to end. Xana asked Vovó to hide her underneath the empty cone that supported the wicker chair where she often sat in the entryway, looking over and over at photographs and magazines, sometimes napping in the afternoon, sometimes doing needlepoint, weaving, and knitting more stockings. To be on the safe side, Xana, with her hands folded in prayer, asked her aunt then to sit on the chair in order to hide her under her long skirts.

That way no one could know where she was. Although she now felt safe, at the slightest noise her fragile heart rattled like stone after stone thrown into a well.

In hushed tones the men plotted to do away with bug-eyed Arregalado. They all vowed to put an end to his life, but none of them had that much courage. They foresaw that if someone wound up injured or killed in the confrontation it would not be Arregalado, but one or more of the many village men. And the harm would be dramatic: children and women would starve.

"Just imagine the justice system bringing back that criminal who has the power to destroy families," all the women shouted. "And at a time when hunger is ravaging a large segment of the population and stomachs are rumbling like active volcanoes."

Indeed, many people were starving, literally starving. Vovó instructed Tia Luísa to take some sandwich fillings and bread to those who had been robbed, in particular those suffering from tuberculosis. They had hardly begun to eat when they started coughing up spurts of blood that blended drop by drop with the brown-green of the walls. And always, that chill anticipated icy death.

Tia Luísa left quickly in response to her sister's request and hurried her pace. She strode lightly with satisfaction, bringing with her the willingness to devote herself to those who needed her most. Along the way she saw a great many shacks with nearly depleted stocks of corn announcing hunger for an endless winter. That was Tia Luísa's greatest concern: seeing so many people "drying up on the vine," just skin and bones, spitting up their lungs, and the oldest and sickliest losing their teeth, their shriveled lips receding into their mouths, their sunken eyes buried in the misery of the mold that climbed walls and entered their very beds.

When my aunt returned home, she had nothing else left to say. She was tired. Vovó sensed something. She realized that Tia Luísa considered that burglaries in a hunger-plagued community like ours were in a sense almost a necessity, a matter of survival. So they were understandable and excusable. But what was inexcusable were the abuses committed by the bug-eyed Arregalado who on that night took away what little bread they had from the many who would then have none.

❋

Autumn was at the door.

At sunset that afternoon the north wind brought an unusual wave of heat to São Bento. One could feel a crumbling that was not from an earthquake, houses, or even land. The entire populace perked up its ears like rabbits, trying to detect any sound, to understand what was strange about it.

All at once the locals noticed that the evergreen trees were curling up their leaves, to the naked eye withered looking, and then they fell shriveled to the ground. No one knew whether it was a plague that would wipe out the flora or, worse than that, a heat that would scorch everyone, human and animal alike.

Pico da Vara soon turned the color of fire. The sun became a half watermelon. Then, toward the southern region, a sudden flash traversed the skies, leaving a vast swath of red that rendered the mountain blood colored. A beautiful spectacle, a horrific panorama engulfed in a coagulated hemorrhage. People were thinking that hell had arrived, then deduced it was something else. Perhaps a flying saucer. The more optimistic wanted to believe it was a sign from Our Lady of Fátima come to save us. And they all knelt and lifted their voices in prayer. To the most skeptical, it might have been another plane crashing, burning like a fireball, rolling and devouring the heavens, seven years after the first one, in more or less the same place but at a different hour.

Arregalado leapt back into the center of the controversy—he who this time had stolen some watches and rings, taken at the cost of severed fingers. The thief had never come so close to such great fortune. Drunkenness, however, led him to squander in short order what had never belonged to him in the first place.

The other village men were not even looking for that monster. Instead, they tightened their noose in order to keep him out. And they tightened it so much that the thief was left talking to himself. He stumbled off, with yellow ooze and pus trickling out of his mouth and running down his chin. He tripped, fainted, and fell into the ditch. No one came to his aid, of course. "That was our daily bread. It was the right place for him to sleep," whispered the elders, anxious to see him gone from the village.

A group of the wisest men were still arguing the possibility that an accident had occurred, while others were inclined to different speculations. They realized, however, that they could not sit idly by and that they had to do something, regardless of what had or had not transpired. So they hurried, in hopes of saving some lives and, if they were none to save, at least to stand guard over the bodies until the responsible parties arrived.

They determined a course of action and set off with sickles slung over their backs, and not another word. They carried axes, pruning hooks, whatever else was at hand, ready to clear brush in search of bodies. The youngest held lanterns. When they reached Pico Redondo they surrendered to the purple silence of night. There was not a single star in the sky. Everyone huddled together, frightened. They waited patiently for the new day. And when dawn arrived, only the birds could be heard.

Traces? Not a one!

Around them, a thick fog more opaque than night rolled in. Nobody knew where to turn. They were all adrift like a rudderless boat. Lanterns were of no use.

They prayed for the heavy milky curtain to lift and a ray of light to emerge from it. And that is just what happened. God heard their prayers and guided them to the village.

They arrived wet, their feet drenched in blood.

But in the long run it turned out to be nothing they'd thought. It was not a plane nor the sun. For those who believed in superstitions it was another sign, along with the falling of the curled leaves and the twigs from fig trees, that Judgment Day was imminent.

And they all stood listening together, under a dark chill mantle.

❀

Sometime later, as my brother further despaired over having to be both "father" and "mother," we found out through others that he was dating Patrocínia, daughter of a very good village family. Nothing would have seemed out of the ordinary, had the news not reached us through other people. However, my grandmother kept silent, as if she had heard nothing. She remained attentive to signs she had been intuiting in recent days, without telling anyone. Vovó knew that sooner or later it would have to happen. There was nothing more natural, she thought to herself, saying not a word aloud and pretending not to notice anything. The fact is that from then on we saw another hole in her expression gape open, never again to heal, never again to close.

She began to sizzle like a frying pan.

"The world is falling apart," our dear grandmother thought, flushed with fever. That delayed moment would have its outcome within a few days. She was sure the island had no room to welcome new couples who wanted to give their children a decent life at minimum. The island was losing all of its youngsters. There was no space to be, no space to live. Even her dear grandson was going to leave. There was no longer any doubt. She did not know when. But he was indeed going away. Her grandson would be leaving.

Heartbroken and perplexed, Vovó could not speak or see, her eyes aswim in the void. Then she muzzled the Earth's sounds, locking them up inside herself, inside herself, feeling the world slip away beneath her feet like a perpetually spinning top. She was not going to say a thing to Tia Luísa; she preferred to postpone the inevitable. On the other hand, she would not ask Daniel anything. It was a matter of time, she knew for sure, a matter of waiting and wishing in the interim to stop the world, to rein it in like a horse and make it turn back, with clock hands running amok more than a million miles an hour counterclockwise.

The rural middle class could no longer find space anywhere on the island. A life of few prospects awaited them. The noose was tightening around them, from which they could not free themselves, even through education. Everything was very hard. It was imperative to leave. To join their parents, to go to a land of redemption. Some mortgaged their debts: they wanted to leave for blessed America at any cost.

When they left they would take, at such pains, the smell of the tides, the strumming of their native *violas* and *guitarras,* the warmth of emotions of family and friends.

❀

But that day came. That day came and the time—which at that point was still bolted shut and dozing lazily on the island—shed its leaves like a tree. The pendulum on the clock went berserk, spinning and spinning wildly like a roulette wheel. And everything was going so fast.

Daniel was leaving.

As soon as he got to America he would deal with obtaining his girlfriend her *Carta de Chamada* so she could immigrate. Once he was there he would relate all the family news and convince our parents either to bury their stubborn dream of returning forever to the island, or once and for all to move the rest of the family to America.

Always being caught in the middle and feeling much more of an outsider was not humanly bearable. It seemed a heresy, a sadism without bounds, inflicted on the weakest family members. "Not like this," Daniel would say, eager to put an end to the madness of a life rent asunder. He had already resolved in his troubled heart to struggle with all his might to convince our parents. He would have to convince them. And only he could undo the snarled tangles of our lives.

My brother was so preoccupied, filled with an intense pain that stung like blade cuts, that he turned to Vovó and said, "When I get to America, I swear the first thing I'll do is kneel before my parents and beg them with hands folded as in prayer to put an end to their stubbornness, to put an end to a life forever torn to pieces. To reunite forever the remnants scattered by the wind, blowing over the sea—be it this side or that, the decision has to be made."

❀

A deathly silence, like a bird with a broken wing sprawled on the ground, hovered over the village. A curtain of rain torn by a shining rainbow lent that autumn morning a mystical mass-like ambience, disturbing people of greater sensitivity who just stood there waiting without knowing why. The leaves were falling, falling from the trees, inert, strewn on the ground. Those at the top whispered, while the others at our feet stuck tearfully.

Tia Luísa insisted on fixing porridge for my brother as usual, a daily ritual. But Daniel was not hungry. What he had was a knife-slicing pain. He was unable to utter a single word. It was raining in his heart, and in his throat was a knot the size of an apple. Tia Luísa, dying of heartbreak, responded with an indecisive gesture, smoothing back her white hair as if to chase away what was bothering her at that moment: a wound that reopened ever deeper. She muttered senseless words, incomprehensible gibberish. Her mind wandered as she tried to hide her wound that was bleeding and bleeding.

For my brother this was a forever farewell, a premature death. Never again would he see Vovó or Titia. The warmth of their affections would remain behind on the island. Ahead lay an emptiness of icy uncertainty.

Daniel, hanging his head, paced back and forth in deep silence. At one point he raised his head a bit, and we saw that his eyelids were dark and swollen. His face was that of a dead man. He hurt, hurt like the blow of an axe felling a tree that lands on the person chopping it down.

✹

In the morning we prepared for a *matança*. Not the slaughter of a hog, but of ourselves.

The taxi was at the door, bound for Santana airport.

Tia Luísa turned away and went to her room. She knelt, bending over so far that she almost kissed the floor. She petitioned the Lord Holy Christ of Miracles for a safe journey for Daniel. She lit a candle and surrendered herself to contemplation. While the wax melted she bade farewell to her nephew. She returned to her spot and sat down on the carpet, lulling herself into oblivion, curled up in a ball.

My brother accompanied all of us, except Tia Luísa, who lately had with some difficulty prepared herself not to cry but swallowed her "tears of oil" (with an invisible flame)—words repeated, timeworn from countless departures.

What we witnessed that morning while the suitcase and two bags were being loaded into the trunk of the car was a veritable amputation.

We were slipping into a sea of castaways in search of a compass.

We were left with an intense loneliness of the highest order. With no boundary or horizon in sight. Just a hole in a void called sadness.

We climbed into the taxi. During the two-hour ride no one dared open their mouth. There was nothing to say. The scenery passed by, and the expression on our faces was falling, dazed. Daniel slid Xana over against his chest and heard a murmur in the depth of her silence, with a wavering moan. She was falling apart, like petals dropping one by one.

"Why don't you take me with you, Daniel?" Xana asked.

"I can't," he responded almost inaudibly, a wave of nausea in his throat. "Calm down, Xana. I'll whisper a secret in your ear that will bind us together forever."

"What is it?"

"It's very simple. It's like this. Whenever you feel nervous or sad, take your thumb and run it over each fingertip, as if you were spinning. It's easy, just go like this: keep running it round and round, as if you were spinning silk very lightly, very gently, until you fly away and feel the serenity of a butterfly emerging from its cocoon. That will be the moment when you remember me and I remember you. Now don't forget."

"No, I won't forget, but what I want is to be with you in real life, Daniel."

"But Xana, what about Vovó? What would become of her? And of Tia Luísa?"

The silence shattered into a thousand tinkling little shards.

A ghastly cry erupted suddenly from her abdomen, as if a demon were leaving her body.

"Oh, Daniel, I don't want to live without Vovó. No; never, ever. But I don't understand why Mamã is stealing you away from me."

"Settle down," Vovó scolded her, somewhat annoyed. Xana was utterly lost, absorbed in that bitter moment, projecting herself to the other side of the world as a way to forget the lies and promises—to flee the weight of death, regain her wings and soar so high that she touched the stars.

She then imagined herself up there on high, keeping house: she swept it, cleaned it, and opened its windows to the senses of the soul, of nard, of unnamed colors, of fuchsias, of the sweet taste of a cantata about clouds made of white, white foam. And she was playing with that tiny doll of hers on the swing on top of the lid of Vovó's gramophone, rocking back and forth, back and forth until the cord wound down. She would wind it up again, and the little girl would rock there under the pink umbrella.

Suddenly her eyes glazed over, unseeing. She had just heard the music of the rain that was falling gently upon the land. From that moment on, my sister realized no wings could enable her to reach her brother, that two-year father-on-loan who was also her first teacher.

Xana remained "out of it" like this, incomparably more distant than in any other situation she had ever experienced before. My brother thought so, weeping on the inside, already recalling with *saudade* the fresh water that landed gently onto the island's ginger lilies, falling drop by drop.

Dark clouds were thickening, threatening to let loose at any moment. A white light flashed across the firmament, and soon thereafter the thunder clapped—rumbling, roaring, and banging from afar. The skies broke open, and the car's roof seemed to be collapsing on us.

We had reached our destination.

⚙

In those days, entering the airport terminal was like going into a morgue. The shouts unleashed there were those of a final farewell, because returning passengers were such a rarity. A strident voice began summoning passengers to head toward the departure gate. The time had come for Daniel to board. Xana entered into darkness. She still tried to grip the handrail that seemed to elude her grasp. Now she found herself at a wake, the lid falling closed on the casket, the room empty with no weeping or candles, just a nauseating smell of faceless orphans. By the time she emerged from it, Daniel was already airborne. I noticed in her little body a tremor like that of someone who gets lost in a blind alley. For Xana that day was the end of the world, an immeasurable blow just like the hollow wounding cut used to prune plants, which brings both life and death—like a yelping puppy licking wounds inflicted by its owner, in a prolonged cry of ow-ow-ow, *ad infinitum.*

A meteorite shower cascaded down from Xana's huge eyes, which bulged like in the head of a stray starling.

For her part, Carolina gave the appearance of something strange, which disturbed me. On her face there was not even a single tear, nothing but a grimace or slight smile. She knew that from then on her little sister would be under her thumb. No longer would Xana have Daniel to teach her so many things or protect her like before, Carolina thought, rubbing her hands together and clenching the grimace at the corner of her mouth—making it clear that from then on she had the right, by distorting or inventing specific situations, to torment Xana in order to put an end to the pampering of that silly girl.

❀

The whole way home Xana sobbed disconsolately. She cried and cried from the airport all the way back to the village. A heavy rain filled her up inside. On the outside, little remained of her as a person. On that day she was a thing, perhaps an animal. She cried her eyes out. Water poured from her eyes, nose, every orifice. There was no comforting her. The neighbors lamented her tears fraught with sorrow and pain. And they continued to make comments, saying that they did not fathom how that child could endure so many heavy blows, one right after the other.

"The granddaughter is suffering, and her grandmother is suffering," the women murmured.

"That little girl was suffering even more than the island itself," one of the neighbor women later recalled. Due to storms in recent months so much rain had fallen that the whole island was disintegrating, dissolving and becoming reduced to dregs—much as Xana was disintegrating and dissolving.

My sister scarcely knew what was going on in Carolina's head. There were fights and more fights. And without Daniel everything was going to get much worse. Some of these fights rose to the level of violence. One such time, Carolina grabbed a knife and with closed fist lunged at Xana, then let the knife fall. Poor Xana turned into a bundle of nerves and went on a hysterical rampage, shattering mirrors, out of her mind, screaming at the top of her lungs, not from anger but out of fear—a fear identical to the one she felt the day she had been in the middle of the bridge that threatened to collapse and crack in two.

Carolina lunged at Xana countless times, until she saw Xana vomit from exhaustion. What's more, Carolina forbade her to speak of it. "If you say anything, if you open your mouth, you spoiled brat, then the game turns serious. I'll wring your neck like a chicken's."

Xana never breathed a word, not even to Vovó. She was afraid of dying.

Just like soaked land, her body could not absorb any more tears. They simply ran off. Her voice was hoarse, her vocal cords swollen, her eyes doubled in size. Xana, feeling faint, slipped into the wall, into that hideout of hers.

❊

Our dear grandmother felt worse than devastated. She lost all control and, desperate to put an end to the silences in the house, buried herself in a sea of pain. Her suffering was so great that she could not bear it. So the house itself was starting to fill up, fill up with noise, with sobs— sometimes murmuring, other times cascading out of control. Her head was bursting; in her throat, a taste of blood. A continual moan pursued her as if someone were killing her. Although a bit softer, it was a cry similar to that of a pig as its life ended on *matança* day.

She talked to herself, as if Daniel were there in body and spirit. She drawled a dark lament, a wail. And again and again she kissed her only grandson's latest photo.

She would never again see him, never again feel the inspiration of his artwork consoling the wounded area in her heart. She returned over and over to his empty room. It was an icy chamber, an abandoned site, a draft, a chill. She would sniff her grandson's clothes again and again, burying her nose in his Bogart-style trench coat and fedora hanging behind the bedroom door. She paced back and forth but was unable to fill the empty spaces.

As for Tia Luísa, she withdrew into the house—she who was always going out to render services to those most in need. But now she was no longer able to do so. Her head felt ready to explode; she would not stray far from her trunk. She'd open it and pull out one of the little boxes that held family mementos: a baby tooth and lock of hair from Uncle Joe when, as a child, he had come to the island accompanied by his mother, our grandmother. A ribbon tied a box for each niece, nephew, grand-niece, and grandnephew: Tia Luísa identified them sometimes by ribbon color, other times by each box's size. She carefully preserved Daniel's last keepsake, knowing she would never see him again. She saved his fountain pen, and unframed pictures carefully rolled up and tied with the most beautiful yellow silk ribbon, the color of a yellow wagtail's breast.

And she stayed there like that for a long time, held captive by the boxes, opening them again and again, touching each object one by one, caressing them with her fingertips until she fell asleep.

❀

After all the commotion to which the house had been subjected in recent times, silence was returning to its rightful place. Quiet reigned once again. Calm no longer emanated just from *things:* it was spread through the old ladies' bodies. And thus from time to time, as the days wore on, a faint and flickering light would carry with it a certain brightness, softening Vovó and Tia's faces.

There was a sign then of something emerging from the depths of the waves, the tides, and even the moon that began to illuminate my grandmother again, etching on her face a smile as fresh as bubbling fountains.

Three knocks on the front door, as though from a knight-errant, signaled a letter. This time, however, the news was unsatisfying. Mamã had little to say about Daniel, only that he had arrived in good health and was already working in a factory and that he ought not to count on resuming the good life of his student days.

Mamã decreed, to my grandmother and Tia Luísa's surprise, that the *araçaleiro,* our strawberry guava tree, was to be cut down in order to turn part of the kitchen garden into a leisure space, a lawn edged with flower beds, and another part into the garden plot. To divide the two parts, the utilitarian from the ornamental, she wanted to erect a beautiful wall of hewn stone that included a wrought-iron gate beneath an arching trellis with a St. John's rose trained up it, and on the opposite side a bougainvillea.

Contrary to custom, the letter had as its aim to drive us all apart, preventing us from talking, and sending each of us to her own corner.

❀

I had never thought about how much I would miss Daniel's presence. And what would I tell Xana and Carolina? And Vovó and Tia?

It seemed my parents were going to arrive very soon. Everything would depend on the house and yard living up to their dreams. Not so much for Papá as for Mamã. She was always so demanding, giving no thought to the old ladies' ages.

The house occupied by Vovó had to be demolished, and in its place a mansion erected. While it was being built, we had to return to the house up at Burguete, where we no longer wanted to go, accustomed as we were to living in the center of the village.

Except for Xana, we all felt the fears and apprehensions that were corroding us.

Vovó came to us and, confiding in the form of a parable, told us a story.

"To everything, my girls, there is a season; to every person, their moment. A time to plant, a time to preach in the wilderness, a time for yellow leaves to fall one by one. A time for new life, with sprouts growing. A time as well for adversities, for life's thorns." And she soothed us confidently. My mother's mother was always watching out for us, for our sense of happiness.

All of a sudden, a great weight dropped onto us. In a split second we realized that others would be coming to inhabit the house, which would no longer be the same. I had never thought about it. Oh, how much I would miss Daniel's presence. And what would I tell Xana and Carolina? And what would the old ladies know of the potential effects of all that moving? And Tia and Vovó, what would they think?

✹

How sad, so very sad, when we heard at the dawn of a new day something sounding like an axe falling heavily upon hard material, tough like iron. We got up and ran in our pajamas to the backyard. Vovó and Tia were standing there transfixed, perplexed. They did not react. The expression on both their faces was stone cold; stone cold too were their bodies. With each hollow stroke of the axe, men were chopping down our *araçaleiro*, in whose shadow Xana used to play with her dolls and pretend to hold christenings and funerals.

After all, Mamã would be sending another letter insisting they cut down the *araçaleiro* in order to make room for a garden in the shape of a half-moon outside the back door. Thus the old ladies, Carolina, Xana, and I saw bits of ourselves stripped away, amputated. We wept, and the sections of tree trunk went to heat the stove. It was nothing short of grief for my grandmother and Tia Luísa. For us it was a flash of betrayal, the loss of our souls.

From that moment on, everything that used to be until then ceased to be. For us there no longer existed any sense of place. It evaporated.

Xana wept bitter tears. She crouched down and began talking to the snails, telling them of that morning's heartaches. "Oh, little *Caracolinho,* tell me your secret. Tell me how you grow your little house, how you hide. Make me a shell like yours, for me to hide in when I don't want to see the light, when I don't want them to know I'm crying, that I cry every day for my brother.

"I'm so sad," Xana continued. "Those men are evil. They cut down our bountiful *araçaleiro.* It's weeping, it's bleeding, and I don't want to see the pain it's feeling. And my dolls are crying, too. And I'm crying along with them."

I looked over toward the old ladies and noticed they were not there, that their disenchanted smiles had disappeared beneath the soles of their shoes. I had heard enough. I felt the pain in my grandmother's quivering voice when she murmured to her sister, "No, Luísa, I don't like seeing things cut down this way before their time, destroyed as if they'd never existed." Tia Luísa remained silent, her eyes sunken and her head tilting toward Pico da Vara.

Vovó turned her back to the scene of the crime, which she'd had to witness, and walked downcast toward the kitchen. She entered defeated, shaking her head from side to side.

A pearl-white butterfly alit on the brim of her hat. The agitation of the sea, in Vovó's head, startled it.

※

That morning, my grandmother was summoned to the school at the teacher's request. She was upset. That had never happened to her.

So I was the one who lent her the moral support necessary at that moment in order for her to face, with difficulty, Xana's teacher:

"What's this about? What's the matter, Senhora?" my grandmother asked anxiously.

"It's just that Xana is having problems," said the schoolmistress.

"What type of problems, Senhora Professora? Tell me once and for all. Don't leave me in this agony, for God's sake!"

"It's nothing to worry about. The problem is that your granddaughter is in fact so advanced in her studies. For instance, although it's only March your granddaughter has already read the entire first grade textbook. I have even lent her story books I had at home, and she devoured them in just a few days. I don't know what to do with her."

"So what should I do, Senhora?" Vovó asked, perplexed.

"Oh, don't get alarmed, don't be worried, please. What I mean to say is that your granddaughter, instead of being promoted to second grade, ought to skip to third. I just want to know, Senhora, if you think she will fit in as easily at that level in both language arts and arithmetic."

My grandmother, her head reeling, turned to me in a plea for help. "Won't it be very hard on Xana's little brain, her being still so young?" she asked me, her eyes empty and uncertain.

"Why the rush?" Vovó again asked.

I stood there not knowing quite what to say, but within a few seconds my grandmother had taken an extreme position that brought the conversation to a close. "I don't want to do this, I don't want to. There's no rush for her to grow up. The higher we fly, the farther we fall. And she's also a frail child, as you well know, Senhora. She's prone to bleeding and frequent anemia. I'm afraid that Xana would find holes so deep she'd never be able to dig her way out of them. I don't want to do that. Forgive me, Senhora."

The teacher grew rather disheartened, but later devised a solution. She called Xana up to her desk, and asked if she would like to play *professora*, helping girls who were having difficulty reading. Xana was delighted, and it kept her occupied the rest of the year.

❀

But things were not all a bed of roses. The following year, in second grade, the professora discovered to her surprise that Xana did not like writing essays. She had an aversion to them, hated them, and they made her tears flow unchecked. She became sad, distracted, and very stubborn. She bit her lip in rage and tore up the handkerchief she carried in the pocket of her uniform smock. She was filled with shame.

Xana knew she could not and should not cry at her age, when her classmates weren't even complaining. But she did not want to write an essay, not at all. She did not want to do what the professora wanted her to.

Xana, who always possessed a huge stubborn streak, insisted on writing in her own style, recounting what was going on at Vovó's house and at Mamã's home in America. But her teacher insisted on birds, trees, the four seasons, colorless and odorless water. And there was Xana, who could see gorgeous colors of the most varied shades in the water and clearly still hear its music, which was white; taste its flavor, which was silk, which was perfume during evenings of São João.

"No spelling errors," her teacher continued.

But her syntax, rather than evolving, grew more tortuous. Her words, many of them, were old-fashioned. There was no logic. Her ideas were scattershot, and she would not stick to the subject or follow to the letter what was required. She changed everything. The teacher no longer knew how to deal with Xana. She sensed, however, that Xana was doing it on purpose in order to defy her. At last she became infuriated, and for the first time gave Xana two smacks to the head.

She placed Xana in the center of the room on display as punishment for being a naughty child who had dared to defy the teacher. But that was not what Xana was trying to do. What she wanted was to recount events on her street, Xana repeated in desperation. She wanted to write about her brother, about the death of our *araçaleiro,* about Daniel's departure.

⊛

But Xana remained in the center of the classroom, as though she were a corpse laid out atop a bier, surrounded by her classmates. She was perspiring, drenched in a cold sweat.

The professora went back on the offensive. "That is not how one speaks. It is not how a young lady should express herself." She lost her temper, then reined herself in by talking to herself: "That's how the old folks used to say it, with words no longer in use, some archaic, others neither Portuguese nor American."

Xana wanted to crawl into a hole and never see the light of day again. She burst into a steady stream of tears.

How embarrassing!

She felt her face getting hot. Her complexion was flushing ruby red and smelled of burning coal.

Then Jesus Christ on the cross came to mind. A cloverleaf cascade descended in sheets unfolding over her frail little abandoned body. Everyone became dark to her and vanished. She seized the opportunity to erase everything around her and felt much lighter. It was as if she were on the other side, unaware of what was happening right in front of her, ready to leave, to board her own airplane for places where there might be no solitude, where the words she was so fond of were unnecessary.

At that precise moment she learned by herself that words could be cruel, angry, violent, and false—but also playful, friendly, and tender, especially under Vovó's wing when she was paging through that magazine with its butterflies of a thousand colors.

The next day she refused to go to school. That teacher was mean, Xana thought, a lightning bolt flashing from her head, awaiting its thunderclap. Her teacher had the face of a witch and a mustache like a palm leaf broom made of *piaçá* stems.

And Mamã did not come, was never there, was only on the other side in the photograph. "A make-believe Mamã, unable to save me from such humiliation."

Lost in an empty space, Xana swallowed the salt of her tears, rough like the strands in burlap cloth. And in place of Mamã what was heard was that hearty laugh that moved the stars in heaven, spangling her forehead, leaving her dazed, feverish.

During a prolonged delirium she stammered, "I'll never tell Vovó about the fear, the shame, the thousand eyes that fell on me at school.

"I don't want to see her sad."

❀

Days later I got word of the situation, through a friend of my sister's. My first reaction was to go see the professora to clear up the facts, but I thought it best for me to keep quiet, unless Xana wanted to tell me about it. And even then, if I knew the details, would I be able to defend her? Oh, if only Daniel were still on the island, we would be better off. But without anyone else up to confronting the teacher, I lacked the courage to do so by myself. The most reasonable course would doubt-less be to keep my mouth shut.

And if Vovó for some reason became aware of the incident, she assuredly would sit like Jacob alongside his well, weeping for her grand-daughter's pain.

※

It was well known.

Lately Xana was growing pale and more silent. I truly wanted to help her. I knew that such humiliation would scar her forever, but she would not open up. She remained elusive and in general played by herself, above all in the summer months when boys and girls were called upon to help their parents in the fields. She did not like adults to intrude on her games. "Shoo, shoo," Xana would always scare off anyone who dared approach her, distracting her from the world she created for herself.

A few weeks later I began to realize that my sister, in addition to her pallor, was losing so much weight that it was visible to the naked eye. Some months earlier, as she raced around Vovó's house in play, it was rare not to see her bleeding, but that day blood spurted out her nose until it choked her, so great was its volume. The hens came flocking in response, pecking at the blood, and Xana almost fainted at the sight of them swallowing a part of her body amid all the droppings. Then she let out horrific screams, begging for help to chase and frighten away death, death that she did not want.

How could her blood have gone to the dung heap, to the hens' craws? And her body, what was left of it? Dazed, she dug deeper into her resolve. She felt as restless as a distrustful dog. She was ashamed of not being strong. She was as humbled as a worthless rag. And for every-thing that was so serious, the likelier she was to seek the other side of the coin—that of laughing, jumping, running, screaming, inhaling life in a single breath.

My grandmother was dissolving in pain. We noted on her facial expression a certain surrender.

"I can't take this anymore. My daughter has to return. What Xana needs is her mother. It's her mother she needs," my grandmother stam-mered in distress.

With pain still boiling up inside her, Xana took to gazing at herself in the mirror and staying there for hours on end. The effect was fascinating, for in our grandmother's bedroom there were two chests of drawers topped by large cloverleaf-shaped mirrors. One stood alongside the bed, the other at the footboard. As a result Xana was multiplied threefold—twice from the front and once from behind, the back view being the most seductive for not showing her face, only her hair and back. She would pull up a chair, clamber up on it, and talk to the mirror in front of her, a fascination that entertained her for hours and hours. She spoke to no one else. With the mirrors she felt safer. She would put on one hat and take off another or do the same with a ribbon or veil. It was in this world of her own making where she felt most at home. She would fantasize, make believe, and transport herself to her parents' America, where she walked down streets she had seen only in photographs. She would go inside their house, full of electric lights, not oil lamps. She would play with their nieces and nephews and go on picnics in New Bedford's Brooklawn Park with her parents, cousins, and friends. She pictured herself skating in the city's Lincoln Park amid the colorfulness of the carousel, the roller coaster, and fresh smiles that were always red and redolent of Uncle Joe's clothing.

The houses were gorgeous, with gardens and broad streets. Compared to them, our houses on the island were tiny as matchboxes, all huddled up, stuck together, some so small that a man could almost tuck them under his arm. They were dark, tormented by island gales, lashed by rain, and cracked by an Earth that shook from time to time.

Then she would imagine seeing her sisters married, their children born. People in the street—many, many people. And everything so fragrant. And she saw waves of shop windows unfolding one by one to infinity. And the roads, the airports. And so many lights, and more lights shining everywhere. And when she was up in the clouds on approach to Boston, she could see a swarm of thousands of flickering little points of light, and even the Earth itself resembled a fireball that rivaled the stars in the sky. Oh, she continued, and white sand beaches! And she too was dressed all in white, riding with her sisters in Daniel's car on weekends. Next, she saw a breathless hustle and bustle of people, fleet of foot and restless of body, always on the run. There was Mamã working at the factory, sewing at home, cooking for her family—and everything was always fast, spinning, running like the jet of water gushing from a garden hose. And there were her married sisters getting up at five in the morning to clear the snow from their cars and speed off on their way to the factory. And she herself was walking from shop to shop downtown, buying a hair ribbon, barrettes, and a beautiful organdy dress for the Holy Ghost *festas* on the island.

And Vovó was walking with her alongside their private pond, showing her their old mansion from another era with its sumptuous façade, and explaining how the walls were articulated to increase or decrease the area of each room according to the season of the year. The fixed walls were lined with books. Here and there, an Edward Hopper painting. And Xana, try as she might, couldn't understand what Vovó was talking about. "But Vovó, the walls moved?"

"Yes, Xana, they were hinged."

Vovó must have been joking, Xana thought. But no, she was not.

The house was exactly the way it looked in the photographs.

The lights were its most attractive feature. "My goodness," she marveled in enchantment, standing slack-jawed. "Such a heaven on earth, so many stars dancing, Vovó."

It was of course hard for Xana to leave the mirror. Whether she was in front of it or inside it, she found space for her emotions and a reality that she herself, though still very little, was creating. Upon entering this world she would wriggle as though she wanted to jump out of herself, like taking off a skintight dress.

When all was said and done, my sister felt good in her mirror-image world in that make-believe house of hers. And every time she left the mirror, the whole thing shuddered.

Next she would run to the foot of the cliff. She loved to see the whiteness of the sea below, when the clouds descended from the sky to slake their thirst.

❋

"It's true that the sea has its own memories. It also affects the wounds in your eyes, my little girl. It goes out and comes in twice every day, and at every tide," Vovó said, her eyes wandering, just as Xana saw them.

A sea of the dead and a sea of the living—and Vovó caught between the two, undecided on either one. The waves were not getting her feet wet. The ocean tide was out, very far away. Its edge, starting at the coast-line that separated it from the island, was farther away for the majority of Nordeste's population than the sky, which was so close to us.

When she woke up and opened a door or window, her eyes would automatically be met by that line out where the water ends and the other lands begin, with no break in either of them from this side or the other.

And it was from that line that boats, dolls, socks, school supplies, crayons, coloring books, roller skates for the sidewalk, and flavored chewing gums emerged. And every time a ship appeared there on the horizon, everyone turned in the same direction.

They would follow it until it pierced the skyline. All that remained of the horizon was a mirrored echo, a tremendous emptiness.

❈

In recent days I noticed our grandmother was more oriented toward sea than land. That morning she had left very early and returned home soaked. She came from the direction of the cliff, with water in her eyes and salt in her throat. Something was bothering her, without her even realizing it herself. It did not take very long to find out.

Soon a gust of wind swept through São Bento, spreading word that her ex-husband was about to arrive. But that was impossible unless the letter announcing his visit to the island had gone astray, my grand-mother fretted. And then she told herself that it could only be a rumor spread by someone with nothing better to do. And Vovó stopped think-ing about rumors, which in those parts were born almost every day.

However, some weeks later people awoke to the curiosity of a ship perilously near the coast. A band of men flocked like wild rock doves to a small boat near the waterfront. One of them asked that they notify his family: Senhor Manuel Fontes was disembarking.

When my grandfather arrived in the village at Vovó's house, he was a fish without a tail. A shadow of his former self. The crowds then opened up for him, so numerous were the women elbowing their way forward to view a scene whose outcome no one imagined.

With his head cocked a bit to the left, perhaps in order to hear better, my grandfather broke away from the multitude and, although still far off, turned toward my grandmother, who was waiting in the doorway. Then there was a brief hesitation, more of a pause than uncertainty.

Xana hid behind Vovó, afraid. Was he going to harm Vovó? And she wrapped herself up more and more, rolling herself inside Vovó's skirt.

They scarcely exchanged a word and barely touched one another. In a brief, almost perfunctory gesture my grandfather ran his hand over our astonished heads, as if smoothing the fur of a newborn puppy.

I saw Vovó fill with a sudden unexpected strength. She stepped forward without hesitation and approached the man who had once been her husband, but no longer held any claim on her. She greeted him with an almost haughty elegance. Distracted, however, she viewed herself as lying prone, consumed by a brief emotion. She walked, or flew, from room to room showing him the old photos of the New Bedford mansion during the good old days, happy times now vanished or perhaps buried.

Our grandfather said goodbye. Xana refused to let him kiss her. She trembled with fear, even though she was clutching Vovó's always-warm hands.

Grandpa departed almost at a run. He seemed to leave behind a trail of smoke. He was a man who had just come out of an oven. He turned away in a brusque motion in order to avoid any temptation, probably dictated by a pain he hoped to frighten away.

There was a jingling of gold coins with his every step.

He turned at the street corner, looked back, and whoever was still there heard what was dancing on his lips. They were words of justice. Then the bells tolled.

"A great woman!" he said to himself.

"A great woman!" he repeated.

And thus departed our grandfather-of-a-few-minutes.

⁂

Afternoon fell.

On the window panes a reflection of fire was warming the "snow" that had lodged in my grandmother's eyes. It melted, sliding down, and she wiped it away with no resentment, no excuses, no apologies. Head held high, she went to the kitchen. It was time to eat, time to swallow a past that no longer existed, my grandmother murmured to herself, somehow disengaged and perhaps nostalgic, for her heart was still warm.

It was Carolina who later discovered in Tia Luísa's trunk the poems to Vovó from my grandfather when he visited the island as a young man and fell in love with her. There were many of them. One went like this:

> Now I shall begin
> Of this I am the actor
> And the one who'll explain to you
> Certain words of love
>
> This young man I speak of
> Is usually in a good mood
> I never imagined
> He could cause so much grief
>
> He says I am flawed
> And takes advantage of this
> Because people do not know
> That I have this imperfection
>
> He is an educated young man
> I'm the one who says so
> The young woman jilted him
> Saying it was because of me
>
> I don't let this bother me
> But I don't think he is right
> If she loved him
> She would not tell him no

The people of the village—always very curious, speculative, digging into everyone's lives—scarcely knew what my grandmother, looking apprehensive, was thinking.

As she used to tell me, there was no ladder on the face of the earth tall enough to span or reach the depths of her intimate feelings, her interior, her peace, and the happiness conveyed by her granddaughters.

Like the moon goddess, Vovó did not need to replace her ex-husband with another man in order to achieve personal fulfillment. She always continued to respect him, remembering the old times and recalling in particular those early years of marriage when he wrote poems in tribute to his goddess, his beloved, as he called her. She also recalled the devastating rumor that shattered her innocence, and due to which my grandfather put an end to a life that had gone from being beautiful to becoming tarnished, as pitch-black as an Azorean goshawk.

After all this, everything had gone downhill. After that, the fact that he had now taken a mistress became an additional pretext for the continued separation, and the children were forgotten by their father, struck off the family rolls.

Forgotten too was his goddess, now dethroned from her "divinity."

CHAPTER 5

Ash Wednesday.

Spring was at the door. The rain was weeping that day.

Xana slept in a lethargic slumber, far deeper than usual. Vovó stayed alert and apprehensive. She thought it all very strange.

Moments later, we found Xana soaked in blood. But this time it wasn't coming out her nose, so Xana would not let anyone near her. She lay there stiff as a board, her eyes riveted to the ceiling. A horrible fear overcame her. She recalled at that moment a story about how babies are born that Carolina had told her back when Daniel was still her companion, her "father." She had never said anything to anyone and had continued to think that Carolina was in fact lying, while fearing the possibility it all was true.

So Xana hid under the sheets, curled up in a pain-filled ball. She stayed that way, becoming more and more stuck to the mattress, ignoring the fact that something might have come out of her—a piece of her body, or a baby?—from between her legs.

"How shameful that would be," she lamented to herself.

All of a sudden a scream erupted that rent asunder the fabric of the universe, parching the land and darkening the skies. There was no doubt but that I had to intervene right away. I offered aid and comfort to Xana, despite my awkward manner. I never knew whether I would find her acting meek toward me, or fierce like a cat with razor-sharp claws. It was necessary to act then, to make a quick decision—while my grandmother, in a daze, mulled everything over and common sense eluded her, as she seemed unaware of where she was. She called the hen and chicks, as if they were running around inside the house. It could be argued that she had gone crazy. She could not bear to see her granddaughter consumed by so much fright, locked as ever in that gaze dominated by waiting for darkness to fall.

So I gathered up my courage, approached Xana and, half out of my own mind, slapped her twice to stop the hysterics. Then I clutched her. A brutal clash between us ensued. I could not stop; if I did, I would lose the battle. And it would be worse for Xana. I struggled with all my might, while little by little her body yielded to my will. I stayed in that position with her for who knows how long.

Once I let go of Xana in order to see her face, to look her in the eye, I spoke to her for the first time in a mother's voice. "Sleep, sleep, my little girl, get your beauty sleep." And at the same time I thought to myself, "My sister is resisting becoming a woman." That was what I realized: a woman warrior tilting at windmills, scarcely knowing what awaited her.

Xana was drenched in cold sweat, listless.

Tia Luísa had already supplied a kettle and a pan of hot water. I then led Xana to the tub. First, I rinsed her face with every tenderness of my being and leached the salt out of her pain. Next I gently washed her neck, where fat unstoppable silent tears rolled down. Then her slender straight arms, and after that her seemingly disjointed armpits. I kept bathing her with all my sweetness. I dried her off and rubbed her body to warm her and make her feel more like a person, more human.

Clean at last.

Between her legs, neither any part of her own body nor a baby—but, inevitably, a cotton pad.

I helped her safety-pin it inside her panties. Her aura came across as transfigured, like Christ nailed to the cross. And it was as if a prison cell gate had slammed down in front of her face, turning it to iron. Her face seemed so weighed down under that torrential downpour of an infinite deception.

To soothe her I fixed some citron tea and again massaged her poor body just emerging from the rubble of an Ash Wednesday earthquake.

I calmed her, caressed her, humming Vovó's song as I stroked her long wavy brown hair, almost the color of copper.

Next I plaited it into a thick braid and at the end tied a beautiful white silk bow.

I determined to dress her all in white, so she could forget the red.

I rocked her on my lap to the rhythm of my tune. Her deep eyes floated in silence. From time to time, a sigh interspersed with sobs wracked her whole body in a dense, long lament. Her pain was anguishing.

Night was falling, serene. The dark at that moment was calming.

❋

After a few weeks Xana was regaining her strength. However, a world's worth of insecurity was visible in her eyes, in that treacherous hurt that had come on without warning. And what right did that monster have to invade her body without so much as asking permission? After which she inferred a fate of forever and ever and evermore.

Once more I snuggled her up against my chest in order to seal our new bond and tried to comfort her by telling her that starting at a certain point all women pass through the same storm once a month for several days and that it is like that for nearly the rest of our lives.

"Nearly the rest of our lives?"

Xana executed a jump that not even a monkey on a tree branch could make. In one leap, I saw her eyes flashing and rolling on the floor, setting the whole house on fire.

Then fear took hold of me. After all, the tongues of fire that our parish priest spoke of were no mere fruits of the imagination. They were indeed palpable, crackling like lightning bolts in midair and leaving a vibration thick enough to cut with a knife. I saw them clearly that day. And while I worried, without Vovó perceiving my fears and concerns, about our Xana's state, her eyes had turned into stars. They reposed soft and serene, and yet somehow far away, wounded. The dryness of her body continued to disappear, however, and in its place water gushed: her saliva already wet, her skin damp and eyes watery. Her complexion was as delicate as pure fine cambric.

Lightly, lightly like clouds, Xana was leaving behind a time of sluggishness, torpor, and death already long ago and far away.

That big scare over, Xana became my friend, but to my astonishment and my grandmother's, she did not grow close to Carolina. It was understandable that at the moment she needed a *mãe* more than an *irmã*. And Xana could not find in our sister Carolina the maternal shelter she needed, nor the essential anchor to keep her down to earth. She always clung to life by a strand as fine as spiderweb silk. But in that embrace I sensed her strength was one of attraction and rejection. It could only come from far, far away, perhaps from a drum in a weightless and immeasurable echo.

Xana bore a somber expression the whole next morning, to the point of scaring me. She approached me all bristly like a porcupine, hair disheveled, her face quite contorted. She was determined to repel me head-on.

She assaulted me like a hawk attacking chickens.

"I don't want this," my sister said, punching my body all over. "I don't want to be a girl, I don't want this pad between my legs, I don't want that monster pursuing me throughout my entire life. I don't want in any way to be a woman.

"I want to play, I want to spin a top, run, challenge the boys, I want to beat them in races around the school, on paths near Vovó's house. I want to be free like a boy. I want to be a girl, but with the same freedom as a boy. And when it comes to men, I don't even want to see them cross my path, Mana."

I was astonished; I dared not make a sound. In front of me stood a monster, a madwoman. I realized that ultimately I did not recognize my own sister—that inhibited girl filled with fears, somewhat insecure, although who if left to her devices would not accept anyone's help.

In childhood that little girl of ours was so frail that when lifted up onto a lap it seemed to us that she would break apart like cracked china—but from then on her strength, in that unforgettable moment when her soul was stirred and she was coiled as tight as a spring, never stopped running until she had again unwound, until she found herself slipping again beneath the dark shadows of death.

"How many rights do boys have?" Xana insisted. "And girls? We have none?"

My poor sister, I thought to myself. Her stubbornness trumped my brother's obstinacy. Fearless, she was ready to change the order of things, and of Nature itself.

Xana promised me and swore (weeping more than Mary Magdalene) that she was going to perpetrate so many, many follies until the monster's curse passed from her at rocket speed. A menstrual period was even worse than the childhood bogeyman.

"The last one's gone, and then another one comes," Xana gasped. "I want nothing to do with this. I prefer to slay that monster before it slays me. I hate it. And yet when 'my monthly visitor arrives,' they say you can't wash your hair, oh, oh, oh! Mana, you know what I think?" Xana told me, her vocal cords leaping from her throat, "All this was in truth nothing but the devil's handiwork."

⊛

So I had to stop that swing of the scythe. Xana was going too far, so I told her, "Now I'm going to talk. It's my turn, Xana." And then a dark, dark silence fell.

"Look, I'll tell you something, my noble little *fidalga*. You're no aristocrat, you're no better than anyone else, do you understand? Why don't you resign yourself to your possibilities? Why do you think you shouldn't have to suffer? Stop blaspheming, for the love of God."

Xana wrinkled her nose at me and replied in a bitter voice, "I don't care for your preachy 'little priest's' tone; nothing good comes out of you. You get so ugly and, moreover, stupid. I know Vovó would never talk to me the way you do in that sanctimonious tone of yours. If I weren't ashamed, I'd open myself up to her and no one else. Not to you."

I felt like telling her, "Stay with 'your' grandmother, then."

In spite of it all, I showed compassion and pulled her to me, stroking her, trying to calm her. She quieted down in an instant, leaned over, and laid her heavy head on my lap while I ran my hand through her damp hair once more.

Like the murmur of counting through rosary beads, a "no-no-no" was perceptible in Xana's stubbornness, until a spiderweb fell over her face and a grimace onto her lips. Within minutes, she surrendered herself to a long, deep sleep.

One warm June afternoon Xana came hopping in on just one foot to be with me and, all happy and with a certain wit, declared, "I learned a new word today. It's very important to me. The word is 'euphemism.' Do you know what it means?" And without giving me time to reply, my sister laughed more demonically than innocently. "'Euphemism,'" she repeated, "that is, using other words as a way to soften what hurts us. For example, instead of saying that so-and-so 'died,' it's customary to say he's 'deceased' or 'departed,' or 'has passed away.' Oh, and this is what I want to get at, instead of saying 'the curse'—the most accurate word to me—people use other terms like 'menstruation,' 'period,' and who knows what else. But why pretend?" she charged, coming closer and challenging me, again exasperated. "So, isn't that a curse, Mana? Or is it delightful?"

"Don't be sarcastic. You're offending me, and you're already old enough to know better."

"Sorry, Mana, but in my case I feel twisted like those old rags the women wring out when they scrub the house."

"Shut up, Xana. You're just talking nonsense."

"It's a curse indeed, Senhora," Xana repeated. "If not to you, then at least to me. Besides that, it's the precise word—the most appropriate one for the reality, which is of suffering, discomfort, a chill called humiliation.

"Don't you think," Xana persisted, "that the word *menstruação* is not the most appropriate? It's a noun of the feminine gender, you see.

"Look, if that were so, then *verdade* would be our ally—and not our enemy, to the point of pounding our bones, muscles, and heads to smithereens. So to me that word needs to be of the masculine gender, contrary to what grammarians say, because only that gender—lord and master of the world—would be able to inflict a suffering on women for which they tell us we'll get our reward in heaven later.

"I don't believe in old wives' tales. Vovó always told me that He and heaven were on Earth, within ourselves.

"'Curse' is the most precise word," Xana reiterated with satisfaction, "because it's devoid of lies and subterfuges. The other is a sophisticated form with a kinder, gentler sound for hoodwinking or pretending—everything except calling a spade a spade.

"Sorry, to me it's 'the curse,' you hear? It's a monster that enters me and tortures me the way nothing else can, like the force of the grape-press, or the roadbed roller that's compacting the dirt on the new street in Nordeste.

"And just like what happens to pigs when they sense their impending doom, I embark on a disoriented flurry of dizziness, vomiting, energy loss. My body becomes a phantasm; my soul, dying; my gaze, sad and wounded. It then rains inside me, like a rainfall, sore and bruising, as if there were two people in me, the outside one and the inside one—just like Vovó's stockings: the thicker pair on the inside, the sheer ones on the outside.

"But while the pig dies only once, I die every month. And that is what's unbearable to endure. Even my head throbs.

"Look, one day I'll tell Mamã everything, if she ever exists beyond her photograph someday. However, the outside world expects that what little strength I have left will return to me. This damned curse likes me so much that from time to time it dares to visit twice in a month. How can I recover my energies when a heavy shadow is cast over my entire body? How can I be equal to males?

"There are few days that I can claim as my own. And I'm always in a struggle, dying to kill the cruel, bombastic monster, the monster that fires everything at me, stealing pieces of me inch by inch the same way that inch by inch the sea washes away the island.

"And I'm dreaming about Mamã and her being so far away, absent, distant. She never arrives anymore. She never comes to my rescue anymore."

❋

There remained, however, the so-called tears of blood that Tia Luísa prophesied to each family member who left for the other side of the ocean. And only then did Xana understand. That was after all a meta-phor, a very powerful image, a hyperbole for an almost nameless pain, waiting to be stabbed until it drew its final breath.

Xana would approach her Mana without realizing she was opening up to me a bit more each time. That afternoon my sister wanted to talk to me.

"Do you feel like listening, Mana?" she confided in me.

"Of course I do, Xana."

"Look, here's what happened: I remember a conversation that's stuck in my head since I was just a child, five or six years old. We were playing hopscotch, and the neighbor women seated on the stoop were embroidering, taking advantage of the day's warm afternoon while waiting for their husbands. Without meaning to, Mana, I heard them talking, talking all agitated about an event that horrified them. And among the babbling of their voices, muffled, I know I heard the word 'blood.' They were speaking in an unfamiliar tongue. To us children, a dead language.

"They were whispering very low and it was said that on his wedding night the groom, Clementina's son, instead of opening his bride's barrier with finesse, went at it like a soccer kick, the brute. He tore her wide open, making her fall to pieces on the floor, and the result was enough bleeding to fill thirty *morcela* blood sausages.

"It was only much later that I came to understand, Mana. At that point I didn't comprehend one iota about anything, but something didn't strike me as right. Their language confused me and threw me for a loop. However, I don't know why, but later I recalled that moment, the way a bouncing ball suddenly rises to its apex. I was sure something was behind all that way of speaking. Thus it told me something that only now do I know how to name: 'barrier' and 'blood' weren't only related, they were one and the same. At that moment, I swore I'd never marry. And I don't want flirtations, Mana, not even in fun.

"I don't like men. In general they make their brides cry and, after they're married, have the right to beat them and disrespect them. They are kings and lords with guaranteed thrones. They speak in loud voices, while their sweethearts lower theirs. And if for some reason one raises hers, it's a sign of weakness in the young man, and the girl mustn't act too clever with him because that would be undesirable. And she winds up carrying a cross on her back under threat of invented jealousies, all to annoy her, sitting there at the windowsill, made to suffer until she gets down on her knees and begs and pleads for God not to abandon her. Her dowry was paid up. And the very next day her beloved broke off their engagement."

❀

He broke it off, the women chattered early the next morning.

But the sunshine was short-lived.

A few days later the same scene, the same weeping, the same gentle words all over again, and always over the top. Never otherwise. "For example," my sister again challenged, "Mana, I've never seen a fiancée sitting in any of our village's many windows who made her boyfriend shed a single tear. Tears are only for women. Men don't have them.

"That's why I'll never marry unless men can become like companions, like friends. Do you understand, Mana?

"And what I'm saying, I've already written down. It's on the first page of my second-year English schoolbook. If you don't believe me, Mana, look for yourself. I don't know how you'll take that," my sister added in a disapproving tone.

"So don't you see how young women as beautiful as you and Carolina and many others are, fresh-faced when they marry, soon thereafter lose their vigor and are totally transformed? Their steps become halting, their faces sallow. They live from one moment to the next, a Cinderella-in-reverse, turning from princess into char-girl. They enter a type of mourning, of modesty, with a kerchief covering their heads, a shawl over their shoulders, bidding farewell to the era of their charms.

"Now take a look at our neighbor Filomena next door," Xana continued, before I could interrupt her. "Do you see how much she's aged in such a short time? How I used to enjoy watching her so much on Sundays. Elegant, well-dressed, behatted, with birds dancing in her green eyes under silky lashes the color of blackberries."

❄

At the end of Xana's lengthy confidence in me, I doubted the conviction with which my sister, despite her youth, affirmed herself regarding the men of that time. I understood her. She had been raised in my grandmother's house without any male figures, save for the sporadic presence of Uncle Joe and the two years spent with our brother Daniel.

One more factor contributed to pushing my sister Xana into her cocoon. She had always been off life's stage.

She was always a spectator, a little girl in the audience. And she stayed that way. Her style was to edge ever farther away.

It was difficult for us to catch her, to approach her. And when we did get near, she would slip away from us like an eel.

After several years of living with Xana, albeit at a bit of a distance due to her stubborn streak, it did not seem to me that she would change. Even when she was very young, she embraced brand-new rights and responsibilities like those of freedom and opportunity, transmitted by Vovó, who had acquired them in America.

It was unfair that some people wound up with the gold ring, others with just a losing fava bean. Upon reflection, I began to realize that Xana would never extend her palm in submission to anybody who wanted her to be servile. Only as equal to equal.

Like Minerva she would wait for dawn to break in order to stage new flights toward other places up above, from the other side of her memory.

One particular afternoon during summer vacation Xana tiptoed up to me. She begged me to teach her to embroider. She did not like that hobby much. She preferred books, she said, but also wanted to learn and experiment with the art, in particular because since childhood she had always let herself "melt" into the colors printed in Vovó's magazines on pages devoted to various species of coral, butterflies, fishes, and birds, which thereafter would be woven into the texture of a linen cloth that she herself wished to feel. She wanted to try some of the stitches: backstitch, which seemed to her clean and very simple to execute; chain stitch, rather more complicated, resembling a rope or Carolina's braid; shading stitch, all blended in variegated harmonizing tones; and the fill stitch, which would transform background fabric into a beautiful tapestry in tonalities approximating a rainbow's.

Needle up, needle down—and little more, just a diversion. Not to be taken seriously, Xana sniffed with her disdainful air: "Now books, those are good! They teach us so many wonderful things."

She sat down near me, her eyes glazed like when you forget yourself. When she at last became herself again, she sidled up very close to me.

Then I began giving her her first lessons in embroidery.

Vovó joined us in order to see how Xana was handling her needle. While knitting stockings from a slight distance, she watched her granddaughter, keeping her company in the complicated exercise between needle and cloth. A stroke of fingernail swished Vovó's silky hair. At one particular moment Vovó concentrated so hard she lost track. She shifted, and the ball of yarn fell from her lap. Her memories of that brief moment fell away, too. She resumed the *click-click-click* of her needles, needles that she may have thought served to stitch up her heart's old wounds, as she cast her glance toward the horizon on the other side of the ocean, where the sun sets.

Right away she stood up, headed for the bedroom, wound up the gramophone, and put on a waltz. She sat in her rocking chair and from time to time would observe Xana, with that smile and braided hair bobbing to the rhythm of the music.

Suddenly the orchestra's melodiousness was drowned out. It was Xana, who had pricked herself. A drop of blood made her tremble. And she flung aside her embroidery with contempt.

❊

I don't know how, but all of a sudden my sister was again recalling her "day of death," as she was accustomed to calling it—a futile obsession already so unbearable to me that it reeked of two-week-old death. Whenever she spoke or heard the expression "being a woman," she emitted a sardonic mucus-tinged guffaw with her teeth gnashing, leaving me concerned yet at the same time infuriated. Sometimes it gave me an urge to slap her so that she would never more speak to me of what should have been buried long ago. But then I would restrain myself so she would not turn away from me again.

So it was better not to cross her. Time could be trusted to put everything in its place, Tia Luísa told us countless times. After all, what I wanted most was to have Xana beside me. So I gave her all the attention then that I possibly could. On her best days she sometimes even yielded, surrendering her whole self, heart and soul, then displaying the sweetness she possessed—despite, if one noticed, a crack of loneliness on her angelic face.

Should she also desire the same thing, I wanted so very, very much to grant a free pass to her often muffled words, to her emotions locked up like the wheels of oxcarts squeaking due to carrying something tightly packed and heavy.

I wanted to put her more at ease, unbutton her, free up her whole body, try to help her accept being a woman, but her reaction always came with an impetus stronger than a volcano, far superior to its forces.

And now, with a giant leap she shot out into the street. She ran and ran along all the paths in the village without stopping, until she doused the fire that was consuming her. Later, when she came in the house, her gaze was calm, with a brief cool smile imprinted on her face as though nothing had happened. What interested her was forgetting, a formula she had cultivated since childhood as a survival mechanism—that was how I understood it when, upon our moving to Vovó's house, I began getting to know her better.

Again she came to me. She still wanted to confide that on the night before menstruation entered her body for the first time, she had been chased by a horrible dream, something to forget. And she began to relate it.

"Oh Mana, it went like this, I don't know really how: I was coming out of a hospital. In front of me on a wide-open field there was one birth, then another and another and another. So many of them were bizarre, as if they were eating each other. Among them, bodies of mutilated people—heads, arms, legs, all going into the middle of a great scrap heap. In the center, on top of that mess, a child's head. It was horrible, with no eyes, and its mouth gaped open emitting a cry not of this world.

"I woke up terrified, drenched in sweat, even after realizing it was only a nightmare. When I then fell back to sleep, I felt wet all of a sudden. Then I noticed a red stain on my shoe, which lay alongside the bed.

"I suspected something that at the moment I couldn't identify, Mana.

"Suddenly, having already slipped from dream to reality, I became aware of a searing heat that was flowing from inside me. I sensed something without a name.

"I sensed the time had arrived. I lay there without knowing which saint I should pray to. I was ashamed to involve Vovó. So, early in the morning I let myself stay burrowed into my mattress, while Carolina laughed in secret. And in my heart of hearts, without wanting to say anything to anyone, I felt as dry as straw or tobacco. My body swelled to the size of a mountain, and not even Pico da Vara was able to protect me. I was no longer myself. I felt my body and couldn't find it. Then

I buried my face in my damp pillow. I couldn't open my eyes. My lids were swollen shut and had dark, dark circles underneath them.

"At that moment, in an effort to see some light, I raised my head, which felt as heavy as a melon. Its weight pressed down on me. I was stuck to my mattress; I was stuck to my pillow. It was like being anesthetized: no body, no head, no legs. Dead.

"And it was then that you mattered to me, Mana. My skin was like fish scales, my eyes as dry as sand. Blood wasn't flowing through my veins, it seemed. I felt it slip through my legs, however, like a river overflowing, forming new streams. My heart seemed to stop. So all that fear of mine in front of a bottomless white void; something was swallowing me, Mana."

✺

Whether they wanted to accept it or not, the truth was that my sister Xana was living with menstrual symptoms a great deal more severe than normal. The doctor attributed it to her nature, with her frequent and at times acute bouts of anemia. There was nothing to do back then. However, there was always advice—a tonic, and sun and ocean baths, to stimulate her appetite. Xana was sometimes so beside herself that she would flee the house, not knowing whether it was out of her need to escape or from pure despair.

She would run and run, climbing up hills and gliding downstream on the currents of smooth waters, only to be ground like cornmeal by the stone at the nearby mill, in order to put an end to so much pain. Not even the water lilies, which opened generously, could ease her suffering. It was necessary to give her an endpoint, to bring it all to a close.

Xana knew that even if her pain were cut into bite-sized bits, it might not solve the state of her nature. She would be better off being washed out to sea, where every particle of her body would dissolve in the salt water.

But it was just an outburst, a rage, some venting.

✺

"Come here, Xana. Sit here with me," my grandmother ordered.

"Tell me your sorrows, my girl. Tell me what's wrong with you."

Her response took an eternity. A heavy silence fell over the two.

"Come here! I want to talk with you. The world doesn't end now. Better days will come, Xana. Believe me when I tell you this. Everything will work out. Listen, pay attention and you will see the world in another shape, another color. And if, for example," Vovó asked patiently, "you didn't have parents or other close relatives, what would become of you, my Xana? It's good to put yourself inside the skins of others, the better to appreciate your own life. Whenever you feel you don't understand a particular person's attitude, behavior, or condition, put yourself in their place. That way you might learn to respect them and yourself.

"Now you're getting older, my girl, and have additional knowledge that I don't. But I also know that when all is said and done, Xana, this is the right time, the time of truth, the time of our connection.

"So I want to pass along to you a bit of what life has taught me. Don't ever forget the good Lord whom our eyes witness at church, He who was our friend and smiled on us when we were sad. That companion of ours on long walks to the orchard, our omnipresent Father and Brother alighting here and there on the garden flowers and the yard of our house. The God who made Himself visible, palpable to us, down to earth. That was how I wanted to offer Him to you, my girl.

"Do you understand then why it is that I refuse to give flowers to the church when it has its own plot of land so nearby in a state of abandonment, with no one to cultivate it?

"Don't you forget, Xana, our God is everywhere. He's wherever you happen to live. Wherever He wants you to find yourself. His breath will always be there, His music printed on a flower's dewy stamen."

❁

"Oh, do you also remember, Vovó, when you lent me the conch shell that transported me far, far away? And how I sat there and listened with rapt attention and without speaking, lost in myself, reduced to a very large ear that appeared to grow and grow endlessly—that brought me distant voices, aromas, even flavors: mint for *sopas,* warm blackberries, salmon-colored peaches, the yellow strawberry guavas we call *araçás,* but not the purple ones that taste acidic to me."

"Listen, Xana. Listen to the silence, listen to the mill's cool waters, the yellow lights flickering like those on an altar with a thousand satiny warm candles. Listen to the dancing shadows—you who want to be a ballerina, throwing your whole body into a pirouette in the middle of the river's round stones, raising yourself to the treetops in woods dense with secrets and mysteries. And in the midst of all this, listen to the God I want to offer to you for your whole life."

And all of a sudden rain began pouring, and Xana worried about the itchiness of Vovó's wet legs, with her thick stockings worn under her thin ones.

That day, Vovó and Xana had left without taking the parasol that doubled as a walking stick for Vovó; they forgot it at home. It was warm and there was no sign of rain. Then one drop, another, and another. The rain was falling softly on the still-green leaves. The drops got bigger. The downpour fell *plip plop* inside her head, heavier and heavier. Vovó and Xana had just left the orchard, more drenched than a wet baby chick that has fallen into a wet manure pile. Xana did not want to see Vovó such a mess; she knew that would depress and humiliate her. So she cut a broad yam leaf to serve as an umbrella and to protect her stockings. She stuck close to Vovó. The rain was easing up. The smell that emanated from the earth inspired in her the desire to taste it.

"Oh, grandmother! The sky is split in two. And the yellow of the sun dances in the blue, landing in the pittosporum branches."

"How beautiful it is, Xana! They're like gold and silver threads," Vovó smiled. "Let's go, my girl; give me your hand. It's time we returned home."

❋

My grandmother and Xana seemed as one. They snuggled up to each other as if they made an integral part of the earth, of the dirt that soiled their feet, the dust in which they sowed seeds, the aroma of green tomato plants climbing the cornstalks out in the back field. On that warm late afternoon they were the same temperature. They felt the same exhalation from the wet earth.

Xana opened herself up, loosening her inhibitions more and more, and soon was filled with enough courage to ask her a question, fearfully.

"Vovó, why do they call you a foreigner, why do they call you an *amaricana?*"

"Oh, that's easy, Xana. People don't forgive it when someone is marked by differentness. They all like others to be cast in their own image and likeness. That's not my case, or at least I hope not, Xana. For example, as you know, your grandfather died in his old New Bedford mansion a few months ago. And I didn't weep, did I? And you didn't notice either anger or pain in me, nor hear even from me one word of disrespect for him, your grandfather. And did you ever see me in mourning? Of course you never saw me in black. Just more somber clothes for a brief period. And it was a great scandal in the village back when, during my return to the island to visit your great-grandparents, the cousin I loved best died and I didn't cover myself in mourning. I don't know how come they didn't kill me. But that was my first and last offense, Xana. People got used to it.

"What's needed, Xana, is for us to be true to ourselves. Don't strive to please this or that person just in order to be well regarded. To others you'll always be whatever they wish to judge you as. As for what you are, you'll need to keep watch over yourself as much as you can. Keep yourself whole. Protect yourself as you would your old playmates, the snails. Don't you remember?"

"Oh, I remember Vovó; I still like them to this day."

"Listen to me. And I'll tell you once more: never measure yourself against others. If you do, you'll be condemned to be their person and not your own, do you understand? Never forget that."

"Never, Vovó. But why are you telling me this now?"

"Oh, there's always a now, my girl. Don't complicate things when they are so simple, Xana," Vovó reassured, spreading her bright smile, white as cotton.

"And I'll tell you what else, my girl. As you know, I went to the city at least three, six, maybe eight times to collect interest on money I lent to the village's former doctor, who left São Bento to live in the city. I always traveled alone, which at that time was considered bad form, something very secret that would drag a woman through a tunnel of endless speculation.

"Back then, going out alone was a venture that reflected ill on a lady. But I brought other habits from America and did nothing to change them.

"Women of that time, my Xana, were barred from places that, even if nearby, required her to be accompanied. But I stepped up and took the risk, I admit. On one of those glorious mornings I fancied going to the seaside. I wanted to take off without knowing where I was headed. I ran madly down the hillside, and the entire village was beyond the range of my view.

"I took off my canvas shoes, Xana, then my thin stockings, and finally the thick ones. I got my feet wet. It was the first time. I liked the soothing gentleness. I sat there a while atop a large boulder. A stiff breeze disheveled my hair. All of a sudden, I was soaked from head to foot. No one else was around. I set off on my way. I was thinking of your grandfather, and of my two children whom I'd left in the care of my mother-in-law (your great-grandmother). But I was already ill. And my diabetes was chasing me, stubbornly not letting go.

"I needed to leave, I had to leave, to return to America, but a demonic force insisted on pulling me back.

"Soon defamation showered upon my head like meteorites, Xana. It fell on my body, my dignity, then on all that I had just lost in seconds."

✻

"The rumor rolled in faster than the tides. Your grandfather had just received a letter with a vile sentence that someone had said disrespectfully about me. He wrote to me.

"His 'goddess,' he called me, must not betray him like that, your grandfather said, full of bitterness. I didn't pay attention to that letter or keep it. Sure, he's the one who cheated on me. I'd never cast lustful eyes on any man—while his eyes, by his own admission, settled on a roster of lovers whom I'd once known well from the many times I visited the island. I didn't stop liking your grandfather, and I always respected him. Then came the divorce and, later, his promise never to remarry.

"Before his death many years later, he begged my forgiveness—just like the letter you read said, Xana. There was nothing to forgive. Your grandfather's gesture was noble, and I remain most grateful to him.

"Do you understand then, Xana, why I told you that you ought never to worry about the image others have of you? Each one of us sees in our own way, and according to our own interests.

"Don't follow others, my Xana. Go your own way, be it road or shortcut.

"That's all I want for you.

"Do you recall when we used to hold hands and dance to waltz rhythms in a slow spin, almost flying? You were such a fragile girl then that a quick breeze would make you tremble. Your slender little hands seemed to flutter, and I took them in the palm of my hand, the better to feel the birds imprinted on them.

"No, you don't know; you'll never know, Xana, how much of yourself you gave to me to ease my soul and restore some joy, like on warm summer evenings when the melody coming from the gramophone would mingle with the perfume of strawberries.

"It was back then that, under an infamous libel, they made me drink from the cup of gall. Much later it was you, Xana, who returned me to the source of honey, solely by virtue of having been born a midnight daughter.

"Your boundless love, Xana—you don't even realize it—kept coming and coming like a succession of raindrops, expressed in the flowers you'd bring me. They didn't come from our garden. It was the wild ones that most attracted you, perhaps for not having *mamãs* and *papás*. Or just by their being similar to your body's fragility.

"I always sensed in the distance, as though standing guard, the dove you would bring in that tiny heart of yours. I would fear seeing it leave, or being left, especially in your first four years of life. And the pursuit by the blackbird strafing our house every day.

"But you endured, Xana. You resisted, my fighter, since the day you were born, for my company."

❁

Lately, dark shadows crossed Vovó's face from time to time. The lie was still alive. It would fall like hail, like the lightning bolt that splits a chestnut tree in two from top to bottom. Vovó suppressed that sad thought, snuggled up to Xana, and whispered in her ear.

"From now on, Xana, you'll have to live another life.

"With your father and mother's return, everything will be different. I'm not saying whether it'll be better or worse, my girl, but it will definitely be something else, another world, another life that you'll have to learn. Prepare yourself to enjoy peace and happiness in this house.

"And no misunderstandings, Xana," Vovó warned, in her big-hearted voice.

"I'm not Mamã," my grandmother smiled, joking to lighten an atmosphere that due to nervousness in recent days had been lined with dark clouds. "I'm *Vovó, Voovóó*, that's it, Xana. And that's enough. Don't let me down."

Then I looked at her. From Vovó's starry eyes poured an immense sweetness.

I wanted, in silent prayer, to attach myself then and there to Vovó's lap, leaving dewy flowers and the impression of my face on it.

❊

On that strange afternoon, surrounded by a dense fog, our grandmother decided to get to the truth, stripping down words the way one peels a banana. She seemed to want to banish cloudy memories, bearing on the tip of her tongue the seed of other fruits.

"I'm leaving them for you for much later, my Xana, when you're an adult, when you cultivate your garden—perhaps married, perhaps single.

"Do you remember a story I told you when you were still very little, I don't know if it was real or imagined, whatever it was doesn't matter now, but it was about people's fates? I told it to you when you were growing up, at three, four, five years of age. I'll tell it to you again. Later on, when you're thirty or more, it will make sense to you.

"Once upon a time a baby boy had just been born. Fairies promptly gathered round, predicting the newborn's future. 'You will be given a father and a mother, and from them you will receive the abundant rains and warmth of melodious spring times. And Mother Nature will be with you. You will work her with your innate strength. As you graze your cattle, you'll find in their midst a pen to write with. You'll build your body and mind. Your brown eyes will gaze on green pastures beyond the time of sirens, and your tears will water the Earth's soil. And the peaceful Switzerland in your heart? It will grow in harmony like a tree and a house, with protective leafy branches under the cool of a dew shaded from the sun. And you'll return to work the fields. And grow a beard. And mountain snow will flood your heart. Coolness under a serene gaze will sow the peace of scattered thistles. And in the stream of your veins your pulse will quiver in the tremor of a late sunset. Indeed. And the Moon will be filled with a portion of your body and your spirit with an incandescent light. A short fluid curve will trace itself in the sky, and the depths of time will sprout a waiting conch shell.'"

"And then, Vovó?"

She flashed a brighter smile than had ever before been seen, stood up, and headed to the gramophone. The music rose, agitated and twangy, filling every room of the house.

"Xana, listen," my grandmother called once more, returning to her big wicker chair while the music continued to rotate in a spiral.

Vovó called to her again, but my sister did not react. She was absorbed in trying to find the meaning in that story, which seemed incomplete and grew more baffling to her.

"Stories are just that way, Xana," Vovó then clarified. "It's not so interesting how they end. What matters is what's in the middle—a long journey into the unknown."

"Oh, that's true, Vovó. I remember you saying so. But only now did I understand what you'd just said. I want to be like you, Vovó, to search and search, like in the game of hide-and-seek; sometimes crying, other times laughing.

"Oh, but you're always right, Vovó. How important is the end of the story? It's much better without one, so we can imagine, invent, think, and even feel tickles in our souls, Vovó, tickles to our heart strings, buzzing in the head, never ever stopping . . ."

Uncle Joe came to our house, surprising us. This time he journeyed by plane. Our happiness was so great that the celestial glass dome splintered into a thousand pieces. Vovó thought her son looked a bit thinner, but his posture indicated good health. She hugged him, straightened his pale gray suit layered over a white shirt, then removed her son's jacket, the better to see him. He had a pleasant face, with that aquiline nose and eyes the color of olive oil. Nothing about him had changed. My grandmother raised her hands to her son's face, brushing back a lock of wavy hair, and then laid her head on her son's chest like a helpless child. In a second, she withdrew from that sign of weakness, then absentmindedly saw herself drawn in again in a joy as expansive as that of a child picking apples.

The house was filling with family, friends, and neighbors greeting my uncle. Carolina and Xana had gone out to play, each with her own girlfriends. They were oblivious. When they later heard that the *amaricano* had arrived in São Bento, neither of them thought it was anyone but Uncle Joe. Xana left everything behind and broke into a sprint that landed her on the ground, skinning her hands and knees. She didn't even take time to complain. What she needed was to get home right away in order to drape herself around the neck of her Uncle Joe, who laughed and laughed in a golden happiness: son of a gun, oh, oh, son of a gun, oh, oh . . .

People were coming and going, and Carolina was going crazy from so much happiness.

"Uncle, dear Uncle," Xana called out in affectionate dulcet tones. "Did you bring the camera I asked for?"

"Look, Xana. Here comes Carolina. Let me give her a kiss, then I'll talk with you."

"I want to know, Uncle, when my parents are coming. I want to know when they'll come back for real."

"Oh, Xana, it's just a matter of months, girl, I'm sure. So you don't know that they're almost here? Your brother Daniel won't let them stay there. Either your parents stay there forever, or they return to the island. That was what your brother told me."

"Oh, please, please, Uncle, tell me the truth. Every year they say they're coming, and every year they never return.

"Please, please Uncle. Help me kill their lie."

Upset and suspicious, Xana turned her back, leaving my uncle in the shade of the wisteria above the garden wall. He crossed the yard, head lowered, brooding.

❂

It was August. A full moon.

My grandmother had been feeling more ill and frail for some time, and it was not due to the diabetes that had dogged her since her forties. It was her heart that was failing her. Perhaps for that reason she thought that by way of farewell it was time to open up to Joseph, as she liked to call him using his baptismal name.

Vovó knocked on the door to his room, entered, and sat down in a chair next to the bedside of her son, who was reading by dawn's light.

"Joseph, my son, I need to be candid with you. It's rare for us to look at one another eye to eye, but it's time to talk in depth."

"What is it, mãe?"

"That letter. Oh, that letter that turned into a cursed tornado!"

"But what letter is that, mãe?"

"Oh, I'll be direct, my son: Is Patrícia your daughter or your sister's?"

His answer came wrapped in a fireball. My uncle slid down under the sheets, hiding his head. A lightning bolt sizzled on the waves. The sky revealed its sunset. The ocean receded, and the peninsula ahead seemed like a cathedral. Uncle then found his mind disoriented, eyes tormented, bewildered; on his forehead, a wrinkle that mixed agitation and humility. A dark tunnel filled him with loneliness. Vovó shuddered. She thought of nothing else except stroking the head of her feverish son, her newly arrived son. She took a washcloth and moistened it in cold water to cool his forehead. It smelled of pittosporum and fennel, mixed with the fragrance of magnolias.

A dark cloud dissipated, slipping away. Vovó then caressed his sweaty hair, the way one smooths the fur of a newborn puppy. With cupped hands, she cradled Uncle Joe's face for an infinite, forgotten moment.

He could not have been more cooled than this.

Xana had just awakened. She ran as always to Uncle Joe's room. When she saw him in that state, she thought he was playing hide-and-seek as usual. Vovó then rose from her chair, heading to the window and turning herself around and around so Xana could not see her face. In the windowpanes a reflection of sunshine warmed the "snow" that had lodged in her eyes. A drop fell onto her nose; it was silvery, the color of her hair. She waited to raise her hand, dispirited.

Unexpectedly, she wiped the tip of her nose with impatience.

"Go outside," my grandmother ordered, helpless.

Xana did not budge a step. She sensed that Vovó was suffering, suffering like the time her nose was broken. And while Vovó buried herself in the curtains with her back turned, Xana lowered her eyes to the ground, where she saw a trickle of smooth water disappearing into a narrow crack in the wood floor—a line so thin it was scarcely visible, barely audible.

Uncle Joe moaned and groaned while my grandmother, plunged in silence, felt helpless. That loss came to her mind—that loss with no return, which at times led to a living death—that living hell, that rumor as dark as the sleek blackness of the hawk swooping down on her body, her soul, wordlessly tracing its own path, its own inner avenues.

❀

There could be no one on the face of this earth able to divine my grandmother's innermost secrets. She always retained her modesty by speaking to herself, lips slightly parted, dry wild eyes, and on her face that morning nothing was seen or heard. However, someone more attentive would have been able to see on the outside of her blouse how agitated Vovó's heart was by its throbbing.

Xana opened her mouth in amazement and was left speechless.

Uh-oh! Uncle was levitating, rising and rising in circles and more circles like a leaf lulled to sleep by the breeze in time to *The Rite of Spring*, babbling strange unknown words fired at goodness knows what. Then, settling down bit by bit, he repeated himself.

"Your grandmother, your grandmother, Xana . . . oh, Xana . . . your, your . . . grandmother was . . . was your m-m-m-mother . . . and the m-m-m-mother I didn't have . . ."

Uncle was still delirious.

Gradually he emerged from that torpor, that nightmare. And as soon as he felt better, he packed his bags and returned to America.

❀

The house that had up until then been rented to Vovó ever since she had returned to the island for good was placed on the market, and my parents decided to buy it. Vovó was glad not to have to move. On Mamã's express order the house was enlarged. So they had the work done, adding here and there until it reached almost mansion size. It was beautiful, but none of us knew how to stand or move around in that five-bedroom house with its living room, very generous kitchen filled with light from three windows facing Pico da Vara, and bathroom with yellow porcelain fixtures imported from London.

In spite of everything, wordless sighs were heard everywhere. It was Vovó going through the whole house over and over, not knowing what she was searching for—probably nothing. She was a hovering bird with no way to find a perch. She stopped alongside each large window with its curtains fluttering in the afternoon breeze, and looked at Pico da Vara, which was bearing down almost on top of her. She moved along and headed toward another room: what lay before her was that blue ocean lacking the white fringe it exhibited almost every day.

She approached another window, and after that another, and another. She saw some figures in the distance heading for our house. They came from afar, from the woods, each with a bundle of broom and logs to heat the oven. The woman was walking at the front, lean and scrawny, and she set the pace. She and a puppy. Her tubercular husband was scarcely able to stand on his legs, and anyone who did not know him would have sworn he was drunk. Beside the father, their children, from four to six years old, moved at the same pace, bunched up tight against him so he would not fall. Their little bodies were almost hidden by the bundles they carried on their backs. They stopped once in a while. It was the father who again had to rest, coughing with a hollow sound that would move even the coldest heart. Playing was not an option for those children. They were sons and daughters of poverty. When they passed by the window of our house, they were no longer four people, they were a bundle of firewood.

❋

Vovó let herself be, as though lost in midair, her eyes rheumy in a time without end.

Then she raised her hand to her hair as if wanting to forget her sorrows and walked away from the window. She drew the curtains closed and turned her head toward the corridor. Her gaze then met mine. I sensed in her a brief flicker and saw her face light up. A toothy smile opened, like someone wanting to speak at the same time. She stepped back with care.

Expressing whatever it was, principally regarding my parents' lives, was something Vovó would never do. From her mouth fell not even one word, only a dewy pearl to moisten her lips from time to time.

Her circumspection was absolute. You could see in her face that she did not feel at ease in her new house. There was something in the air that left the old ladies lost and Xana troubled. For them, everything seemed a sham, a fairytale.

But no. The new house was indeed charming, a joy for us. But for Xana and the old ladies it was a loss, a disorientation, a yearning to go back. The vegetable garden had also disappeared in order to make way for a beautiful flower garden in the shape of a half-moon, in compliance with all the requirements imposed by Mamã, for whom they were still not enough. She had further instructed in the same letter that they remove everything that was old, from furniture to pots and pans. And also going were the old calendars with their Van Gogh sunflowers, Cezanne peaches, and Norman Rockwell street urchins clad in solitude.

So great was my grandmother's pain that she sensed they were digging her grave. It was as if the world were near the end.

She was bringing everything with her to the island, my mother said in her latest letter: a refrigerator, mattresses with *esperim* ("bedsprings," in Portinglês), sewing machines, buttons, fabrics, clothes and more clothes.

The scent of American clothing, perhaps from the power of suggestion, was already invading and intoxicating us. She was going to bring us sunshine and *joie de vivre,* thus scaring away the cursed moldy smell from moisture running through the walls, covered with green slime like most island homes.

In order not to anger her daughter, Vovó hid some of her old-fashioned furniture from America at her niece's house, and the rest at the home of her longtime maid Luciana. Vovó thought that perhaps one day many years hence someone in the family would return to São Bento and be able to find their own history, maybe their own life, there.

Vovó knew full well how to distinguish between junk and antiques—for that reason her eyes were so bleary, devoid of their usual charm. And as the days passed, instead of emotion, joy, and anticipation over my parents' arrival, by contrast the fear, uncertainty, insecurity, and emptiness surrounding us on all sides were increasing, digging an immense icy hole.

Each one of us opted for her own mask, consciously or not, thus resisting the final stage of a new life beyond which neither eyes nor soul nor the roar of the sea nor Carolina's witches could predict or envision in the least whatever might come.

❋

After many years without Mamã and Papá's return, Vovó trembled and trembled, as did Xana likewise, locked between two worlds—one of curiosity and anxiety, the other of reality and fantasy. Oscillating between these two worlds caused Xana's face to break out.

We almost never saw her anymore. She secretly gnawed and gnawed at her fingernails, taking refuge in herself. Her lips were sealed like a tomb, and her eyes bulged more than an ox's. They served as a mirror for other people, and for her they were a way of absorbing the world, shutting it with a lock. Hence her usual seclusion; that necessity of launching into the beyond, where the music had the taste of strawberry; the flower, a way of dancing in the sweetness of the dawn with no wind; the moon, a perfume kissing people's bodies, taming waves that were fading into a sharped note.

Our Xana no longer lived in the clouds. She was a grown woman, like it or not.

To replace her dream world, she created another realm that might afford an even keel, but with endless possibilities, even if walking in a straight line.

She thus adopted Vovó's custom of gazing very, very far into the depths of time, where drums do not drown out sounds, echoes, or tunes—anything emanating from the oldest trails, marked by the footsteps of other eras.

❋

With the sun descending into afternoon, the wind suddenly stirred up and rustled some leaves, which hit the windows and left a fragrance of dampness. Then a rain shower struck without warning. It fell furiously, while water splashed from the eaves onto the roadside gutters.

The ground, turned into gullies by the very dry summer, was pounded by every drop. Hydrangeas, already past their prime, were yielding to agapanthus and golden ginger, which spread through the island's walls.

Next we heard a sudden clamor like agitated chickens. It was the women running, coming to help, some to bring in the laundry from the clotheslines, others the crops spread out to dry on mats, old carpets, and large sheets. And all the men and children were helping.

Xana persisted in her childhood habits. She would lean out the window and stay there, listening to time without the tick-tock of the wall clock while water splashed onto the gutter of the eaves, forming bubbles of iridescent colors that would soon burst and reform into a bubble, then burst again to the identical rhythm of women and men in their day-to-day routines.

The lazy rain was still running off the eaves. Xana's eyes turned upward, fixated on the bubbles in the gutters. They appeared to be made of crystal. As soon as the rain let up, part of the moment's magic dissolved. So she abandoned her windowsill to search for Vovó.

My grandmother was there on the first floor of the house, heading toward the terrace. She stopped and looked toward the damp meadows. From there one could take in everything: plowed land, seeds sprouting in the fields; in the streets, the din of the children, like bees swarming, or birds of prey on foggy days over choppy seas.

"Look, Vovó," Xana called out in delight, "the books have arrived already. Not all of them, but at least the French one. I want you to see it. I want you to hear the sounds, music, and smells of other letters. Look, Vovó, see how the colors are named: *bleu, blanc, et rouge*. It's a fresh, melodious language, Vovó, unlike American English and our own tongue."

"Oh, but you shouldn't think that way, Xana," my grandmother interrupted. "I've already told you, each one has its own music, so it's unnecessary to diminish some in order to enhance others. The same happens with people, Xana. The tendency is to raise some up and bring others down. Let go of this and listen to me again: the most important thing is for each of us not to allow ourselves to take the measure of others. I've already told you this a thousand times.

"And what I'm telling you, Xana, doesn't necessarily come from books; it comes from our ancestors, from those who'll be leaving their footprints so others might tread the same path with more pleasure, more speed, more depth. Don't forget, Xana."

"I won't, Vovó; I don't quite understand what you're saying, but I know I'll follow in your footsteps forever."

❁

Outside, the sun continued its dance beneath a rainbow. It insisted on insinuating itself between storm clouds—some brownish gray, others black, some milky, and still others snow white creating an effect of a bottomless abyss. Then the clouds broke and soon thereafter were reduced to nothing. The sun emerged bright again. The same ritual was repeated. Once more the *tremoços,* wheat, beans, corn, and fava beans came out. On every house's balcony, pumpkins emitted waves of heat, so intense was their yellow-orange color.

With the tolling of the church bell it was again time to bring in the grains, subject to humidity at day's end. The next morning we resumed the same project, and again we brought them outdoors into the sun, until they reached the "sweet spot," rattling like pebbles polished by the calm waters of the village streams.

That morning contradicted all of our expectations. The day was not all that bad. Occasionally a thin drizzle hung like wheat flour, which despite everything precluded field chores. So the women returned home and found other tasks to do—sewing, embroidery, weaving straw hats. And it was fun: they told stories and jokes, and laughed and laughed, in stellar outbursts of mirth that could shatter mirrors. They sang and sometimes danced in the middle room of the house.

The buzzing of sticky, stubborn flies on that warm drizzly afternoon annoyed the women and children.

In our house Vovó and Tia Luísa despaired, for they did not want to see flies fouling their new home. Then there were other worries, other cares to be taken into account. The house, being new, caused a deafening echo, so we had to speak very low. The shutterless windows did not guarantee our privacy. They did not fit in with our customs. They belonged to another world, to the America of our fantasy and pleasure.

"Total prudence is necessary," my aunt whispered. "Watch out for the doors, Carolina. Hey, you little devil, get out of here. Be careful of the air currents, so you don't break the glass."

The heavy atmosphere left Carolina exasperated all the way down to her cuticles.

"Hey, Tia Luísa? Is the purpose of this house to serve us and give us happiness, or is it to bury us?" my sister asked with her head pounding, and ready to disappear outside.

So many prohibitions were making her feel unwell and nauseated, with a need to raise the toilet lid.

Now she confronted the matter head-on. "Why a palace, why so much land, Tia Luísa, why girls in hats, girls decked out, having everything and having nothing?"

"Oh, you scamp, I'll tell your grandmother everything, you ingrate."

Carolina turned her back, and burst out the door, shaking her head in disapproval. On her face she bore a stamp of sardonic laughter, bewildered, almost demonic.

❦

With the days passing so quickly, we lived on sighs, each longer than the last, seeming to enter a tunnel with no light at its end. Discretion was the order of the day, both in our own home as well as at everyone else's, and much of what happened was done in hiding. Everything was a secret, a mystery, a murmur being extinguished like a match. Of all five senses, hearing was the one that remained sharpest. We were reduced to speaking in whispers so not a word would fall on the floor . . . those voices at the end of supper that, at the onset of an already cool autumn, were mingled with warm ashes from the American stove, a slight vibration in the air remaining from it. At the slightest wind gust in that direction or a hissing of green wood—announcing the cold north winds of the first months of autumn—the stove with its mother-of-pearl crest was overwhelmed by the hole in the lock of the kitchen garden door. While still warm, it could make an irritating noise. Afterward, it went in different directions from daytime. It was embarking on the night, leaving a trail of bodies heavy with sleep and dreams.

They would arrive the first week of October aboard the ship *Queen Ann Mary*.

And despite our fears and concerns, there were enough reasons for euphoria entrenched throughout the house to rip the veils from the firmament.

CHAPTER 6

Back, at last!

After so many promises, so many bags packed, so many assurances that they would return, my parents had at last arrived in São Bento. They were coming with no intent of ever returning to America, except to visit.

✳

It was on a morning in the first week of October that we drove to the city for our parents' arrival. The wind was gentle, the sun hidden, and warm drizzle sprinkled over a broad spider web.

Laughter and smiles burst in air like rockets in flight. We all wore our Sunday best, except for our aunt, who stayed home. She walked with great difficulty, shuffling her feet; her face, with its tired, vacant, sunken eyes, was growing more wizened. Outside, a strident uproar grew unbearable. Our taxi had just arrived, and local children ran up to the car. They trampled over one another trying to touch it, feel it, get closer—to possess it, if only for a second.

Since it was still rare in rural areas back then for an automobile to show up, it became a symbol of insatiable desires for young and old alike—they felt a fierce, unsustainable greed, and their eyes grew awestruck in the dazzling presence of that vehicle. They would just stand there until it disappeared, bound for other destinations.

Our ride that day was surely one from the city, coming from its docks filled with every boat, every dream, every illusion.

⚙

We were all going, except Tia Luísa.

A certain lightness, like a bird on the wing, was noticeable in the atmosphere; patchy blue sky contributed to the reflected joy of that morning. Xana flaunted her beautiful pearl-colored nylon dress edged with wine-colored velvet butterflies, a hat in the same shades, and a white cardigan. Carolina had donned a dress that attracted glances from everyone who saw her: salmon-colored taffeta skirt, and above the waist a long-sleeved black velvet bodice. I wore my new suit: vest, jacket, and straight skirt in pale blue. Vovó looked radiant, bearing sunshine on her lips, although a light shadow obscured her forehead a bit. She was wearing her favorite turquoise dress; over it, a lightweight midseason jacket in pale gray. Xana laughed and laughed, and was unable to stop. She almost choked, on the verge of nausea. And her tears flowed, she was so filled with fear, and shivering from the chill.

I continued to keep my eye on her, but from a distance so as not to intimidate, much less humiliate, her. I realized that Xana's nerves must have been just under the surface of her skin. She would walk from one side to the other, sometimes going to Vovó, then back; then she would come to me and, within minutes, wander off without telling anyone. Her fingernails were bitten down to the quick, some bleeding. Her face had broken out in angry red pimples.

Xana sidled up to my grandmother. "Look at my face, I'm getting uglier and uglier. I look like a bat. How shameful! They won't like me, and I don't know where to hide my face."

"Of course they'll like you. Don't act like a child; you're old enough to have some common sense."

"Oh, but I'm so very, very scared, Vovó!"

"No more drama, my girl," my grandmother retorted with an incisive air.

"You'll like your parents. You'll see how they hug you and smother your face with kisses, never noticing the pimples."

I continued to accompany Xana in her restlessness and began to understand the weight that must have fallen onto her shoulders. She was the only one of us who did not know Mamã and Papá personally. That must have been why the world was spinning topsy-turvy around her and she was bewildered, feeling that the ground was swallowing her up.

Perhaps Vovó did not sense it, perhaps Carolina noticed nothing, but to me that was a sign of Xana's lack of control, her helplessness, her wanting to run off and find a little corner where nobody could see her. Had she been able, my sister might well have climbed into a hole and pulled it in after her, bumping up against the chilly surface of death.

⚙

We managed to reach the city on time. The *Queen Ann Mary* had just docked. There were so many people waiting on the wharf that it resembled an ant colony scavenging for crumbs of family, friends, and neighbors. A celebration. We didn't know where to look. Then we heard a hollow clanking of iron against iron. "They're lowering the gangplanks," someone shouted. "The first one's for passengers, the other for unloading cargo."

A loud shout suddenly arose nearby, above all the dock noise; it was someone who from a distance had just spotted coming down the steps a relative who had left many, many years ago, gesturing and gesturing frantically.

There was utter confusion. Scattered everywhere were suitcases, boxes, bags, and tears of euphoria mixed with shipping containers that would only be arriving at their destinations a week later. In one of them would be our new furniture, sumptuous sheets in a variety of colors, satin curtains and damask bedspreads, and so many other things for our house. Our feelings of satisfaction left us breathless due to everything that was coming from the other side of the ocean, from the land of our uncles and cousins in America—that word so magical it filled our home and the lips of our island's people.

⚙

"There's Mamã!" we shouted over and over. I hooked Xana under her arms and hoisted her up so she could see the face of our Mamã, who was waving her white handkerchief in our direction from afar.

Xana entered a trance, lost within herself. She thought she was dying. Not of pain, but of astonishment and awe.

"Is what I'm seeing real, Mana? Oh, I didn't realize she was so beautiful!" We could see her plumed hat and, beneath it, a forehead as lovely as Elizabeth Taylor's; her white teeth dazzled from the distance.

"How tall Mamã is!" The feeling that inspired her at that moment was one of immense pride.

In spite of everything, I noted on my sister's face an unnamable suffocation squeezing her throat. Upon spotting our mother as she emerged from the crowd to descend the staircase, though still far from us, Xana moved away, imagining that Mamã would be very sweet—and even fantasized that Mamã, being taller and larger than Vovó, perhaps could do something about her body's unprotected holes; perhaps she could ask Mamã to remove the pain and slay her menstrual dragon forever.

We could see Mamã, still off in the distance, giving orders left and right. However, we did not know Papá's whereabouts. There was no way for us to see him. Mamã was taking the lead and it was obvious, even from such a distance, that she was the one who made the decisions, controlling herself and exerting command over those who impeded her exit from that tangled human ball of yarn. She looked a bit nervous, irritated, what with so many people elbowing one another, trampling and stepping on each other's shoes. Space was becoming tighter, and sweat soaked her face, dripping over her upper lip, which she wiped countless times with her handkerchief. We waited in expectation; Xana, however, felt she was sinking, searching within herself for an anchor to grab. She said nothing to Vovó, much less to us. But I saw her slipping inside herself, curling up tighter than a snail, in a blend of mixed emotions. Her confused mind transported her to the zero slot on a crazy roulette wheel.

Her mind still racing, my sister heard her heart pounding at a gallop, resonating on the roof of her bitter mouth and leaving an anxiety made of sticky greenish saliva.

She looked at Vovó, who was pale as whitewash.

It seemed the time would never come for us to embrace. I think at that moment there were none of us, even Vovó, not grinding our teeth. We didn't know whether to laugh or cry. And Xana clung tighter and tighter to Vovó—begging, for the love of God, for the two of them to be intertwined as closely as a pair of zipper coils.

My sister all of a sudden felt herself on the brink of a precipice.

"Vovó," she called out, disconcerted.

"What is it, Xana?"

"Oh, Vovó, you don't know, you can't imagine how much I need you and your warmth, to lean on you like on a walking stick, but don't say anything to anyone. All this is strange to me, it all comes down to a grueling solitude by the name of Babel, Vovó."

"What is it, Xana? Calm down, girl. Why are you so nervous? Remember the secret that Daniel left you. Use the tips of your fingers, like someone at a spinning wheel, and let yourself keep turning and turning them for a few minutes, until you find peace within yourself."

A few seconds later Xana realized she was losing her senses. The smell of her clothes from America, the touch of the old ladies' soft wrinkles, the freshness of the streams—she was losing herself, devoid of ideas or emotions, not seeing or hearing—all of it already so distant, so outside her grasp.

To steady herself, Xana tried to find a walking stick or something else to lean on, perhaps a bush, but the only thing around was the chill of the dark void.

When she came to her senses, she headed straight for our grandmother. She swallowed a tear and mustered up her courage. She reached out her hand and, trembling, surreptitiously clutched Vovó's soft hand just the way she did as a child. That way she again felt the rhythm of her heart, as rapid as a yellow baby chick's.

Xana closed her eyes and inhaled deeply, wanting to deposit there in Vovó's palm a tightly shut little box that would seal the two of them forever. At that instant she thought she was weeping for Vovó, but soon realized it was likelier for herself.

My sister was in effect being tossed into unknown worlds and languages, down a figurative well echoing in the darkness, while she felt as though she had no parents.

"I wonder what they are like outside of their photographs?" a perplexed Xana wondered. "I've never touched them, never felt them. I don't know what their skin smells like, whether it's coarse or smooth, their hands are soft or calloused, their hearts warm or cold."

Next my sister thought of her orphaned girlfriends. In those days, to have no father or mother was to be at the mercy of the compassion of close relatives, and often at that of other people who took advantage of the situation. Xana came right back to her senses, drove out that thought, and begged Jesus for forgiveness.

That was decidedly not her case, she mused. "I do have a father and a mother, yet at the same time I feel that I don't have any, and I think nobody understands me, perhaps not even Vovó."

In that moment my sister felt even more entangled than if in a cobweb, quasi-orphaned, lost in a forest filled with dense opaque mist, transformed into an unfocused photograph like one of Uncle Joe's when it came out blurry.

Now Xana found herself bogged down by thoughts that were coming from above even faster than clouds blown by a cyclone. In despair she wiped away the present moment like someone erasing a blackboard at school and flashed back to that episode when the ax had chopped down our beautiful *araçaleiro* and to another time that occurred somewhat later when a similar blow felled our yard's only white camellia bush.

❁

The unexpected loud tumbling of a huge crate snapped our attention back to the pier. My parents, in the midst of so many people, insisted on searching for more bags, more suitcases, more crates. And Xana was still looking without seeing, submerged aimlessly somewhere inside the wreckage of her body. An emptiness took control over what little she had left, without the adults noticing. She edged away a bit in order to find some space, amid the whirlwind of everything that was racing through her head, to think and to force a smile that might distract from her pimples.

In that frame of mind, my sister wondered, "Where will I stay, when I've lived with Vovó ever since I was five months old?"

Disagreeable thoughts were confusing her to the point of not knowing to whom she should turn. And again she wondered where the boundary would begin between Vovó and our parents. The answer came fast, as fast as a lightning bolt—with Vovó.

So Xana left us and ran to our grandmother, who sat resting in the cab. "Oh Vovó, I think I have a fever."

"I don't think so," my grandmother said, running her hand over Xana's forehead. It's only nerves, fears that give you no respite, my girl.

This will soon pass. Look out there to sea, let your eyes float and set sail."

"Oh Vovó, this is no joking matter. What I'd give, what I'd give to be tiny, made of nothing; I wish I could go back to our room dividers in order to hide the way I did as a child, or return to our old backyard and inhale the scent of every flower, sniffing the peach tree's lilac-pink blossoms and savoring guava strawberry blooms the color of sunflowers on our *araçá* tree. I want to disappear from here, Vovó."

"Hush. You're not acting like yourself. Look, I don't like any of this. I already warned you."

"Sorry, Vovó. I'm not myself, but what can I do?"

"Run along, Xana. Go be with your sisters, for the love of God."

It was already getting late.

A ball covered by a crimson veil, tacked up in the sky along the horizon, was sinking into water robed in blue satin.

Papá showed up, at last.

"He's here, he's here," Carolina and I shouted.

"Him?" Xana pointed, incredulous.

"That's my father? Oh no, he can't be. This must be a joke, a mistake. A mistake," Xana repeated, perplexed, talking to herself. "No, it's not possible, he's so small, and I'm filled with shame." My face flushed, my thoughts once again in disarray.

"An affront, like being splashed with a bucketful of cold water, disillusion. No, it can't be. They're toying with me. It's impossible. It's normal for the man to be taller than the woman. What will my girlfriends say?"

Xana felt her assessment spinning in circles, topsy-turvy, on the brink of something, under the glare of an intense light. She wanted to throw up, she wanted to turn herself inside out.

She turned around and once more went to be with my grandmother, who was still sitting in the taxi. For a while they held hands: Vovó's were warm, Xana's cold. From time to time she had a mind to tell Vovó of her disappointment at seeing how tiny her father was; on the other hand, she had the self-control to rein herself in. It was better to keep quiet so as not to worry Vovó. Xana leaned her head on Vovó's shoulder and within a few minutes fell asleep with gasping sobs. She dreamed the ship had left, taking her parents back, and Carolina with them.

She awoke with a start, not knowing where she was. Then she came to her senses and sighed with relief; she felt calmer now and went over to Carolina. Without knowing how or why, she indulged the desire to run her hand through her sister's fine wavy hair, luxuriating in a silken moment. Carolina then leaned her head against Xana's, in a tap-tap like when they were little, a gesture Xana appreciated with a wholehearted smile at that moment when she was feeling lost.

※

I do not know how, but something unexpected and illogical had happened to my sister, something that touched her so deeply that she could not find the words to express herself.

In seconds she undid the image she had formed of Papá, and turned him into a big satin bow. After all, he was handsome, serene, made all of seafoam like the ocean at São Bento. Easygoing, he radiated a beaming smile that did not emanate from his lips but from his dark, dark eyes. His face was almost beardless, his hair soft and thinning, resembling a baby chick's down. White teeth and tiny feet made him look like a ballet dancer or a mannequin. He moved like undulating piano keys.

She wanted right then and there to run to Papá, but she was afraid, so stopped short. She backpedaled, in search of a barrier, a wall, a daisy bush. Too late—her expansive gesture was almost leaving her bones. She felt a certain chill.

My sister had just realized that words, like Papá's face, were round. His gentle, affectionate gaze at times became despairing, like when Mamã stopped him from speaking, lest he mangle his grammar.

And Mamã continued barking orders like a drill sergeant, or a rider astride a rearing horse. She dug in her spurs, lacking only a whip. Xana, meanwhile, recalled once again that thudding sound of our noble peach tree, dead of old age, falling and rolling on the cold ground.

She withdrew and went to be with Carolina. "Aren't you afraid of them?"

"Of them? Who, Xana?"

"Oh, Mamã and Papá."

"My God! You're being so silly, a whole lot worse than I thought, Xana."

My sister cloaked herself in sadness. It seemed no one understood her.

She was, as always, an outsider. Alone.

Her head was spinning like a top.

At last free from all that crowd, they went to greet the travelers with hugs, weeping, and singing.

✦

Xana clung tighter and tighter to Vovó, for fear that Mamã might not be so sweet after all as she had thought at first sight. Mamã's kiss was very quick, somewhat brusque, and Xana felt a shudder. She sought Vovó's attention.

"Look, look, Vovó. Mamã looks like she's wearing a gold brace around her throat, the way Grandpa did on his crippled leg. And all this is tearing me up inside."

"I'm going to snap you in half. It seems as though I really don't know you, girl!"

"Oh Vovó, you know how I feel, for heaven's sake. Before, I was complete with you, but with Mamã everything's falling to pieces inside of me, don't you see?"

"No. Don't be a diva, Xana. I don't like anything, anything at all about the way you're reacting. Trust me. You'll see, everything will fall into place; it's just a matter of time. Be patient. Or have you already forgotten everything I taught you?"

"Oh, don't scold me. Don't speak to me like that. You can't imagine what's going on inside me."

"Well then, my girl, save it for another day, when we have time to speak the same language. OK, Xana?"

"But it's all so different, Vovó: I don't know why, that laugh of Mamã's always had the power to strike terror in me; it's not real 'terror'; perhaps it's better to say 'fear.'"

Even when I was a child, whenever Tia spoke of Mamã with total affection, that guffaw could be heard for miles around, and I didn't like it.

It reminded me of sandpaper, abrasive, something coarse that irritates or scratches, or something like that.

On the wharf, Xana meandered through her shadowy thoughts, not knowing what to feel about Mamã, having lost her way in a sea of confusion. She was starting to get the picture, and no longer liked that fur coat of Mamã's, nor even her hat; they were suitable for winter, but not for early autumn.

Mamã no longer seemed to be from this side of the ocean, she was so different from most of the people there on the pier. She brought the New England autumn cold with her, as if that were the chill of the whole earth. "Sure, because America is in fact the world, wouldn't you say?" Mamã was a metaphor for a woman outside her place and time, Xana thought in shame.

And while the hours continued to unspool on the dock, my sister experienced amid the disorderly crowd moments of great, great tension. Her eyes, lost and misty, followed our mother without missing a beat.

She wanted to know who that mother of hers was, in order to learn how to be her daughter.

I did not want to hurt her, and did not know how to breach my parents' closed circle without offending them, given that our different languages could lead to ambiguities, disagreements, and misunderstandings.

On second glance, now quite close to my sister, Mamã's gestures seemed to Xana angular like a sharp rock; her words were rough, her movements rapid and jerky.

My sister was disappointed; she had never imagined Mamã would be like this. And Mamã was in perpetual motion, arranging and rearranging things, giving orders to everyone, and acting more agitated. Xana had always expected much, much warmth from Mamã. But it was her chilliness that enveloped her at that moment. Then Xana tugged at Vovó's coat. Vovó turned her head toward her granddaughter.

"What is it?" Vovó asked anxiously.

"Oh, it's Mamã. To me she seems cold, and I feel myself swimming in a swamp of fear."

"Don't worry, that's natural. It's going to take some time to warm up to her, my girl."

"But look, Vovó."

"Oh, I don't see a thing, Xana, so let's stop this nonsense," my grandmother despaired. "Not another word until you get some sense into your head, do you hear?"

"I'm sorry, Vovó."

"Gracious! See here, what you need is a couple good swats across the face."

❀

Unlike Xana, Carolina and I wore on our faces the pride and pleasure of starting to call her Mamã every single day from then on.

Again, Xana was the outsider. So I kept a watchful eye on her, drew her close to me. I sensed that she did not feel a part of all our euphoria. Her hands sweated. She did not move, did not say anything; with haggard eyes, she seemed perched on the brink of an abyss.

Mamã continued to be exuberant.

She came up to us again, with quick kisses amid all the confusion. And Carolina and I were practically hanging from her arms, resembling milk cans dangling from a horse saddle.

Xana squeezed my hand tighter and tighter, as if recoiling. Then Mamã imposed order on the chaos at that instant. She stopped and kissed us all, but Carolina did not quit; she demanded Mamã's full attention on her. And Xana was pulling away, retreating as always, dropping my hand and standing outside our circle. Perhaps she sensed her identity was less as a daughter and more as a granddaughter.

All of a sudden, my mother looked around and did not see Xana.

"Now where did she go, where is she?"

I intervened immediately. "Don't worry, Mamã. She must be with Vovó in the taxi."

What else could I do or say to minimize her state of abandonment, I wondered. Our Xana always lived in the shadow of a Mamã in a photograph—and so she found herself lost, disoriented, plunged into a cold, dark solitude. The Mamã beyond the picture frame was who her real mother was, but it would take some time for Xana to feel comfortable with Mamã, her scent, her skin, her siren's voice and beautiful honey-colored eyes.

❀

Papá sauntered over toward us, greeting friends he had made on the voyage. He conveyed a serious yet informal air—his gray felt hat banded around the crown by a black silk ribbon and tilted ever so jauntily, a cigarette dangling from his fingertips, conveying a careless elegance that only happiness could lend. He had stepped out of the photo as soon as he arrived. Everything about him was authentic, from his luminous expression to his perpetual broad smile.

Mamã moved about among the throng in order to collect a missing suitcase she had just located. There were no others. Five bags in all.

At last she went over to Vovó.

Both women had difficulty disentangling themselves from so many people, and proceeded with uncertain steps. With a compassionate look on her face, Vovó reeled and almost toppled onto Mamã, her daughter, in an intense embrace of pain and joy, of nostalgia and reunion at long last.

"Oh, my dear daughter, it's been such a long time! There's so much that I don't know where to start," said Vovó. "Let me feel your body to see if it still exists, if it's real, my God! How much you must have suffered in America, my daughter, without me to help you!"

"Don't say that, Mother, for the love of God don't say that. Let's go, let's go, Mamã. I'm anxious to get to São Bento."

❊

After so much laughter, tears, and hugs, I noticed that my father was keeping his dark eyes on Xana, always watching her, perhaps as though wanting to protect her. But that bothered her, inhibited her, and filled her with nameless fears.

Poor Papá! Perhaps he was searching for that "girl interrupted" of his; he could have been trying to get her back, to breathe new life into her, weave her a new garland, and, after so many years, talk to her at last in a common tongue.

Xana turned to Vovó: "Papá's so sweet. He doesn't make any noise, Vovó, and his feet almost don't touch the ground."

"Oh, I see what you're trying to say, Xana, and I know as well what you're driving at, and it's very, very ugly. You'd better think again. I don't want to see you acting this way."

"It's not that, Vovó. What I mean is that Mamã repels and Papá attracts."

"I kind of understand you, Xana, but give them some time, my girl."

"Oh, perhaps Mamā is tired, right? I always dreamed she would be like a honeycomb or a pinch of cinnamon."

"And she will be like that, Xana; you'll see."

We departed for São Bento. Afternoon turned to evening, and the sky was sprinkled with stars—some hot, others cold. The journey was long, and our weary bodies, filled with so many mixed emotions, toppled over one by one.

❀

In those first days following my parents' arrival in the village our euphoria rivaled, even surpassed, the chirping of the bird population. The excitement in that buzzing of bees was extraordinary, with people coming and going almost without being able to distinguish between night and day. My parents' many years away from the village of São Bento demanded it.

Mamā was pleased with the house that she herself had dreamed of and designed. Everything was according to the schematics she had sent from the United States. Nothing failed to live up to her expectations, so our dear mother was happy. The windows, which were numerous, three to a room, admitted streams of sunshine like a braided maypole, so everything shone. On the house's large terrace, Mamā, who had always been poetic, admired the scenery that could be enjoyed from there: to the north, all that vast sea; to the west, a long peninsula whose snail-shaped contour gave the illusion of another island ahead; to the south, hills and more hills, some rounder, others more rugged; to the east, mighty Pico da Vara, which, from our terrace, loomed over us. It was always in our sights, and we looked at it from morning until dark, when there was moonlight.

❀

More than a week after their return, the big trunks arrived at last, around nightfall.

The next morning we awoke to the buzzing of a swarm of bees. The household was in pandemonium: old things into the trash, and new items taking their places in the house; the rearranging of rooms, new furniture—and lamps and chandeliers that would have to wait for electricity to reach São Bento. New items were being added every day. We could hear the nailing up of pictures on all available wall space. One room or another was being touched up and painted, because mold was unavoidable even in new construction, taking over walls and ceilings, annoying my mother, who had become unaccustomed to those yellow-green spots that turn Azorean houses old in no time flat.

Mamã contorted her face to convey displeasure. On her shoulders weighed a certain nostalgia for American homes, public utilities, shops, etc.—all with no trace of mold.

I noted in her a tremor, a shudder.

❀

This always happened whenever the taxi headed to our house, sometimes for a drive, other times to go shopping in the city: children would lurk around our house hoping for some American candy, far sweeter and prettier in its assorted colors and flavor than local confections. Even those who were older, walking by like pilgrims on a *romaria,* also came past with a tendency to crane their necks out of natural curiosity.

For days on end the people closest to our family dropped by as though on pilgrimages, offering their services and wishing us happiness in our new life, which was adopting an air of normalcy.

The month of October was waning and remained golden.

For a while everything seemed fine. Sunlight filled the house and it was a party: prosperity all around, joy, and a great need to show off everything they had acquired in America.

❀

But as life continued to unfold, conflicts began taking shape—some more serious, others less so—but without major disequilibrium. Then one day an alien element entered our house, and there would never again be any peace. Her name was Rosália, and she was the sister of my mother's best friend in America. Being poor, she spent her days at our house. She was old enough to be my mother's mother. And everything would have been fine, had she been sensible and grateful. But step by step she went about seizing the reins. Feigning solicitousness and sub-servience, she gradually invaded our house, our intimacy, making herself at home the way a *lapa* latches onto a rock.

In a trice she and Mamã became fast friends, while Rosália insinu
ated herself more and more into our lives. There was no room for either
Vovó or Tia Luísa.

Curiously, that creature was very astute. For example, she dared not
accost me, much less Carolina.

The victims in the midst of that confusion were the weakest of all
us females: Xana, still very young and at that point helpless; and Vovó
and Tia, due to being too old and without much strength. Their influ-
ence was depleted, especially my grandmother's, who kept her head
held high and her body erect no matter the cost. Vovó wore no apron
and rarely a headscarf, although it was obligatory at church back then.

On weekdays she wore a scarf only when it rained; the rest of the
time she flaunted her soft silver hair, caught in a bun clipped by an elegant barrette made of whale bone from the old days, back when Vovó
was still the "moon goddess" beaming in her splendid New Bedford
mansion. Wise and quick, my grandmother from that moment forward
summoned her few flickering powers and found the quiet courage to
defy the creature that Mamã had moved into our home.

Vovó's posture spoke volumes. Once again, it was worth the flight
of her silence.

As for Tia Luísa, we almost never saw her. Becoming more hunch-
backed, she would drag her slippered feet along in that slip-slip, slip-slip
shuffle of hers that irritated my mother no end. Tia Luísa, realizing the
trouble she was causing her niece, took refuge in the storeroom early
in the morning. She would sit in the chair beside the trunk and spend
the day there piecing together family memories—sometimes dozing off,
other times looking again at yellowed photographs from a time already
very, very long ago.

Tia Luísa was from good stock, always healthy, unlike Vovó.

❀

In no time, Rosália dominated and contaminated every facet in the life
of Mamã, who was becoming more annoyed by everyone and everything except that creature.

One fine day Xana was startled when she suddenly realized a coincidence. She ran to the photo album and in a fury searched for a specific
picture that in childhood used to distress her and scare her to death.

Once she had her hands on the album, she opened it with pounding heart and experienced the same sensation as when she was a little girl. That figure, seemingly human, more resembled an animal's snout—so dim and mysterious, gnawed away by mold, the only picture in such a state, differing from all the other photographs and, despite all this, without anyone even having dared remove it from the magnificent album.

Xana said nothing to anyone. She was afraid. She kept her secret and tried to think, but not even one idea came to her mind. It was empty.

An unaccustomed rage moved her to rip up the picture.

She sighed with relief.

She put the album back in the same spot and went into the parlor, where Mamã and Rosália would sew and tell jokes, giggling and giggling like timid little bunnies. Sometimes they went for long walks without telling anyone. At that moment they had just returned from going out and sat down to resume their usual tasks: Mamã embroidering, and Rosália cutting patches for quilts. They were seated on the floor on the Persian carpet. Then, like bolt out of the blue, Rosália's raw look met Xana's, leaving the girl petrified. It was then that my sister realized the woman's eyes were sour as vinegar, hotter than a furnace. Xana was livid, gape mouthed as if an earthquake had just struck.

Rosália made a gesture, an effort, a movement, with some difficulty, and stood up. Xana looked her up and down, and was aghast. Her mind was pervaded by fear, shock. She was terrifying, that woman. "I've never seen such a sight," Xana thought, fearing a woman who possessed the gift for tormenting one and all.

That creature resembled a Gothic arch: her head was shaped like a cucumber; her eyes were unsmiling and served only to accentuate her frown; her lopsided nose drooped over her upper lip; her sagging shoulders were veritable clothes hangers; her elongated arms almost scraped the ground; and her fingers were bent like the devil's. It seemed she never ended, that woman; she went on and on forever, reaching and reaching up toward the roof.

Fear led my sister Xana toward Mamã, with her feet scarcely touching the ground in order not to distract her. Xana waited a bit, then sweetly asked for a kiss. A kiss Xana then pulled away from.

"Yes, yes, it's a false kiss, like Judas's. And don't come at me with sweet talk."

"Tell me what you want, Xana."

"What do I want, Mamã? I don't want anything."

❀

Xana was speechless.

My sister just wanted to experience the touch of her lips at long last on an unwrinkled cheek; she wanted a taste of the honey that gave color to Mamã's skin, her eyes, and likewise her beautiful hair pulled back in a ponytail. Above all she wanted to feel the trembling of a smooth hand.

"That's all it was. Oh, mother."

Disappointed, she ran wilder than ever before.

She felt cold and naked, donning a long cloak of solitude.

❀

"How ugly, Mamã! What a disappointment to me! And it was here that you killed me, and it was also here that I killed you, although I called you day and night, night and day, always shouting your name over and over, while Papá sought in me the art of unconditional love, without anything in exchange, any price or expectation."

Papá came to my sister's aid and began stroking her, repeating with nostalgia that last farewell ritual of his, when she was only eleven months old. That moment then became more vivid for him. And he again blew a playful kiss to his daughter that would nourish her for her whole life. Xana then puffed herself up like a balloon, giving life to all the fragrances of crisp dawns.

My father's eyes twinkled like little stars from the sea on a sky-blue day. He was a silver light dancing on satin-clad waves.

Xana went over to be with Vovó.

A peaceful hush blanketed the plane tree branches that the breath of a light, cool, late-autumn breeze had set to dancing. Darkness fell over the rest of the day.

Vovó sat there motionless beside the American potbellied stove on its turned-out feet, all in pale yellow glaze trimmed in sage-green, with six cast-iron burner grates.

In spite of everything, my grandmother got along very well with the shadows, and from them radiated the arched vault of her smile, a bit vexed in those days. She left her place by the stove and went to fetch the lamp. She lit it.

The oil lamp spread a warm yellow light across the entire kitchen, illuminating the new wall-to-wall china cabinet with its twelve glass doors, filled with porcelain brought from America by our parents. Without saying why she did so at that exact moment, Xana leaned her head ever so lightly on Vovó's shoulder, like grass quivering below the springtime morning breeze.

It was a mere stroke of sky-blue wing that she felt. It was birds flying. Their feathers brushed face to face; Vovó was kissing her, with a smile so tender it seemed divine.

"Vovó, where are you?"

"I'm here in the bedroom; what do you want, Xana?"

"I want to listen to music, Vovó. I want to hear your Chopin mazurkas, just like when I was a child, always at your side. And now everything's so sad."

Vovó's reply rang hollow.

There was a long pause, a deathly silence. And to my sister's surprise Vovó stammered, blurting out unconnected and disjointed words, unable to satisfy Xana's request. She shot a compassionate look to her granddaughter, pleading for her understanding at a moment when ambiguities and confusion were multiplying at home. She feared the music might disturb her daughter, for whom even the most sublime of arts turned into "a 'noise' like thunder rattling her head and nerves," Vovó confessed with a heavy countenance.

She sighed, and sighed some more.

A fissure cracked open from top to bottom. Xana heard what she thought she would never hear. It was a muted echo repeating scalding words fraught with anguish and despair. And these words came from Vovó's mouth.

They came from Vovó's mouth, and she said, "No, it can't be—that one's not my daughter, my daughter was made of silk and satin." And, amid the murmur of the sea, we heard the incessant tolling of bells.

"She's died, my daughter; my daughter has died," Vovó whispered, looking wounded, her suffering heart bleeding and bleeding.

"No! That's surely no longer my adored daughter. I don't recognize her, she's a stranger to me. The blood transfusions she received at New Bedford Hospital turned her inside out. That's it, that's what must've happened: blood from someone cursed with a bilious disposition, a foul nature." My grandmother sought an explanation at all costs to absolve her daughter—long ago beautiful, beautiful to love, and later sour, bitter, alienated from everyone and everything.

"Could it have been America?" my grandmother brooded once again, adding, "Could she have been too ambitious? Was it because she'd forgotten the tempo of island life?"

"I've lost her, truly lost my daughter," Vovó kept repeating desolately, more desolately than any tolling bell, on that face of hers passed over by a dense fog and rain.

Life had clipped her wings. And at that moment Vovó called to mind the shudder she had felt when, on the eve of the wedding, her daughter had wanted to run away where nobody could see her. But it was too late.

With heavy steps her daughter trudged through life, bearing a cross of triple weight. Nobody had heard, nobody had noticed anything. Not even a sigh. There were no blooming flowers—rather, just wilted petals.

Half-dead from fatigue and disappointment that night, my grandmother dreamed about the old shortcuts that led to the mills; those same paths that led to the center of the next town—something of a small city, with its pharmacy and men sitting around reading the only newspaper that, although days old, circulated among those who wanted to read it. They would speak low, and even seemed to be preparing some sort of political maneuver. There were still poets, doctors, and judges who would flock there on summer vacation. And Vovó dreamed . . . dreamed that she was reading, reading, reading, savoring the perfume of words and hearing the music of writing.

❀

Contrary to our usual household custom, the volume on the record player kept being turned down lower; sometimes we were prohibited from playing it at all, depending on Rosália's scowls. That tall piece of furniture called a gramophone was our companion, above all Vovó's and Xana's. It sat smack in a corner of the bedroom where my grandmother and Xana slept. Its music would waft up in heavenly circles and mingle with the scents of wisteria, roses, and lilies, principally on feast days like those of the Divine Holy Spirit.

It was already quite old, and it scratched and popped agonizingly through the whirl of Chopin waltzes and mazurkas, nocturnes and polonaises.

In its place a huge radio entered the house, just purchased in the city, the most expensive model at the time, to compete with one belonging to a neighbor who came from noble lineage: "A *fidalga* to be sure, but without a penny in her pocket," Mamã gloated.

Rosália disdained that twangy music consisting of shouts, shrieks, scratching and gnashing of teeth. Yet her own voice was twangy, Xana charged indignantly. Rosália? That creature filled her nostrils with snuff from morning to night and had rotten black teeth, nothing like Vovó's, which were always clean. And we would cover our mouths so as not to catch a lethal whiff.

Moreover, Rosália was aggressive and would act like the lady of our house.

The old woman butted in again. "Oh, that old piece of junk. It's worthless. Who wants to listen to those needles scratching and scratching? The radio, yes. It has a cheery voice, clear as window glass. And then come those beautiful *cantigas* in improvised-song competitions; *fados* on request, the serial 'Marcelino, Bread and Wine'; it's a joy that brought together almost all the people of the village around the few radios that existed here."

"Now, is there any comparison?" Rosália prodded.

And Mamã conceded she was right, that the gramophone was more noise than music.

Xana leapt like a cat into the midst of the conversation, shouting until her vocal cords turned blue with rage, attacking the woman who had seized control of our home. Xana became a veritable hot stove, shooting flames out her mouth.

"Get out, get out of this house!" Xana spluttered, awash in tears and at that moment fearless. "Go away, you witch. This isn't your home."

Mamã, who had been engrossed in her embroidery, heard the racket and went to the door to find out what was going on. When she saw that nonsense, she flung a shoe, which hit the hallway door.

"Xana, Xana, come here now. What kind of joke is this? Just who do you think you're talking to?"

Xana fell silent. She was stunned.

Rosália said nothing; she was getting a foretaste of what could come to pass.

"Look, my girl, settle down," said Mamã. "Next time you dare to act as ill-mannered as you were just now, you'll get a good thrashing. You see, these are not beads from your rosary, and don't forget what I tell you; get this straight in your mind, if you don't want to get into big, big trouble, my shrewd little girl. I'm the one in charge here. Understand, Xana?"

"Yes, Mamã. But I don't like her."

"Oh, yeah? And why? Can you tell me why?"

"Yes, Mamã. You're trading Vovó and Titia for that woman."

"Of course I'm not, girl! What sort of thinking is that? What do you have in that head of yours? You're way out of line."

"No, Mamã. She's the one who gives the orders."

And so Xana took off at full speed on the shortcuts toward the cliff, looking at the sea that was gentle as a lake, smooth as a mirror that day.

My sister returned home filled with consternation. She did not feel like talking. She did not want to eat. And she was weighed down by her disappointment, her bitterness.

"Oh, is that you, Xana? I'm getting ready for bed. Where did you go?"

"I went up to the cliff to listen to the sounds of the sea, in order to clear my head, Vovó."

Without registering a thing, Xana dwelt upon Vovó's gaze and sensed birds in flight. She was not quite sure what she had seen or felt, and there was no sign to allay her doubts. Something crept into Vovó's eyes, which as an amulet always possessed the trait of changing color, according to cold or heat, morning or afternoon, shadow or light. When limpid, they turned from honey brown to gray, an indication of some reservation on her part.

Worried, Xana plotted and sought to make sense of it all from back to front and front to back, and she seemed to understand.

Xana realized then that perhaps Vovó might have been suffering from neglect.

✦

In a flash, my grandmother called to my sister, "Listen to me well, Xana. I beg of you, be gentle with your mother, whatever the cost. She is your mother, the mother you always asked for and who will forever be 'your' mother."

"Oh, and was I the one who wanted her so much, Vovó? Would that it were so! You don't realize it, but there's no way for her to break the ice between us. No way for her to warm my hands."

"Yes, I understand, my girl," Vovó said. "In cases like these, only time can take care of stoking the coal until it's red hot."

"But Mamã doesn't listen or pay attention to me," Xana insisted.

"Oh, don't be so stubborn. What the devil is this now? I want you to be strong, but I also want you to be obedient. And what I most desire is for you not to cry in front of anyone. In the state that everyone in this house is in, we have to exercise good sense, we have to be patient. It's best to pretend we have no tongues, do you understand?" my grandmother warned, with her sly twinkling look.

And so it was that at this exact moment Xana grasped that she had just experienced her clearest insight, as clear as spring water, as clear as its sources.

No longer was my sister a child, stripped as she was of her innocence.

✦

Rosália, who paid close attention to everything around her, did not like seeing such a level of intimacy between my grandmother and my sister, when she had already given Mamã to understand that they should not spend time together. She took advantage of what she had heard the day before and, secure in the role she was scheming to play in our home, she stepped in to give my mother advice. "The first decision that must be made," Rosália proposed, "is to separate granddaughter from grandmother right now. Xana's already a young woman, so she shouldn't keep sleeping in the same room as the old lady anymore. It's not healthy," Rosália repeated, with her sour pickle face.

"Now my friend, look at your daughter's face, stunted from being spoiled by her grandmother." She continued, "Besides their being separated in the bedroom, what you should do is work out a way so they're not often together. Put an end to all this, and throw Xana to the wolves, so she learns for herself how to be a woman, to face life's difficulties, and do something besides just read books, I don't know what good they do. But it's up to you. If you don't take my advice, my friend," she continued scolding my mother, "you won't have a daughter anymore. You'll have a pile of miseries, unsuited for marriage. And instead of one, you'll be saddled with two old maids. I won't say three because your Carolina, that one's on fire, woman. She doesn't even know what home is. A pistol, that daughter of yours, who just wants to flirt; a shameless hussy. I don't know which one of them is worse."

"And see here, my friend, there's no shortage of folks who whisper; I don't know if you've ever noticed these people. Everyone knows," she continued in a masculine voice, "that your mother wasn't the best choice to raise your daughters, especially the youngest, who's always done as she wished; and her grandmother, in spite of everything, always handed her the reins, always handed her the reins—and the result is that we see her crippled, a beanpole. Now that you're here, my friend, deal with your girl; you've arrived in time to get some eggs down her still: raw, boiled, fried, poached, any style whatsoever, you need to stuff them down her throat, which if nothing else, with a few slaps was the least her grandmother should've done, but didn't."

And Mamã's laugh rose up like a cyclone—a wooden clapper during Easter Week, helping satisfy that creature's whims.

Rosália, who kept a sharp eye like a hawk watching its prey, resumed her offensive. "Your mother always thought more about herself than about your daughters, my friend."

"Oh, don't say such things, Rosália," my mother replied, rather offended. "It's true they were very spoiled, but it's best we not speak of that, please."

"Poor thing!" the creature insisted, piqued. "Your mother used to stroll around acting all high and mighty like a *fidalga*, like some wealthy noblewoman, always dressed up, with her nose stuck up in the air. A city woman, traveling three, four, six times a year unaccompanied by anyone.

"And she wanted so badly to rise very high that she fell very low. I don't know why she was so haughty. After all, we all wind up below the same ground," Rosália gloated. And soon that uncontrolled nervous laughter arose again, noisy and rolling like thunder—and Mamã choked on being beside herself, as if she owed that woman a great debt or there were a price on her head like at a guillotine in olden times. The more nervous she got, the louder the peal of her usual laugh. And this time her laughter was so strident that Mamã cupped her hand like a conch shell to her mouth in order to stifle the hysterics. At times she almost managed to stop, but whenever she lost her bearings laughter overtook her, pointing her directly toward Rosália, as if to tell her that the reason was all her friend's fault.

❋

Xana felt as though she were dying that afternoon. Without meaning to, she had heard everything that came out of Rosália's mouth. The door was ajar. With her heart in her mouth, racing a mile a minute, she absorbed the whole stream of inanity. How could that creature speak of my dear grandmother in that insulting way she wondered to herself. Her pain was as intense as that inflicted by the sickle on those loveliest of flowers called golden ginger, which spread throughout the woods, along all the edges of the paths and on the island roadsides.

That night Xana buried her head in her pillow and wept bitter tears. Then she imagined hacking Rosália to pieces with a hoe.

To her surprise, she disliked the idea. What a dreadful thing! Such cold darkness! It was better to hang her on a cross beam, upside down like hogs after they are killed. It was the only way that creature could muster a smile on her face. With her legs in the air, her expression would go from concave to convex, making her scowl less pronounced.

❋

Anyone paying attention to what was going on in our house would have observed that day by day my mother was turning into the subordinate, while Rosália arranged and rearranged our lives. My father, however, failed to notice a thing. He was out of the house more than in it, working in the fields, giving orders, or playing cards at the tavern for entertainment.

Carolina, as always more inclined to go out than be a homebody, sought out female friends ranging from her own age to the oldest ladies, with whom she related better—if for no other reason than that they had told her many of the stories about witches that she had loved best in childhood. As far as anyone was able to determine, Carolina could not abide facing that creature either and therefore sought by all means to chase away anyone who tried to get close to Mamã, who was so absorbed in the art of embroidery that she essentially shut out the world around her.

Fearfully, Carolina tiptoed into the room with a lightness only ghosts possess. She sat down with care and snuggled up along Mamã's right side to watch her and let her continue with the embroidery she held in her hands. She said nothing; the warmth emanating from Mamã was enough. For that reason she was afraid of Rosália appearing unexpectedly to spoil her few moments with Mamã. Despite Carolina's craziness, she had always been attached to our parents that way, insecure, and she thought that no one liked her, which was untrue. What she wanted most was to be equal, equal to Mamã—so she always said—from the time she was a child until she was an adult. She became the most mischievous of us sisters, but also the most complicated, caught up in her Electra complex, the one who was separated from both our parents at barely seven years of age when they left for America, and who stayed behind in the care of one or another family member, whether on Mamã's or Papá's side. It was a difficult situation for each side to handle in its own way—Vovó was wasting away, not knowing how to cope with life, although embracing it as much as possible. Never had she left the girl in the hands of others, although susceptible to a heart that sometimes betrayed her.

Carolina had always been jealous, and wanted Mamã all to herself, but Rosália left her no opening. Whenever Rosália came up with shady deals, she would go into Mamã's room and lock the door. What they said or did, no one knew.

So great then was Carolina's curiosity that she peered through every hole in order to see and hear.

Xana continued to hide and would only come out when called.

In this case, she was the one who wanted to bare her soul. She reached for my hand and warmed it for me. She confided, "Oh Mana, I really feel like laughing, if only to keep from crying. What that creature doesn't know is that despite her cleverness and diabolical airs, to me Vovó will forever and ever continue to be my coat, my blanket, and above all the Moon that has illuminated my entire childhood. And there's no person who can extinguish her. Only death."

"Oh Xana," I replied, "I heard everything. It's just like that, my child. Vovó is the force that you must always keep inside you. Don't forget her." Vovó went out into the street, nodding her head in a sign of satisfaction.

❀

Lately, Rosália was no longer even going home. She stayed with us day and night, a hindrance to us, "a pebble in one's shoe." How much we would have liked to be close to Mamã. But she would chase us off: "Xana should play outside with girls her own age," the creature objected. And Carolina, for her part, was going downhill, not knowing what to do if not for Mamã's badgering. Our dear mother was running and running away from her, her illusions piling up and weighing on her. And Carolina was rehearsing faint after faint in order to scare Mamã—who, not knowing if they were fake or real, would then wipe her down with alcohol. Her swoons served especially well to garner a modicum of affection.

CHAPTER 7

We were going our separate ways, grain by grain. Each one of us to her own island.

Xana had to leave for the city in order to continue her studies. She was sad over being separated from Vovó, yet at the same time she was happy to be going, since she would be learning more. After all, the separations were brief, because my sister would come back to São Bento almost every weekend. She took along Vovó's old blanket in shades of the rainbow, light, light as a cloud or as foam—and a new one, as new as if it had been saved just for her.

❃

Whenever Xana returned from the city and did not see Vovó, she knew where her grandmother would be: at the home of her close friend Dona Amélia, from one of our village's most esteemed families. It was in that house that my sister spent hours and hours on end playing alone in a corner, from the time she was a tiny girl up until five or six years of age, in the company of Vovó, Dona Amélia, and her daughters.

That house was disturbing, but sad and solemn without its head of household, who had died young. The three daughters of the house, three hothouse flowers, were true sprites—always gentle, always affectionate. They toiled from dinnertime until nightfall. The rest of their time was devoted to their respective trousseaus, without which no man would ever approach any of them. Those young women were so fragile, made of a translucent porcelain. That was why they scared off men, who in those days desired robust women with broad hips atop strong legs, ruddy faced and ever-ready to help their husbands with field chores.

However, unlike field girls, Dona Amélia's daughters had deathly pallid faces. They avoided sun exposure by always using a parasol when they went out. They did not work the soil, and enjoyed a distinguished upbringing. They made no noise, to such an extreme that it was believed they were ethereal, surrounded by the buzzing of persistent flies. From morning to night, always the same routine. They were Penelopes in a long dream-filled wait, never reaching the end of the ball of thread, but their hope would not die there. They waited and waited, certain of one day meeting a minimally polished young man for a potential solemnization of a much-dreamed-of marriage. And as time evaporated they saw their dream fleeting more and more, further and further away. However, they did not despair. They were accustomed to the slow pace of their household, the rhythm of the tick-tock and the click-click of needlework and knitting—needle up, needle down, on a piece of fabric stretched over a hoop, which enabled more precise execution of the embroidery in their hands.

❋

No one knew why.

That week, when Xana arrived from the city to spend another weekend at home in São Bento, I saw that my sister bore a portrait of sadness imprinted on her face. She lingered by the door. She did not relish entering the house, all of which was becoming more disturbed than disturbing. It was a house divided, devoid of any soul, Xana reflected. The sweetness of its affections was being replaced more and more by vinegar. The house was no longer hearth nor home, nor a nest. It was a pile of debris superimposed upon Vovó's old house, with only sighs on the one hand, hatred and revenge on the other—in Mamã's way, frustrated as always in her desires ever since that answer of her father's, heavy as a stone, dashed her dreams of becoming a teacher. "Money doesn't grow on trees," he had told her in English. Period. Without remorse.

And my poor mother, she who had been rocked in a golden cradle; she, the daughter of the great businessman and politician; she, who always had everything as a child in America. And then, an entire life down the drain . . .

❁

However, it did not take long for my mother to start entering into an
even fiercer competition with a neighbor lady. Xana became embarrassed by, and even developed a certain fear of, Mamã. Xana had not
been accustomed to violent conflicts. She was close friends with the
neighbor's son. The same age, they were like siblings. He had always
been a good friend to Xana. As children they would always, always play
together, because unlike most of the other children they had all day long
to play, sometimes at Vovó's old house, other times at his mother's,
where a swing hung from the corral's crossbeam, and there was a beautiful red toy car almost as big as a real one that provided the greatest fun
for the two of them. It defied comprehension, that hatred my mother
harbored against this neighbor and her son. My grandmother, without
saying a word, hid her indignation so as not to hurt her own daughter—
who, unfortunately, continued to irk the dispositions of those she chose
as her enemies.

"They're all envious!" Mamã boasted with pride.

At Rosália's instigation, my mother had to do everything to defeat
that big *fidalga,* once and for all.

Mamã hurried to the city in order to trade in our radio for a better
model. "There's nothing else like it in the village," she bragged. Later on,
Mamã decided to buy a garden hose many feet long that served not only
to water the vegetable garden and yard but also to wash the windows,
which sparkled thanks to the powerful water jet spraying the glass.

My mother exulted once again when she spotted her neighbor,
under cover of darkness, washing windows with a watering can: with
it firmly in her left hand, she gripped the neck by its nozzle with her
right, shooting a water spray insufficient to make the glass windowpanes sparkle. Its pressure was only strong enough to cleanse a person's
colon. Mamã then whispered word of this throughout the village, and
the woman was mortified.

But when, to everyone's surprise, the village's first car appeared days
later in front of our neighbor's house, my mother just about keeled
over. It was an old jalopy, but all the same a real automobile. This simply could not be! Disheartened, my mother began huddling with her
girlfriend. They debated back and forth and arrived at a conclusion.

"An old car like that is worse than disgraceful, my friend," Rosália sniffed. "Look, not even folks barely scraping by would want to sit in that old rust bucket. They know they have to get out to push it, and, to top it all off, they get a black cloud of smoke in their faces.

"Just what we needed," men and women murmured.

To Mamã, who saw her money running like water through her fingers without mentioning a thing to Papá, it was better to hire a good cab from the next village than to ride in that junk heap.

When our family needed to go to the city for shopping, or wanted to take a ride in order to familiarize themselves better with the island, all they had to do was call the taxi, which was in fact well maintained.

❄

During festival season our competition turned into a *tourada*, only fiercer than a bloodless bullfight. The more fireworks shooting into the air, the more prosperous the home. Papá began scratching his head in a sign of disapproval. He needed money for more useful, more important endeavors: clearing the Fogo forest, which was of great value, for example; and having at least two household servants and cash on hand to support our family in comfort. He was prudent and disliked taking risks. Thus, whatever they acquired on the island would always be paid for with cash on hand, he warned, shaking his finger at my mother.

"Look, woman, exercise restraint. Things aren't going well for me. The island seems to have gone topsy-turvy, and we no longer even know how to manage our lives. It's like being in a foreign land."

The disenchantment on my mother's face was obvious. In America she did not know what fear was; she went out alone at will, and when she spotted a good buy she didn't even consult Papá. She only informed him once the entire transaction was completed.

On the island she was bound hand and foot, unable to do anything. For her it was the end of the world, an irreparable mistake.

Amid all the confusion, in weather as turbulent as twenty-foot waves, Papá began feeling that the aforementioned Rosália had entered his home only to put an end to his way of life. He sensed something in the air, something one could feel without being able to see or smell it, something similar to what had happened at the house in the village of Burguete following Xana's birth, when witches made noise all night long until they drove our parents crazy.

At that moment Papá wanted to chase away the ill-fated memory and, looking around, saw fit to get out of there, far away from that creature. From the bitter scowl of this woman, who did not even give him so much as a "Good day."

Papá thought he had seen the devil incarnate. He turned around and went out to get together with his hunting buddies.

He needed to unwind.

❀

The next day, early in the still dark predawn hours, my father, Xana and their friends got underway—all but Carolina, who chose to stay with Mamã, knowing that Rosália would not be at our house that day because she was off traveling to a village far from ours and would only return days later, her business completed.

So they began their ascent to the public brushland, under a drizzle as fine as flour. And as soon as dawn began breaking amid patches of blue and white, they entered the woods looking for tracks, burrows, and other signs of rabbits nearby. Despite the three shotguns he owned—two of Uncle Joe's plus his own—my father never made use of any of them. To him hunting was a sport, a clearing of the cobwebs, a cleansing of body and soul; hunting was turning his back on everything that troubled him. For that reason the firearms stayed home. He and his pals only needed the dogs, the ferret—and the vastness of nature, all of it fresh, towering, almost touching the sky. Throughout the hunt, which had been productive that day, there had been time to relax and joke, to eat and drink well, and then to rededicate themselves, alert, eyes wide open, deathly quiet. Suddenly the dogs' ears pricked up like canine candles lighting, indicating something very nearby. In a second the dogs all ran to the same burrow and stopped. The men did not move, and neither did Xana. Everyone stood in suspended animation, humans and animals. Suddenly the silence was broken. And the frenzy was of such magnitude that it startled rabbits and birds alike. It was our last catch of that waning day.

"Oh, here comes Coimbra with one more rabbit," my father called, beaming.

"Unh-uh, nobody beats this dog, do you hear me, *compadre?*"

"Yes, but mine too, nobody beats him in a race, do they?"

"But Januário spoils his dog more. Watch out for that critter."

※

The others were still waiting for one more bunny, but they too joined the conversation, each with his own brace of rabbits. Each one, the biggest and best.

They prepared to leave. The return trip was long. Their steps were heavier but effervescent joy persisted, while Xana enthusiastically gathered a variety of dried leaves from plants and shrubs to add to the many she already had in her herbarium for study in classes.

Afternoon faded as night descended.

Their pace picked up with each step. Papá wore his rabbits suspended from an American belt suited to the purpose. The other men hung theirs on a stick, which they carried over their shoulders.

Flocks of birds filled the damp tree branches.

When they reached the village, Papá and Xana bore a luminosity on their faces that puzzled many without their saying so, because they did not know what name to give it, but certainly they smelled of pittosporum and cryptomeria, broom and eucalyptus.

Next they skinned the rabbits, gutted them, removed parts that were of no use, and then set the meat to marinating with wine and garlic in a large clay crock, in preparation for cooking *vinha d'alhos* the following day.

※

Sometime later we were wakened by a heated argument we inadvertently overheard between Papá and Mamã. His soothing voice was barely audible, while by contrast it was Mamã moving in for the kill, and her voice carried a long way. They realized they did not have as much money as they thought. What they had amassed over several years was almost all sunk into this "palace" better suited for housing fairies than real people. The insanity of competing with neighbors and other folks had made my mother spend far beyond their means, neglecting to total the expenses racked up in so little time.

"The old days have evaporated. I've already told you and now I repeat it, woman, get that into your head."

Then a sudden, inopportune hush fell, leaving us hanging in a vacuum. We were terrified. Xana trembled. Carolina set about looking for ways to find out what they were saying. The minutes seemed an eternity to us. Very quietly Carolina crept around the outside of the house and crouched down along the back window where Papá and Mamã were, so no one could see her, enabling her to detect something, albeit garbled. Carolina then turned her ear in order to get a better angle, amid a whirlwind of verbiage. From one moment to the next, a single word leapt up that stood out above all the rest, strident and repeated, coming from Mamã as well as Papá. It was "Brazil." And there was no other word, it was "Brazil" this, "Brazil" that, but we could not determine what was being discussed. The world was spinning like a top at our feet.

Carolina emerged from her hiding place on tiptoe. She made no noise and did not want to hear anything further. Everything had led her to believe the worst was yet to come. And it didn't take long.

Soon, even Xana came to understand the meaning of the word "Brazil." It was no longer necessary to keep it a secret. Quite to the contrary, "Brazil" became the word most often spoken at home in the coming months.

"We're going to leave, my girls. And not for America. For Brazil," my parents said in unison.

"We're going, my daughters, we're going to depart for Brazil, a nation where the currency is far weaker than Portugal's *escudo* and much lower than the U.S. dollar. We'll sell our land for good money and take the few dollars we still have left in America. We're leaving, leaving for a new life."

Xana stood there slack-jawed. To her it was a judgment day.

"Vovó, Vovó? What tragedy is this? I for one will not go with them."

"Shhhh, Xana," Vovó whispered. "Calm down, my child. Everything's going to be fine, it's just a matter of time. You'll see."

"No, Vovó. I won't wait for that time. I'll go, but it will be right now, and in order to hide myself."

❀

Poor Xana fled at a run. She stumbled, fell and hurt herself, screamed and yelled—possessed by a noise most resembling the roar of beasts, surpassing by far the crazed howls of our neighbor Maria da Estrela. She bawled and bawled both night and day, and her eyes, already naturally prominent, assumed dimensions large enough to frighten even the bats. Almost blind from so much crying, Xana came to realize at that very moment that pain possessed color, yes indeed. It was the color of Christ's blood, the color of the executioners' bile that they gave Him to drink.

Out of her mouth emerged tongues of fire. My sister's hair loosened and covered her face. She was a porcupine.

Xana knelt down in a deep sleep, her head lying on the big wicker chair, but without Vovó's warm lap.

The next day at lunchtime my mother rose from the table and went to speak with my father. She was all flustered, prodding and provoking him until he reached the point where he could no longer contain himself.

"That daughter of yours," my mother said in desperation, "needs her face slapped, and you're the one who's got to do it, otherwise she'll never shut up," my mother decreed, staring at Xana.

"It seems this little *fidalga* runs our lives. Haven't you realized that yet, man?"

Without thinking, my father cocked his arm back, then brought his hand up very close to my sister, but in the end he lacked the courage to follow through. His hand remained momentarily in suspended animation, experiencing a tremor. Ever so slowly he dropped his limp arm. He was terrified, livid. And she, his daughter, stood there with fear in her eyes, unblinking but dazed.

Papá wept.

His whole body trembled with remorse. He shifted the blame onto my mother: if she were not so ambitious, their life would be on a more even keel, and the family happier. It had been an entire lifetime of going backward, of falling little by little, without anyone realizing it.

"It's your fault," my father charged, shocked by all of this, turning again to my mother to explain to her that Xana was not resisting them. Xana continued gasping for air, so as not to drown or sink.

"Yes, that's right, woman. Calm down and see if you can exercise some self-control. Our daughter is never going to leave her grandmother. Get that into your head. But if you want, take your mother along with us and that way we can all be happy."

"But we can't, man! You've always got your head in the clouds."

"No, you're the one whose head is stuck in the clouds, woman. Of course it would be a burden further complicating our lives, but then again it lets our daughter fulfill her desire, which is to be with her grandmother. And how sad this all is. How sad this is, woman!"

"What can we do?" Mamã asked Papá.

"Nothing, there's nothing we can do. We can't expect anything from our daughter. We have to realize that we were the ones who wound this tangled ball of yarn made from those broken strands called life, so we're the ones who must untangle it."

"That's not true," my mother interrupted.

"Yes, it is," my father replied. "You can't do this, woman. I myself will not let you separate our daughter from your mother. That, never. This is not some card game like *Sueca* or *Bisca*. It's our life and, like it or not, we've lost our Xana. And I was the one who wanted so much for our family to be together; you didn't want it. Now it's too late."

Mamã turned her back to him.

Tears were pouring down her face.

With nothing more left to lose, it was then that my mother decided to use elderly Rosália as a lifeline. She would pay her a good commission if she could sell, outside our village, the fabrics she had brought from America, the hundreds of buttons, the fine and heavier threads in various shades, the remnants for blankets and small bits of fabric for patchwork quilts that delighted one and all. And for those needing to buy sewing machines, ten in all, they would have to come to our house in the dead of night in order to load them onto donkeys or horses, all very hush-hush, for Mamã did not want anyone in the village to know we were in dire financial straits.

However, the more Rosália sold, the more compensation she demanded in return, not so much in money as in imposing her say on everyone. She took over our house, and we and the old ladies were left living at the mercy of that woman.

We had to keep up appearances, my mother insisted during an argument in which Papá wound up losing his temper. He threw almost everything. One of the lushest ferns decorating our hall got hurled at my mother, missing its target. Xana and Carolina cried in terror. It seemed their world was closing in around them. Lightning flashed from Mamã's eyes.

Vovó and Tia Luísa had already gone to bed, but that night Xana just wanted to lie awake and dream. She begged God to make her parents go away forever, to the ends of the Earth—to hell if need be, she fantasized in desperation. At that instant what she wanted was to hear the chanting of *Lembrar das Almas,* which she no longer feared. They were tender hymns, gentle, soft, sweet, pure and smooth as moonlight. She was indeed afraid of the tumult roiling in our household. Never before had she lived through moments like that night's. She was a bundle of nerves. Her poor face was a mass of angry red blemishes, and the skin all over her body was covered in gooseflesh. Her world seemed to have been turned upside down, with Xana flung out of it. She did not want to return home. It would be better to stay a few days longer in the city, after so many misunderstandings.

The whole family was enmeshed in a tangled ball of yarn so snarled that no one was left untouched. Equally complicated were the feelings that were playing themselves out there and that were tossing us all off a precipice called perdition.

❊

Some weeks later, after things were calmer, my parents shut the door so they could talk and talk. Rosália stayed in the living room as usual, cutting patches, sewing, and mending. That woman was strong. "Carry on" had been her watchword, performing whatever jobs came her way in order to support her children of unknown paternity. It was so amazing, because instead of thanking our mother for her hospitality, Rosália continued to be demanding and to exploit her. All that power to impose herself with no shame derived, after all, from her knowledge that her sister in America had taken in our mother for a time after her father (our Grandpa) had thrown her out of the house at his mistress's behest. For that reason, perhaps Rosália felt she had every right to collect reimbursement for her sister's generosity to our mother.

In the previous weeks, my parents had seemed to grow closer and closer to one another. They began working things out. Perhaps the next harvest would enable them to raise some cash that might leave them a bit more flush, Papá thought. Summer was still a long way off, so with luck and sound judgment whatever little money that remained could, if well managed, perhaps cover the most important necessities.

And Papá pleaded to Mamã, "No more taxis coming to the door for any and every reason. Only in an emergency."

While returning from Dona Amélia's house, Vovó called to Xana to ask if she wanted to go with her to the old orchard, in order to distract themselves and view the flower buds. The sky had a purplish cast, and birds were raising their songs to the still-bare treetops. They entered the orchard. They sensed a profound desolation.

For some reason Xana enjoyed seeing the leafless branches that blended into the milky color of the sky on days when the fog was bright. And while Vovó caught her breath in the hut that Daniel had long ago built of wheat straw, Xana lay on the ground face up, as she had in childhood, so she could see things from a different angle. Some of the last dry leaves, survivors of autumn and winter, fell, covering Xana. She wanted to stay there forever. But Vovó, with a ceremonious gesture, indicated to my sister that it was time to return home.

❀

In the distance a dog barked, and its echo rippled the waters of the stream below. A breeze disrupted the serenity of the rest of the day. Xana arose and helped Vovó up, giving her the longest kiss ever.

They set out on their way.

From time to time Vovó stopped and sat along the edge of the path, listening to the rustle of the eucalyptus, cryptomeria, and pines and to the sound of the cascading waters rushing down to the stream on its way to the sea.

"Oh Vovó, may I ask you something?"

"Of course, Xana, go on."

"I need to talk to you so much, Vovó, the way a mouth needs bread. I still don't know how to deal with Mamã, or what to say. There's something between us that separates us. Sometimes I start to wonder if it's in fact a deep purple abyss. It's something you want to catch, but then it escapes in a second. I know she likes me and wants what's best for me, but she always keeps her distance. And I myself want to help her, but I'm shy and, in truth, so afraid."

"Afraid of what, Xana?"

"Of that creature Mamã likes so much."

"Oh, I don't know. I don't know."

A cold heavy silence quelled the babbling of the stream waters.

Vovó raised her finger to her lips: "Shhh shhh shhh . . ."

Xana obeyed.

Some clouds quivered, others broke apart, and the lightest ones disintegrated, intertwined themselves and danced.

※

It was almost nighttime.

Back home, not a living soul.

Mamã wasn't there, nor was Rosália, nor Tia. No one anywhere. It was all so strange: people were whispering at the end of our street, speculating—maybe appendicitis, a heart attack, gall bladder or liver trouble. Others inclined toward a blood clot. Vovó was losing her mind. What else will befall us?

And now it had been all for naught, all that hard work in America for so many years in order to create the right conditions for them to return to the island and lead a comfortable existence, enjoying a new life in a land surrounded by the sea and breezes on all sides, but with clocks still running on a slower time, one of relaxation and memories—some forgotten, others restored to an easier tempo, an accomplice to good and evil. A disoriented time with its hands running clockwise and counterclockwise. And the old ladies did not even realize that the winging away of their lifetimes was, like time, also dying.

"It can't be," my dispirited grandmother said.

Tia Luísa, who had been out, when she learned what was happening picked up her pace as she came hobbling. She wanted to arrive as soon as possible in order to kneel before Lord Holy Christ of Miracles, praying to God to take her and instead leave Papá and the girls.

Mamã and Carolina had accompanied Papá to the hospital in the city. Nobody felt like sleeping. It seemed the ground was being pulled out from under our feet, and there we stood on the precipice of a cliff, surrounded by hungry hawks that mistook us for hens.

※

My parents just arrived. They had come by taxi from the city.

Papá bore the pall of death all over his face. He had lost a great deal of blood en route to the hospital. Three hours to the city.

The doctor readily diagnosed a duodenal ulcer brought on by stress, which for lack of treatment had proceeded to rupture and bleed. And so Papá was ordered to lie on the living room sofa, confined to total bed rest—a torture for someone like him who never stopped. Those times when the entire family was together came to mind then. And as he lay there reflecting for hours on end, he started brooding, burying himself deeper in the horrors of his fears in those recent weeks since he had realized the money that had once seemed a fortune was in fact quite short, in particular for projects they had dreamed of while they were in America.

Papá's dream was not to have to go back to working in the fields. His dream was to be the lord of his inherited lands and of the other real estate purchased while in America by the sweat of his brow.

After a while, my father began regaining some strength, but he was no longer the same. We would typically see him standing with his back to the rear of the house, beside the wall that divided the yard from the garden, looking off toward Pico da Vara. And when Xana came home to São Bento, he would be there in that same place, always with his back turned, head tilted, perhaps dreaming, or perhaps digging his own grave.

In our house a whiff of death was growing. It came from the corners of the house, it came from the cracks in the windows, filtered through curtains that seemed to evaporate.

From the swollen walls, patches of mold emerged. Emotions, tears, and singing oozed out; pieces of an old puzzle from America, difficult to reassemble, some so minuscule that at the slightest breath they could vanish, leaving the puzzle incomplete. And when that happened, it was like a loss of life—a curse that fell upon us, separated as we were from all the other pieces of our family.

A dark void opened up then, an irreversible absence, a separation that left us frozen.

That afternoon was warm and mild. Spring was just starting.

Over by the wall, our elderly neighbor who lived directly below us headed up toward my father. They engaged in conversation for quite some time. Xana saw them and approached the old man, who always brought her a treat: in summer, blackberries; in autumn, sweet corn stalks that she sucked on eagerly; in winter, moss to decorate our nativity *presépio;* in spring, abandoned bird nests.

A broad smile spread across the weary lips on Papá's pallid face, as soon as he recalled once more the times when the family still gathered around him at the same table, and the irretrievable affections that left him shaken because of all he felt he had lost during so many years in America, due to their separations and absences. He thanked the old man for all he had done for his daughters, especially the youngest, who had stayed with her grandmother since the age of five months, so tiny.

The afternoon was pleasant. The old man came even closer. His mouth seemed to recede into the knotted hairs of his frizzy beard, as he sought the most dramatic position to savor narrating all the juicy details of things that kept crossing his mind. He then plowed through a whole series of events, some noteworthy, others less interesting. He stroked and stroked his beard, and prepared himself.

"It was in the month of August," he began recounting a certain story.

"That day the moon was so large, so warm in its color that it resembled a sun. Men and women were sitting outdoors along the streets on woven mats. The night was very still. There was no breeze. Some were already sensing the airlessness. Others went into a panic. It felt as though the heat of an open flame were pouring out of the mouth of hell. Some wondered if there was a wildfire over by Burguete. Everyone fell silent. No one wanted to move, and their fear was not so much of the heat as of a stillness that was in fact engulfing one and all. The silence remained absolute. People's hair bristled like barbed wire. Something was about to happen, that was for certain. Then a growl that was not of the earth or moon, nor from the skies, arose from within the bowels of a hidden world. Never before had such a thing been witnessed, nor did anyone even know for sure what had happened off in the direction of Caldeirões.

"I've never seen anything like it," the old man marveled, stroking his long snowy-white beard.

"Oh, but neighbor," my father asked, "why did you remember that story at a time like this, at the start of spring and with summer still so far away? Could it be that you're prophesying something?"

"No, sir," replied the old man. "I know that your little girl goes to school, and when the mood strikes me I haul out a tale for her perhaps to tell others someday, or to write about everything that God has sent our way. These are scarcely tilled clods in this midocean of ours, so tiny that almost no one's heard of them. And to what small extent they have, it's that sometimes they crumble, other times they tremble with all the fury of hell.

"Dammit, I forgot the rest of the story already. My mind no longer speaks coherently—'So it was on that day that the sirens all rose up from the sea, and the entire island caught a glimpse of them . . .'"

He stood up with great difficulty, leaned on his staff, and carried his small bundle on his back up to his house, right near ours.

Xana followed our neighbor to his door. When she returned, she saw Papá still in the same position, his back to the rear of the house, daydreaming.

❋

Within days, Papá's detachment, his lack of interest in life, his already distant absence had become well-known. He was a lost man. All he had left was his kindness, and his compassion for Xana, Tia Luísa, and especially his mother-in-law. He did not know how to change his life around. He regretted having left Mamã in charge of the house. And who knew why?

He anchored himself for days along our "Wailing Wall" as if chained to it and reviewed his entire life in America. He concluded that they had failed, that returning to the island had been a mistake, a disappointment. He grew more and more nervous, and his hair began falling out, leaving him partially bald. After so much soul-searching, so much fretting, such a great strength arose from within him that it knocked him to the ground. Then he called my mother and declared, "We must leave, we must return to your land, since the idea of Brazil is out of the question."

"And why?" asked my mother.

"Because I don't want to. I'm not going to have some of us in Brazil, others in America, and the youngest in Portugal bearing up under the island because she won't let anything separate her from her grand-mother," my father replied with enormous sadness—realizing, however, the hopeless bind in which Xana and her grandmother found themselves.

❊

My grandmother called to Xana, "Come here, I want to talk to you."

"What is it, Vovó?"

"Look, let's see if we understand one another, my girl. Tell me, Xana, did it ever cross your mind that I won't be here forever? That I have very little time left to live? That I'm already a very old lady with little strength? Or do you still think that, like when you were little, I would remain in this world forever and ever at the same age? Despite your twelve years, you continue to be confused, or rather, in fact you want to be confused—that's how I see it and how it seems to me.

"I understand, Xana, but don't do that. Vovó is your grandmother and Mamã is your mother.

"Go, go, my princess, go with Carolina, with your Mana Isabel and your parents. Go be with your brother Daniel, who's your great friend and teacher, and don't be stubborn, I beg of you."

"No! It's not stubbornness, Vovó, it's love, it's *saudade* for you. It's that I can't detach myself from this wounded bird of yours and mine."

"Go," Vovó prodded. "Go see all those wonderful things you imag-ined in the mirror. You're already of an age at which to start subtracting a bit from so much dreaming, my girl, so you can add a bit of reality to your life."

A tear slid down Xana's face. "I see, Vovó. You want to say goodbye to me, and now I know that not even the snails can protect me any-more. I'm all alone."

"No, Xana, that's not true. You have great inner strength, my com-panion. Sooner or later, whatever the cost, I'll have to release you like the doves in our coop. I'm weary and you need to leave."

"No, no!" A strident scream of pain tore through the sea itself.

All of a sudden Xana bolted for the woods, trying to hide from a world that was propelling her toward death. Using leaves from golden ginger and pittosporum, she fashioned a bed and rocked herself to sleep on waves of dreams. She saw a lady carrying a child in her arms, picking fragile mimosa blossoms along the sides of island roads. They trembled at the slightest noise—and the lady, after smoothing them, wove them into a crown, setting it on the little girl's head.

❀

As time passed, our parents remained disoriented; their dual disappointments kept fermenting. Mamã and Papá would repeat, "The island is no longer the same, the island is no longer the same. Things here, no matter how much they evolve, do not guarantee a brighter future."

"It was a mistake, woman. Either there or here, but never both here and there. And, let's put an end once and for all to that story, so very badly told."

To our surprise, Mamã let him speak that day, and her voice was not heard. They were lost, dangling in the darkness from a tightrope.

Mamã headed for the house. It was apparent that she was crying. And Xana saw her.

The tears poured down her face.

Xana was silent and swallowed hard, thinking, "Oh, how much I would like to cheer Mamã up; to lick the salt from her eyes, to leach out all the pain that's eating her. And how many unlived *saudades* I have of smelling and touching her body, fragrant with rosemary; from softening it with oils, from then laying my head on a lap of cotton."

❀

Days later there was a commotion that made the whole house shake. It was another earthquake, another deep fissure.

Carolina was to blame for Mamã's wrath, while Papá exited into the street out of a sense of self-preservation. Let his wife be the one to deal with the girl, since he was never called on to calm tempers that were hard to soothe. What had happened was that Carolina was in the habit of getting out of bed at certain hours of the night in order to check on the noises, squeaks, and giggles emanating from the direction of her parents' bedroom. It disturbed her to the point that she wanted to find out and investigate what was going on and how it was happening. Carolina's curiosity increased until she was unable to fall asleep. The previous night she had gathered the courage to go ask Xana to keep her company. But Xana wanted nothing to do with that. Carolina tugged on her, trying to drag her out of bed in order to listen to the creakings of a rocking bed. Xana, who was groggy, rolled over onto her other side and went back to sleep.

She dreamed of one of her favorite toys, that little girl doll dressed in pale blue, swinging under a pink umbrella, turning and turning until the cord played out. And she was always alone, riding round and round on top of the gramophone lid. A flash of light faded behind frosted glass. Xana saw a very large airplane, which was looking for their white camellia bush, now dead and gone. Like a hawk, the plane circled over and over in search of a place to land. Xana reached her hand out and rang the bell, the way she had as a little girl. Suddenly, like a sack of clothes from America, out tumbled women and men, faces smashed, rotting teeth falling out, and skulls minus bodies, through the leafless red camellias.

She woke up drenched in sweat from head to foot. Her eyes burned with fever.

Early the next morning Mamã was in a rage, and beat Carolina, threatening to send her to reform school.

During the night Carolina had mustered the courage to head toward her parents' room. Their door was slightly ajar. The crack was very narrow, so she was unable to see anything. Her curiosity, however, was so great that she pushed the door open, the better to hear and watch. As she approached, she forgot the small step and tripped, opening the door all the way. She went sprawling on the floor, where she had time to think about how to extricate herself from that predicament. So she faked a convincing faint, as though she were nervous and suffering from gall bladder trouble—her *modus operandi* in similar situations, which left her shivering from the cold. Papá believed his daughter, and worried about the state of her health. Mamã was unconvinced. She was beside herself and continued to threaten Carolina: "You ill-bred girl."

Rosália gloated, taking advantage of the moment, triumphant as ever. "Well, didn't I warn you, my friend, that your mother never made the effort to raise your girls right?"

My mother then rose from the couch, left abruptly, and went to talk with my father, scolding and scolding him, and blaming him for everything.

"A situation as serious as Carolina's," my mother shouted, beside herself, "requires nothing less than a good thrashing." And she thrust her finger right into my father's face.

"What she deserves is a good paddling from head to toe, so she'll remember never to poke her nose where it doesn't belong."

Papá hit the ceiling and, with a livid gaze, spoke peremptorily.

"Shut up woman. I'm sick of all this."

Mamã bit her lip until it bled, and then vanished.

⚙

Some months later it was clear that Papá was still unwell, but he never unburdened himself to anyone. He seemed to suffer in silence. At that moment he resembled one of the patriarchs—Prometheus, perhaps. He held his head in his hand as he squirmed and writhed against the wall. He rolled on the ground, as if his body were woven of cords; he suffered cramps all over. He resembled Rodin's sculpture "The Thinker" in one of Vovó's magazines. He looked very much like that.

Tia Luísa, meanwhile, emerged from her refuge, and when she saw his condition, she raised her hands to her head and began moaning and groaning, crying much like a kitten's meow. Papá was all sweaty, and his clothes were soaking wet. Then, like a woman in labor when her water has broken, the same thing happened to him at that moment. And while Xana and our aunt stood there bewildered, unable to comprehend a thing, it was apparent that his haggard face had taken on a shiny shade of pink satin. Papá calmed them down and asked them to keep quiet about it, not to tell anyone, for he was accustomed to having such spells, so they should not worry.

Days passed, and it seemed to us that our parents had buried the hatchet.

All was quiet on the home front.

The recent noise from the breaking of thrown china and flower vases had abruptly ended. However, the silence grew heavy and, at the same time, stupefying. No one knew which of these alternatives was better. So we remained alert, distrustful, on the lookout like rabbits when they leave their burrow.

⚙

Xana had just arrived from the city. She went up to her room, set her briefcase down and fled the scene, which left her not only perplexed but also afraid. The calm had already gone on too long and we feared its opposite: a potentially devastating storm, Xana wondered. And she went right out to be with her closest girlfriend. Xana told her about her studies, her new friends, but it was plain to see that she was sad. She had no desire to go home. But it was already getting late. She said goodbye and, with heavy steps and drooping head, slowly walked home. She did not even want to eat.

She came in, and immediately her body trembled.

No one!

The house was dark. Silent. Dead.

Xana went straight to the kitchen, where she beheld a terrifying scene: Mamã at the head of the table, and Vovó to her left. The two of them propped up, with vacant expressions. Between them, "not a creature was stirring." And neither one blinked. They looked like cutouts from a page in one of the magazines in the china cabinet. In the middle of the table, uncovered, sat an untouched piece of roast pumpkin, Mamã's favorite dish. Indoors nothing moved, and outdoors no cat was heard meowing nor dog barking—not even a slight trace of a breath, nor a brief gentle breeze that might rustle that lock of honey-colored hair covering Mamã's face.

Xana surreptitiously watched all of this, terrified. Everything was so different than usual.

Here and there, a slight movement. And again, everything stopped.

Vovó sat with her head bent forward, heavy like a stone. Mamã, with a somber expression, was looking down at her shoes. Both remained mute. Probably caught amid a past that already told them little, a present more virtual than real, and a future to be feared since its name was unknown.

When Xana, already at some distance, went numb from fear, she turned her back to leave, but soon stopped.

At long last a sound was heard.

Their words were few, falling suddenly, like an ax cutting the white camellia, white like Tia Luísa, who went by the nickname Luísa Branca.

"I'm leaving, mother!" Mamã said to my grandmother.

Vovó did not answer her, and Mamã's eyes, at the moment ashen, settled on the bowl beside the uneaten pumpkin.

Vovó stood up and went into the bedroom. She sat down in the rocking chair between the corner of the window and the gramophone. In front of her was the large mirror on the dresser.

She fell asleep.

Xana tiptoed into the room, caressed her, kissing her whole face, her every hair. That night, Xana took care of herself. She slept with Vovó's pain, in the same bed, but with no more Rosálias, no more ghosts.

⚙

Early the next morning, without warning so as not to hurt Vovó, the taxi was waiting at the door.

Vovó had understood. The land was cracking open and it was not raining.

She stayed in bed, making herself sleep, breaking the pain the way someone breaks branches off a withered fig tree.

Xana came to the doorway, arms outstretched as in flight, clutching the door like someone clinging to life.

TRANSLATOR'S NOTE

"Call me Isabel."

Had she wished, Adelaide Freitas could have opened her novel *Smiling in the Darkness* with this sentence in English, because as a scholar of Herman Melville's epic *Moby-Dick* she knew the famous line "Call me Ishmael" that opens its first chapter. And just as Melville's mysterious survivor Ishmael relates his account of Captain Ahab's obsessive pursuit of the whale that had severed his leg, so too Isabel narrates *Smiling in the Darkness* about her mother's struggles to avenge the amputation by her own father of the only family lifestyle she'd known.

Both narrators' names notably share most of the same letters—I-S-A-E-L—and in the same order. Further, in *Smiling in the Darkness,* Isabel's aptly-named emigrant grandfather Fontes was the font of his family's tribulations for decades to come, starting in the 1920s after a visit to his native Azores to find a bride to marry and take back to Massachusetts. As a self-made man, he prospered and advanced in New Bedford while his uneducated wife kept their home, bore his children, and turned a blind eye to his adulteries in return for an increasingly wealthy lifestyle and the respectability of their marriage's false façade.

Then disaster struck when one of Fontes' mistresses insisted he evict his wife and children, and install her in his mansion; his family returned to their native village in northeastern São Miguel island. This parallels Hagar and Ishmael being expelled by Abraham except that, unlike in the Bible, exile was to the middle of an ocean rather than a desert. Over the decades this expulsion precipitated one family member's career-ending near-amputation as well as a succession of emotional ones—Freitas even had narrator Isabel use the term "amputate."

However, unlike the whale's victim, Fontes' wounded wife was no obsessed Captain Ahab. Although illiterate, she had learned of a wider modern world, progress, and humanism in America, where women had greater legal and cultural rights than in Portugal. Thus, upon her return home she would lead a more independent life than the village women who had never left, think more rationally and less superstitiously about natural and physical phenomena (including frequent major seismic activity), and behave more pragmatically in relation to societal rules. She went unchaperoned about town and occasionally to the island's main city, refused to wear the widow's weeds expected of divorcées, capably husbanded her own money, refused to be cowed as others were by authority figures like the schoolmaster or village priest, and dared teach her grandchildren that God lies within each person—a deity of tolerance and joy, not hellfire and damnation.

It was instead her daughter who—upon being suddenly stripped of her dreams of studying to become a teacher, having her own piano, pursuing her various artistic inclinations, and generally living the wealthy lifestyle she'd known in New Bedford—felt most keenly the consequences of the figurative amputation, becoming as obsessed with her lost money and materialism as Ahab had been with the whale that took his leg.

After marrying a local man and giving birth to five daughters (one of whom, the frail tot Serafina, joined the seraphs) and a son, she found herself pregnant again late in life, suffering complications and illness that necessitated medical treatment as well as money to pay for it. In a society still largely based on subsistence agriculture, hunting and fishing, cash was scarce, so following daughter Xana's difficult birth in late October 1949—only days after an airliner slammed into massive nearby Pico da Vara, killing all on board[1]—and post-partum complications, the next April ("the cruellest month") she decided to return to America long enough to earn sufficient money from factory work to put her family on sounder financial footing, and left her children's upbringing to their *Papá* and both grandmothers. However, six months later her husband joined her in New England to earn even more money for the family—and over the years she would force their two eldest daughters to come work in American factories upon completing their basic schooling (while their only son came to find a better-paying job for himself, and obtain a visa card for his fiancée, since employment opportunities for both in Azores had worsened).

The three youngest daughters were raised by their grandmothers, especially their maternal *Vovó*. Many years passed before the couple felt financially able to return home, *Mamã* believing she had at last vanquished her whale of money and materialism. While still in America she'd begun planning grandiose renovations to their house in the Azores, and aspired to a status comparable to the birthright she'd long ago enjoyed in Massachusetts. She insisted on outdoing any neighbor's challenge to her economic supremacy; she wanted her family to be the Joneses with whom no other villager could keep up, let alone surpass, an obsession leading inevitably to further familial "amputations."

Like *Moby-Dick*'s Ishmael, the cipher Isabel lived to tell the tale. However, by her allusion in English on the first page of the original Portuguese edition of *Smiling in the Darkness* to the opening line "April is the cruellest month" from T.S. Eliot's classic poem "The Wasteland," Isabel signaled that she survived to become erudite, even if the other relatives lived in a familial and cultural wasteland, damaged by the latest amputation for at least another generation.

A final note: Freitas created a stylistic tic to characterize the narrator's voice; Isabel sometimes repeats the same word twice, for emphasis. An example from early in the novel: "Overhead, for the child's amusement, hung a wreath made of wildflowers; wild, too, were her dark, dark eyes." The translators have strived to retain such repetitions whenever feasible.

This book could never have been completed without support from many people. Above all I wish to thank author Adelaide Freitas for writing a masterpiece, and her devoted husband Vamberto Freitas, who has stood by this translating project through her illness and death. Also Diniz Borges, who fifteen years ago gave me my first break as a translator, for drawing this novel to my attention; and Betty Bispo and the late Jonas Waxman, for finding me a copy of the novel on their travels.

I must thank my co-translators, without whom this project never could have been completed: Bobby Chamberlain, my long-time professor and translating collaborator, who has been correcting my work ever since my first day in his Portuguese 1 course at the University of Pittsburgh; and Reinaldo Silva and Emanuel Melo, for extensive corrections, re-translations and suggestions to successive drafts, as well as their invaluable insights into Portuguese culture and language.

Thank you to the University of Massachusetts Dartmouth's Tagus Press and its Executive Editor Mario Pereira, and his Bellis Azorica Book Series co-director Onésimo Almeida, under whose aegis this translation is published; and Anthony Barcellos, polymath professor, novelist, eagle-eyed proofreader and morale-raiser.

Finally, thanks to Adelaide's cousin, singer-songwriter Amy Correia, for her enthusiasm and inspiration; and to Adelaide's numerous friends for encouraging this project and waiting through many drafts for its completion.

And above all, boundless gratitude to John Baker for his love and support—and patience in living with a translator!

Katharine F. Baker

Pittsburgh, Pennsylvania

January 2020

NOTE

1. Bettencourt, Urbano. "O Último Voo Do Constellation F-BAZN." *Comunidades* blog, 9 Feb 2015. www.rtp.pt/acores/comunidades/o-ultimo-voo-do-constellation-f-bazn--urbano-bettencourt_41788; and, de Sá, Daniel. "Um Stradivarius no Pico da Vara." *Comunidades* blog, 28 May 2017. www.rtp.pt/acores/comunidades/cronica-um-stradivarius-no-pico-da-vara-de-daniel-de-sa_54089.